Other books

Historical Romance

Winter's Heat
Summer's Storm
Spring's Fury
Autumn's Flame
A Love for All Seasons
The Warrior's Wife
The Warrior's Maiden
The Warrior's Game
Lady in Waiting
Lady in White
Almost Perfect

Co-written
Men-ipulation

From Award-winning, best-selling author
Denise Domning Santiago Canyon College
Library

SEASON OF THE RAVEN

"In this medieval mystery of stunning
realism, Domning brings the English
countryside alive with all the rich detail
of a Bosch painting. With well realized
characters and a depth of historical
detail, she creates a vibrant mystery and
a layered, engaging protagonist. CSI
12th century style. I can't wait to see
more."

Friend of the Library Donor

Donated by
Lana Wong
SCC Librarian

© DEMCO, INC. 1990 PRINTED IN U.S.A.

A MILLER FOUND UNDER HIS WHEEL

It's 1194 and Sir Faucon de Ramis, the shire's newly appointed Keeper of the Pleas, must do his duty and make an official declaration of the cause of a miller's death.

Saddled with a clerk who names Faucon his 'penance', the shire's first Crowner must thread the tangled relationships between the sheriff, the village of Priors Holston and the priory that once ruled it. As a simple task takes a turn to the political, what seems obvious isn't and what appears safe turns out to be more dangerous than he could imagine.

Season of the Raven

by

DENISE DOMNING

SEASON OF THE RAVEN

EDITED BY: Martha Stites

ORIGINAL COVER ART:
Ms Sloane 2435, f.85 'Cleric, Knight and Workman representing the three classes, illustration from 'Li Livres dou Sante' (vellum), French School, (13th century)/ British Library, London, UK/©British Library Board. All Rights Reserved/The Bridgeman Art Library

DESIGN: Denise Domning, Refined by ADK Designs

Printed in the United States of America, First paperback edition: February, 2014

Dedication

To all of the readers out there who have enjoyed my historical romances. Thank you for reading and I hope you like this mystery just as much.

My Apologies

My apologies to the people of Warwickshire. I have absconded with your county, added cities that don't exist and parsed your history to make it suit my needs. Outside of that, I've done my best to keep my recreation of England in the 12th Century as accurate as possible.

Michaelmas, 1194

"Tonight you sleep with the angels, my sweet," I tell her and press a kiss to her forehead in blessing.

As I sit back on my heels, I sigh in appreciation. Such beauty! Her skin is fine and soft, spared ever knowing the corruption of lust or the degradation of time. The rain that spits down from an overcast sky settles jewel-like in her dark tresses and on the ring of bright blue flowers I wove as her crown. Her hands are folded sweetly upon her chest, resting atop the posy of meadow flowers I presented to her as her final gift. Now that her nails are pared and her fingers are free of dirt stains, there is nothing to mar their elegance.

The simple white shift she wears is not as fine as those that adorned her spiritual sisters when they made their journey to the gates of Heaven. For that slight I made my apologies to her, assuring her Saint Peter will find no flaw in her plainer attire, not when she is every bit the equal of those I sent on ahead of her.

Nor could I have chosen a more perfect site for her translation. Tall meadow grasses rustle on this treeless hillside, tossing their golden heads in gentle rolling waves driven by a persistent wind. As they bow to Heaven's breath, I catch glimpses of scarlet, white and blue—poppies, daisies and cornflowers, remnants of summer past.

Of a sudden, the clouds part and a single shaft of sunlight sings down. The beam comes to rest on this exact spot.

For breath after breath, the light persists. Tears fill my eyes. My heart soars in joy. I am not forgotten!

I know I have always been the most grateful and caring of His servants. But it has been years since I last felt the call to send Him another one pure enough to serve Him in his heavenly house. If that quiet period could not break my faith, I will admit to feeling tried by His silence.

At last the holy light dims and the time to leave is at hand. I start to turn away only to have my gaze catch on her throat. A tiny rusty smear remains upon the wound that finished her.

I tremble. Was His light blessing or warning?

Not so much as a fleck of earthly smut can defile my offerings. Should I fail in this, neither hairshirt nor scourging will save me from roasting in hell forever. Nor should I be saved, for without His blessing, what I do is naught but murder, pure and simple.

Kneeling at her side, I remove my capuchin. The woolen hood is well-moistened with the rain. Using it, I wipe away the last bit of crusting blood, then survey her once again, seeking further signs of my carelessness. There is nothing.

"Hold me in your heart, little one. Soon enough I will join you and all your sisters in service to our Lord," I tell her in farewell.

I sing my prayer as I tramp back to the road, willing her soul safely and swiftly heavenward, while begging our Holy Master to let her body make an easy return to the earth from which it was created.

Chapter One

Hungry, tired, and crusted with so much dried muck that his chain mail more crunched than jangled, Sir Faucon de Ramis watched the ravens as he rode. At least a dozen of those foul carrion-eaters turned wide circles over the grassy hillside at the far edge of this long low valley. Faucon's lip curled in disgust. Bold creatures those birds were, as quick to feast on the dying as they were to consume the dead. So many in one place always spoke of death, be it human or animal.

Faucon scanned the treeless slope, then followed the line of the Stanrudde Road to where it crested the hill. There was no sign of human habitation. So, it was some wild creature that attracted the birds this time. Nonetheless, he was grateful to turn his shoulder to them when the time came to urge Legate off the muddy road onto the even muddier track that led to Blacklea Village.

After nearly two weeks of constant rain, the sky had finally cleared. Now the descending sun stretched gentle not-yet-rosy fingers across a low defensive mound and the village that spread along its top and sides. His view framed by the arch of his helmet's nosepiece, Faucon eyed his destination in surprise. Why in God's name was his auspicious great-uncle calling him to such an inauspicious place?

The small settlement could contain no more than four hundred homes, if hovels made of mud and manure topped with thatch could be called homes. As in any other place of this sort, the fields that supplied its daily bread were close at hand, just beneath the mound. And just like in any other village, the furrows in the fields as well as the hedges that surrounded them went every which way to take the best advantage of slope, sun and water. In the orchards the trees—be they apple, pear or walnut—were yet heavy with fruits. Harvest time was at hand.

At the next turn of the track, Faucon came upon a crowd of villagers as muck-ridden as he. They were gathering up their tools. With all the rain, their wheat was too wet to harvest, so it seemed they'd spent the day seeding in next year's crop.

Although a lone armed man, even one in full armor, wasn't usually a threat, no one called for him to stop and declare his intentions. That suggested Blacklea had a strong protector and had long known peace.

Shouting and whooping, a gaggle of boys raced from the field and onto the grassy verge. Bare of foot and dressed in brightly-dyed homespun, each one carried a sling and had a sack of stones hanging from his belt. They'd been keeping birds from consuming the newly-sown seeds before they could be covered with soil.

In their native English, the boys threw goads at each other, daring one another to get closer to the knight. They leapt and hopped over clumps of grass, trying to outrun the trotting horse. Legate gave a snort.

Faucon grinned as he understood. His big-hearted boy wasn't as tired as he'd been pretending. He gave the courser his head.

His steed curved his neck in a pretty bow of gratitude, then stretched his legs. In an instant, the boys all bellowed in frustration as the horse left them well behind, his easy gait swiftly eating up the distance to the base of the mound and the flimsy gateway in the village's wholly inadequate defensive wall.

Legate was almost into the opening before Faucon caught a glimpse of the flock of sheep on the other side.

He brought his mount to a sliding, dancing halt, just before overrunning the shepherdess. With a cry, she stumbled back from the horse and his deadly hooves. Her sheep scattered, baaing and milling about the narrow lane until it was blocked. The noise brought several housewives to their doorways, their arms crossed and their eyes narrowed against the possibility of livestock invading their front gardens.

"My pardon," Faucon called out in her tongue as the shepherdess caught her footing and straightened. "Are you hurt?"

Dressed in rough gowns of vibrant green, the young woman looked up at him. She wore no head covering, and strands of gentle brown hair straggled and curled out of what had once been the sober confinement of her plaits. She seemed plain until she smiled. The turn of her lips was so compelling that Faucon couldn't help but smile back.

"Ah, racing with our boys I see," she replied in the French of England's ruling class, as the lads who'd tried to outrun Legate streamed into the gateway to thread through her flock as they made their way home. "Would you be Sir Faucon de Ramis?"

"I am," Faucon replied, as startled that she knew his name as by the fact that she spoke his native tongue with but a hint of an accent.

At that, she put her hands on her hips and studied him as boldly as any whore. Her gaze measured the breadth of his shoulders and the length of the sword buckled at his side, as if she could gauge his strength and prowess by eye alone. Apparently he fell short, for she gave a disappointed shake of her head.

"Crusader or not, I fear you're too young to be pitted against Sir Alain. Our sheriff will be sucking the marrow from your bones in no time," she told him.

Faucon frowned at her. "What are you talking about? How do you know me?"

She only cocked a brow at him and smiled once more, sharp amusement filling her blue eyes. "Oh, I shouldn't like to spoil the surprise. By the by, your bishop awaits you at the house, not at the church."

She offered him a bold wink, then put her fingers to her lips and freed a whistle so sharp that Faucon winced and Legate danced. A dog, deerhound-sleek but the same dusky brown color as her sheep, appeared from the back of the wayward flock. Tongue lolling, it darted silently from one side of the track to the other, nipping and snapping, knitting the sheep into a unit. It drove the reformed flock past Faucon and his horse and through the gate within a breath. The shepherdess followed, taking up a position at the rear of the flock this time.

"Which house?" he called after her.

"Follow the track to the green. You'll know it when you see it," she called back without turning, her voice still warm with amusement.

Now, as befuddled as he was tired and filthy, Faucon urged Legate up the rising track, which quickly became no more than two well-used ruts in the ground. It took but a few short moments to reach the village green at the top of the mound.

Studded and rutted with the rocky remains of some ancient construction, the grassy expanse played host to a dozen horses, palfreys all, save for one churchman's donkey. Among them was the graceful gray Faucon recognized as his uncle's favorite mount.

The men who rode these horses were also in the green. With the rain at an end, some had thrown their cloaks onto the piles of rocks to lounge in what sun they could catch, while others crouched in tight groups on the wet grass and gambled, that being the thing most men did to pass an idle hour or two. To a one they wore rough brown and green hunting garments beneath their leather vests.

Blacklea's church sat on one side of the grassy expanse. It was small, but built of stone, its square tower lifting above a gleaming slate roof. Directly across the green from the church was a house.

The shepherdess was right. This was the only abode in Blacklea that could possibly serve his uncle. Made of reddish stone blocks set in thick white mortar with a roof of dark slate tile, the house was three times the size and twice as tall as the largest of the cottages it overlooked. Although its door was on the second storey, accessible by a set of wooden steps that clung to its exterior wall, there was no keep tower for a final refuge.

One of the waiting men came forward to greet him. "Sir Faucon?"

"I am," Faucon replied. How did everyone here know him when he knew them not at all? Although this man did look familiar. Then again, after traveling to the end of the world and back again, Faucon had seen so many faces that everyone seemed familiar to him these days.

"I'll take your horse for you, if he'll allow me," the man offered.

"He will," Faucon reassured him. Although more than capable of carrying Faucon into battle, Legate was no nobleman's deadly destrier. "He's only a courser, and calmer than most at that."

As predicted, Legate tolerated the stranger's touch after a reassuring pat from his master. Faucon dismounted, only to groan as his feet met the earth. Almost a full day astride with only a few short breaks left pins and needles in his legs. Leaning against Legate, he pulled off his helmet and hung it from its tether on his saddle. After pushing back his mail hood, he removed the leather coif he wore beneath it and stuffed the cap into his helmet. As he reached for his pack, which contained his finest attire wrapped in oiled skin to keep it dry, the man holding Legate's bridle gave a jerk of his head toward the house.

"They're impatient for your arrival, as they hoped to be gone from here by now. You're to present yourself immediately. Go, knowing I'll see your mount is fed and watered."

They? Then again, his uncle rarely traveled without at least a few men near his own rank to bear him company, or some storyteller. William of Hereford was especially fond of men who could spin a proper tale.

Faucon grimaced as he looked down at his mud-stained surcoat and filthy chain mail. It did his father's name no honor to present himself to his betters looking like this. But if the choice was between being filthy or irritating his uncle by delaying him, well, that was no choice at all. He started up the steps on still-clumsy feet.

The thick door at the top was bossed in metal and scarred as if more than one army had tried its strength and been rebuffed. He reached for the latch, then hesitated. What if his mother was right, and the handwritten note from Bishop William commanding him to ride at all haste to this meeting meant an advancement in Faucon's fortunes?

Until this moment he hadn't dared believe it possible, even if he was eager for any purpose his powerful kinsman might find for him. Anything was better than the sorry half-life he'd been living of late. That made presenting himself so completely covered in mud impossible.

Tucking his stained gloves into his sword belt, Faucon ran his fingers through his matted hair. After rubbing as much of the muck and dirt as he could from his surcoat, he opened the door and stepped inside.

The chamber within was so small it hardly deserved the name 'hall.' At the back of the room, a man knelt in prayer at a modest prie-dieu set beneath a narrow window. Enough light streamed through that opening to reveal the shaved skin on top of his bowed head and his black habit. A Benedictine monk.

At the center of the room, two other men sat at a simple table made of planks set on braces, a chess board on the tabletop between them. Faucon paid little heed to the man with his back to the door, other than to note he was dark of hair and wore a leather vest atop a rough tunic. Instead, his full attention was on his uncle.

Bishop William of Hereford stared at the board in front of him, so lost in concentration he hadn't yet noticed his nephew's arrival. Faucon had not seen his august relative since departing England for the Holy Lands with England's king, Richard, Coeur de Lion, five years past.

If new silver threaded his uncle's black hair, his face seemed the same as ever. Like Faucon and his mother, William's features wore the stamp of the de Vere family. His brow was broad, his cheeks lean and his nose long. And then there was that chin. Faucon hid what he considered a far-too-pointed chin beneath his neatly-trimmed beard, but the bishop had sculpted his facial hair to a narrow thread that accentuated the acute line of his jaw.

When another moment passed and his granduncle remained focused on the chessboard, Faucon cleared the road dust from his throat. "My lord uncle, I have come as you requested," he said in quiet announcement.

Chapter Two

William lifted his head, a smile already bending his narrow lips. His opponent shifted on the bench and looked over his shoulder. Faucon gasped in surprise.

"Lord Graistan! What are you doing here?" he asked of the man who was the elder half-brother to his cousins.

Rannulf, Lord Graistan, came to his feet. Taller than either Faucon or William, he was in his middle years but maintained the form of a man who counted on the strength of his sword arm to hold his livelihood. "That is something I've been asking myself all day, Pery," he replied, a quick smile bringing warmth to his gray eyes and banishing the native harshness of his roughhewn features.

He used Faucon's pet name, a name devised by Lord Graistan's youngest brother. Pery was short for Peregrine, a play on the meaning of 'Faucon.' Faucon had welcomed it. Far better to be called Pery than *Falcon*, even if his name supposedly came to him from an ancestor—one of the men who had followed Rollo the Viking into Normandy—as his mother claimed. Indeed, Faucon would have preferred a simple Thomas or well-used Robert, since neither of those names inspired taunts.

"Truth be told," Lord Rannulf continued, "all your uncle and I have managed to do here this day is waste hours waiting for your arrival."

"Waste them, indeed," William of Hereford snorted, fond irritation filling his voice. Although Lord Graistan wasn't blood kin to the de Vere family, he was among William's greatest supporters, as had been his sire before him.

The bishop's bench chittered across the wooden floor as he came to his feet. Like the baron, William was also dressed in hunting green, although his tunic was trimmed in golden embroidery at the neck, sleeves and hem. He pointed at the chess board. "You call this game wasted time, Rannulf? I have you on the run. I've almost got you!" he gloated.

"Hardly so! I'd never let you catch me, not when your win would result in you stealing my son's inheritance from me," the nobleman retorted, his tone more taunt than complaint.

"My lord, have a care how you speak to our lord bishop!" Filled with outrage, the chide came from the monk at the back of the tiny hall.

Startled that one so humble would dare so much, Faucon watched the black-robed brother come to his feet, his prayer beads clutched tightly against his chest. Outrage pulsed from the man.

Lord Graistan's expression could have been carved from stone. William lifted a warning hand without turning to look at the monk.

"Brother Edmund, once again you overstep yourself," the bishop said, his voice cool and low. "For the sake of your abbot and your sire, I have been patient, but know you there is precious little left of my tolerance."

"But my lord bishop, he calls you a thief," the monk protested.

William stood as he was, his hand raised. Chastisement filled every line of his body.

The monk bowed his head. "I beg your forgiveness, my lords." There was no meekness in his tone.

The bishop continued speaking as if there had been no interruption. "All I want is what is my due, Rannulf.

19

I have helped you, now you must do the same for me. Did you not say you wanted marriage for my grandnephew Gilliam?"

Faucon blinked in shock. His cousin was to marry? When? To whom?

The better question was how. Gilliam was a third son. He had no inheritance or means of supporting a wife. Then again, neither did Faucon, and he was a second son. One day he'd own the land his mother had brought with her into her marriage, but that wasn't enough wealth for any man to ever give him his daughter.

"You know I do," the nobleman replied, "but not at the cost of Blacklea."

"Then keep Blacklea and tell the hundreds to elect you to the position, as you know I wish you would," William retorted. "The Keeper of the Pleas should be a man of substance and some stature in his shire. Rannulf, you are such a man here."

Lord Rannulf's smile suggested that he and William had chewed this bone so well between them that there was naught left save the joy of fighting over it. "I can't. Your new position will take me away from home far too often, when my greatest need is to make a legitimate heir with my new wife. Remember her? She's the one you made me pay an additional fee for marrying, because I didn't invite you to officiate at our wedding."

"Pah! I'm also the one who made sure she got her rightful inheritance, which means you're rich enough that you won't need Blacklea's income until your bastard son comes of age years from now," William retorted. "If you won't take the position, do as I request and give Blacklea to Pery, so I may make him a keeper in your stead."

Faucon rocked back on his heels in shock. He looked from bishop to baron, wondering if he had fallen asleep in the saddle and dreamed. This had happened to him in the past.

The nobleman paused as if considering, then bowed his head. "As you will."

William's smile was slow and pleased. "Then you will lease Blacklea to Pery at no cost for this year, letting him collect its profits as his own?"

"Only if Pery agrees that he will return Blacklea and all its rights and rents to me with no prejudice, either when my son comes of age or at the moment Pery ceases to serve court and crown," Lord Rannulf replied, haggling.

He paused, then added, "And only if you allow me to marry my brother to the woman of my choice, at no cost to me. I'll not budge on this, William."

The bishop made a low noise in his throat, then sighed. "So it will be."

Lord Graistan grinned. He reached to the chess board and laid one of his bishops on its side. "This game has been much more interesting and satisfying than the one on the board, my lord bishop."

William groaned. "What did I miss? What were you holding in reserve, Rannulf?"

"You'll never know, William," the baron replied with a pleased laugh, then walked to Faucon, his hands outstretched before him as if in prayer. "Give me your oath, Pery."

Too confused to question, Faucon dropped to one knee and put his hands between Lord Rannulf's. "I am your loyal man."

Graistan's lord nodded in satisfaction, then helped Faucon back to his feet. "Then I hereby elect you as Keeper of the Pleas for this village as well as all the other villages and hundreds over which I have dominion. Take good care of my son's patrimony, Pery. You'll have all Blacklea's income as your own for this first year, as William requests, but you must feed and house the steward and his family if they choose to stay.

Any salary you wish to pay Sir John can be negotiated between the two of you. Should you remain a Keeper of the Pleas after this year, you will pay me one sixth of your profit as rent, and continue to support the steward's family for as long as they remain."

Faucon's shook his head, trying to wake himself. "What is this Keeper? Why are you giving me Blacklea? No man just gives another his property and his income."

Lord Rannulf smiled again. "You're wrong, Pery. Not one man gives you income, but two. You'll not only have the profits from Blacklea, but your dear uncle is giving you the sums he claims from one of his benefices." He nodded his head toward William. "I do believe you're to receive the income from the Priory of St. Radegund, which lies not far from here. You see, to serve your uncle and Archbishop Hubert Walter as they wish, you need an income of twenty pounds a year."

Faucon gaped. Twenty pounds! That amount went far beyond any hope of advancement his mother had cherished for him. It was wealth enough to encourage a nearly penniless second son to do more than dream of marriage and a life as no man's servant.

"As for why, you heard me say it's not convenient for me to become a servant of the crown just now," Lord Rannulf continued. "Of all the men we could conjure up to take my place, yours was the one name that kept recurring between us, and one we both trusted."

Beyond stunned, Faucon looked from one man to the other. "Me? Why would you even consider me?"

"First, because your mother's dowry lands lie within this shire, and you are her heir," his uncle replied, coming around the corner of the table to stand next to his noble friend. "That ties you here. Also, you read and write, but that is not as important as your nature. You are a careful man, slow to speak, but not slow of wit, being quick to learn. Your foster father continues to take great pride in you, in how you came so late to squiring, yet swiftly mastered the skills required of knighthood."

Faucon swallowed uncomfortably. He had mastered those skills because he'd loved learning them as much as he'd hated the studies required of a scholar.

William was still speaking. "Since your return from the Holy Land, letters from your lady mother often relate how well you do as your father's steward, how you have a gift for calculating the value of lands, structures and harvests."

So she would say, since her goal had been to remind her uncle of her son, hinting that a comfortable position might be found for her heir in the vast estates held by the bishopric of Hereford.

"But mostly, it is because both Rannulf and I have seen the care and concern you've shown your brother and his inheritance these past years. We agree that you have no ambition in that regard. That you should lack all avarice or impatience when your brother is so obviously incapable of being your father's heir, despite your parents' protests to the contrary, is admirable," William finished.

Although meant as a compliment, his words struck Faucon like a bolt through the heart. He'd been nearly ten-and-four, two years younger than his brother, when Will had taken a blow to the head while practicing at arms. It had rendered him unconscious for days, and when he'd finally awakened, it had been as not-Will, a man who walked and talked like Faucon's brother, but wasn't the same at all. This new Will held tight to rationality for long periods, long enough to achieve his knighthood, but the relentless head pain never left him. There were times when it drove him into the darkest corner of the hall, made his words jumble and his thoughts go astray. Other times he'd explode in towering rages, spurred by nothing at all, the anger driving him from home and hearth. He could disappear for weeks before returning, thin and wild-eyed.

Worst of all, Will understood he was damaged. It ate at him, as did the knowledge that their father had made Faucon a knight instead of a churchman because of Will's injury. Will hated Faucon for that as much as he hated himself for being incapable of rising above what had happened to him.

His uncle smiled. "You are an honest man, Faucon, and honest men are just who the Archbishop of Canterbury and I wish to become our new Keepers of the Pleas."

Here, Lord Graistan gave a scornful snort. "Keeper of the Pleas. I think me it would have been better if you and Hubert Walter had named the position 'the sheriff's bane,' for that is its true motive."

The shepherdess's words rang in Faucon, about how he was too young to be pitted against this shire's sheriff, and how she thought the man would eat up his bones.

"And so they should become the sheriffs' bane, if those sheriffs are lining their purses with stolen royal income," William retorted. "King Richard wants all his due, and that is his right no matter what you say, Rannulf."

"All I've said is that the king of England is a far higher honor than the count of Anjou, or even the duke of Aquitaine or Normandy. A king should keep his attention on his kingdom," the baron replied flatly.

"I'm sure His Majesty will spend more time in England once he's settled all the challenges to his continental holdings which arose because of his imprisonment," William replied quietly, but his voice lacked conviction.

Lord Rannulf smiled tightly. "I pray you're right. Now, have your servants gather themselves while I find Marian. Before we depart, she must know that Blacklea has a new master."

Then he grinned at Faucon. "She especially needs to

find your new Keeper of the Pleas a tub and some soap. Your new royal servant is a solid clot of muck."

William looked at the nobleman in surprise. "We're still riding out? It's almost sunset."

"What?" Rannulf retorted. "Do you intend to waste tonight sitting idly by and chatting? I thought me that was why you brought that monk of yours, so he could do the explaining to Pery, leaving us free to track boar. There's still light enough for us to reach my hunting lodge. That means we can be out with the dogs and beaters as early as dawn on the morrow."

The nobleman's words sent the longing to hunt washing over Faucon. He loved the chase, from the careful search for spoor to the stealthy tracking, the discerning of false trails from the true, and the discovery of every hidey-hole his prey sought out while trying to escape him. Unlike most men, joy came for Faucon when the creature he'd tracked was cornered with nowhere left to hide. If it were up to him, he'd happily turn away at that point, letting his prey escape to be hunted again another day.

William's grin was slow and pleased. "You're right. We've wasted far too much time on this issue as it is. Pery my lad, meet Brother Edmund." The bishop didn't turn his gaze to the monk as he made his introduction.

"He will be clerk for all those who serve the crown in this shire, which makes him yours alone for the time being, since we've not yet recruited the two other knights required. Brother Edmund is well-versed in the laws of our land, and will act as your right hand,"–the bishop gave odd emphasis to his words as he paused to shoot a look at the brother before continuing–"as you make your assessments and hear the pleas that might come your way.

"As for the Priory of St. Radegund, aye, you will now collect its income on my behalf. I had suggested to the prior this would happen when we arrived at Blacklea yesterday, and have told Prior Lambertus to expect your visit. Brother Edmund will confirm with him that you are to receive that income when he retreats to the priory this night to take his rest. Pery, do not fail to present yourself to the prior on the morrow. When you do, remind him one more time that he has my best regards."

With that, Faucon's auspicious uncle drew his grandnephew into a brief embrace, the press of his arms around Faucon's back dislodging another shower of dirt. When he stepped back, his hands still on Faucon's shoulders, his eyes were filled with warmth and not a little relief.

"You will do well with this, lad. I know it, aye."

Then he turned and left the room.

Chapter Three

Faucon watched in stunned surprise as his uncle departed, still not certain he hadn't fallen asleep and dreamed all this. But surely not even his wildest dreams could have conjured up such a turn of fortune.

The monk came forward to stand beside him, his footsteps echoing hollowly on the wooden floor. "After years of loyal service, a single mistake and you are now my penance," Brother Edmund said harshly.

That brought Faucon firmly back to earth. A great turn of fortune, aye, but one not fully in his own hands. At least not yet.

As the animals and men in the green below the house stirred into action, horses neighing and huntsmen whistling and shouting, Faucon studied the monk his uncle had made both his mentor and his servant. The monk's clean-shaven face was well-made, with a strong jaw and high cheekbones. Indeed, he might have been accorded handsome, despite the impressive thrust of his nose.

"Your penance, am I?" Faucon asked quietly. "Should I be sorry to know that? Or perhaps you will someday be sorry you said as much to me," he replied evenly.

The monk blinked, his expression suggesting he hadn't expected a response to his jab. Then he recovered his arrogance. Faucon guessed the resentment that twisted Edmund's finely-drawn lips and befouled his dark eyes beneath their gently-arching brows was a long and closely-guarded habit.

The monk looked down his big nose at Faucon. "I am an honest man. I refuse to engage in the false compliments and fawning phrases others use to manipulate their betters. Instead, I have chosen to always speak only as my heart directs."

"A worthy trait, if a hard path to walk," Faucon acknowledged with no lack of irony.

Then, weary to his core, he dropped to sit on the bench Lord Graistan had vacated. "So what is this Keeper's position I've been given?"

Brother Edmund crossed his arms, tucking his hands into his wide sleeves. "At the Michaelmas court that ended a week ago, our dear Archbishop of Canterbury, may God preserve him, did decree that every shire of this realm shall now employ three knights and one clerk who will keep the Pleas of the Crown."

"Pleas? Do you mean the pleas for justice and redress that folk bring before the royal court when they have had some violence or wrong done to them?" Faucon asked.

"Exactly. Until this summer past, when our archbishop saw to it that the justices in Eyre visited every shire to resolve all the pleas waiting to be heard, it has been more usual for years to pass between the circuits. Because of that, much information was lost. When that happens, a goodly portion of the king's potential revenue disappears through the loss of fees and fines that could have been collected. The archbishop determined that, if written records were kept of these pleas, the royal court was far more likely to collect all His Majesty's rightful due. That is what you, and me through you, are to do. You will have me note the amounts of all fines, fees or amercements that might apply to any plea for justice, as well as all sureties promised or paid by those charged with wrongdoing. Also, we are to hear and note the confessions made by all felons.

"And as *coronarius*"–here Edmund used a Latin word Lord Rannulf had used earlier which translated to the phrase 'servant of the crown', although from what little Faucon yet retained of the Church's tongue, his translation would have been 'crowner'–"you will also be responsible for discovering and noting the details of all acts of murder, burglary and rape, as well as the theft of anything valued over a shilling, or any foul act, such as treason or outlawry, where property or goods might be forfeit to the king."

Faucon choked on a laugh. Holy Mother! No wonder Lord Rannulf hadn't wanted the position. These tasks could keep a man in his saddle for a good part of every week as he went from village to hamlet to town, meeting with all those who had been wronged in some substantial way.

"So I am to be a tax collector for the king?"

"Not a collector," Brother Edmund replied swiftly. "That is still the sheriff's to do. We but assess and make note of all, or rather, I note and you, along with whatever jury you have called, confirm.

"And from now on, only you, and the other two knights who will soon be serving this shire as *coronarii*, can call the hundreds to attend inquests over those who die by unnatural means."

Faucon leaned back on the bench to look up at the monk. "What portion of the shire's revenue is dedicated to compensating this new royal servant?"

The monk met his gaze with a narrow-eyed look. "None at all. It is the archbishop's intention that the new coronarii should never be tempted to line their purses the way the sheriffs do, taking what belongs to their king and country. That is why each Keeper must have an income of twenty pounds a year."

"And who pays you for your trouble?"

"You, for the time being. The bishop has arranged for me to stay at St. Radegund's, being fed and housed from the income he has directed to you."

This time Faucon let his laugh fly. And this was why Lord Rannulf had pushed to leave so swiftly. He didn't want to be in the room when Faucon realized the whole of what he'd been given.

In that instant, Faucon felt his life turn full circle. After gratefully escaping a second son's usual fate of a life dedicated to the Church, he had just accepted a position in which his limited ability with pen and parchment and even more limited knowledge of laws and courts were more important than his significantly greater skill with sword and dagger.

Twenty pounds, Faucon reminded himself. He'd have it for at least this year, and earn not only his granduncle's gratitude, but Lord Rannulf's as well. There was nothing wrong with that.

"When do I begin pursuing my new duties?" Faucon asked.

Brother Edmund cocked a brow at him. "You just have, even though you were not actually elected by those you are to represent. Then again, with every freeman and bondsman in these hundreds beholden to Lord Graistan in some way, if he says you are elected, you are. It doesn't matter to the nobleman that his actions subvert the archbishop's wishes. All he cares about is his own comfort and futtering his wife."

The insult tore through Faucon. His hand flew to his sword hilt. In the next instant, he breathed out costly rage and opened his hand. Long experience with the stranger who was not-Will had taught him it was safer never to reveal his true emotions, especially to an angry man. Besides, Faucon had weapons more suited to this sort of battle.

Cocking his head to the side, he said, "Do tell me of this honest path of yours, Brother Edmund. What event set you upon it? Better yet, relate how it is that your superiors have managed to leave your tongue intact in your head for all these years."

The monk's eyes flew wide. Bright color flooded up his neck to stain his cheeks. His mouth moved as if in speech. No sound came forth.

Faucon gave a slow nod. "You are right. Such a tale will wait until we know each other better. I shall give you your first lesson of me and mine, so you will have insight into who I am. Lord Rannulf is my cousin by marriage, and I am fond of him." Aye, so Faucon remained, even after this strange gift of his. "If we're to have peace between us, I suggest you keep your opinions of him to yourself."

Brother Edmund's jaw tightened and his eyes narrowed. "You have my apology, Sir Faucon." He spat out the words. "If we are finished here, I will depart for St. Radegund's to bear company with my brothers for the night." Not waiting for Faucon to give him leave to depart, the monk pivoted and crossed the room, a most unservile servant.

As the hall door slammed after him, Faucon turned his gaze to the toes of his muddy boots. Did he really wish to trade the comfort of his family home, even burdened as it was with his raging damaged brother, for twenty pounds a year and the burden of a churchman just as angry? There was still time. If he rode out now, he could yet catch Lord Graistan and his uncle and refuse their honor.

Across the room, the door creaked again. He looked up. Much to his surprise the shepherdess entered. With a cheeky grin, she offered him a quick curtsy.

"Well come to Blacklea, Sir Faucon," she bid him. "I am Marian, wife to Sir John, Blacklea's steward. My husband apologizes for not greeting you personally, but he ails of late."

That brought Faucon abruptly to his feet. "My pardon, Lady Marian," he said, offering her the honor due her rank. "I didn't realize," he started, only to catch himself before he admitted he'd assumed she was a commoner.

She laughed, and in that instant she looked younger than he'd first judged her, even younger than his own four-and-twenty years. "I know what you thought. Admittedly, I don't look as I usually do." She held out her rough skirts, then patted at her wayward hair. "We were culling the flock today, and in all the running and dodging I lost my head scarf. Should I assume you will be staying on at Blacklea?"

Was he staying? Faucon eyed her for a long moment. In the end, it wasn't the wealth or the possibility of winning his uncle's favor that spurred him to speak. It was this woman's certainty that he was no match for the sheriff in this shire. For no reason he could name, he needed to prove her wrong.

"I will be," he said.

"I thought as much when I saw you," she said, pleasure and the offer of friendship filling her voice.

"So, in case you have not already confirmed it, your chamber is there," she pointed to the door at the back of the hall. "The bed within it is among Blacklea's assets, so it is yours to use as long as you are master here. We don't have a bathing tub, but I've already warned the laundresses of your need since the laundry serves as our bathhouse."

She waved for him to join her as she turned and walked to the narrow window above the prie-dieu Edmund had used. When they stood there together, she pointed through the opening at the long thatched building at the back of the house. "The laundry is at the right end of our kitchen."

"My thanks for arranging all this on my behalf," he said, and meant it. Then he offered her a rueful grin. "This is especially so since I wager my coming has expelled you and your family from your home."

Twenty pounds a year, an angry mentor, no

recompense for what sounded like a great deal of work, and now he'd cheated a man and his wife of their comfort. Somehow, this wondrous event was feeling a little less wondrous with each passing moment.

"You have not," Marian retorted stoutly. "As I said, my husband ails. It has left him incapable of mounting the outside steps. Last month we left the house for a cottage that does not challenge his legs. In all truth, I'm grateful for the change. Lord Graistan has been good to us, but he knows well indeed that my husband can no longer protect Blacklea as is his duty. Dare I say I hope your presence here might delay our eventual departure for a little while? Blacklea has become home to us and I know not where we might go after this," she added wistfully.

And with that, Faucon knew what his uncle had missed when he'd allowed Lord Graistan to name another Keeper in his stead. It was incumbent upon all noblemen to support their loyal servants until the end of their days, but given Blacklea's small size, Faucon was certain this place didn't have income enough to pay two stipends, one for the new steward and one to maintain Sir John and his family. Now, instead of losing money on this insignificant piece of his holdings, Lord Rannulf made the steward's stipend Faucon's duty along with the upkeep of Blacklea, whatever that amount might be. Aye, and if Faucon stayed another year, he'd add a rent payment to his costs. On top of that, Lord Rannulf got the wife of his choice for his brother without incurring the king's usual fee for approving a marriage contract, which was substantial.

And, the nobleman avoided the work required of the Keeper's position without ever threatening the love Bishop William held for him.

Faucon's eyes narrowed, even as he once again fought the urge to laugh. Until this moment he'd had no idea his cousin's elder brother was such a cutpurse.

Apparently there was more than one man among the FitzHenry brothers who owned the urge to pull pranks.

"Oh look," Lady Marian said, once more pointing out the window to indicate a pair of racing children. She sent that amazing smile of hers in his direction. "Best prepare yourself. You are about to meet my sweetlings."

Together they turned to face the door. A moment later, footsteps pounded up the stairs, then a lad of no more than six and a lass a few years older hurtled into the chamber. Pushing and shoving at each other, they raced across the room, each trying to reach their mother first.

The boy, a handsome child with fair hair and his mother's blue eyes, won the race. "Maman, it's not fair that you said Mimi gets to sleep in the loft with me."

"Why should I have to sleep on the floor just because I am a girl?" his sister complained as she stopped just out of her brother's reach, her skirts still swinging about her legs.

Faucon caught his breath in admiration. Unlike her plainer mother, Marian's daughter was beautiful. Thick dark hair spilled out of a loose braid to frame her fine-featured oval face, set with bright blue eyes she'd inherited from her dam.

"For shame," their mother scolded both of them, taking each by the shoulder to give them a shake. "You have embarrassed yourselves before our new master, Sir Faucon. What sort of hellions must he now think you?"

"I think they are children," said Faucon, extending his hand to the lad. "I am Sir Faucon de Ramis, knight of the realm and son of Thomas de Ramis. Who might you be?"

The boy glanced nervously at his mother, who nodded and released him. He took Faucon's hand, his tiny fingers surprisingly firm as they gripped Faucon's larger ones. "I am Robert, son of Sir John, steward of

Blacklea, sir. Well met and well come to Blacklea."

"A fine name, Robert," Faucon said. "And you are?" he asked of the lass.

She shot him her mother's dazzling smile, but there was a sweetness to the way her mouth curved that tugged at Faucon's heart. "I am Marianne, daughter of Sir John of Blacklea," she replied, offering a quick bob, "but everyone calls me Mimi because my name is too like my mother's. Well come to Blacklea. I know you will like the bedchamber here because," she slanted a look at her brother, "it doesn't have a dirt floor."

Marian shot a look heavenward. "I pray you, blessed Virgin, have pity on my hopeless daughter, who will never marry because she cannot learn to control her tongue. Come," she took her progeny by the shoulders once again. "We will leave Sir Faucon to the peace of his own thoughts."

She looked at Faucon. "I've already seen to it that your steed be taken to the stable and cared for. Our cook knows you will require a meal, although I fear it can be just soup, bread and cheese. With two noblemen and all those huntsmen here for the past two days, and it being the harvest season, we've no meats left in store at the moment, although there will be fresh mutton on the morrow," she added with a quick lift of her brows. "I'll also send a man to help you disarm. Should he bring up your saddle pack? Have you any other belongings?"

With her final question everything in Faucon shifted. He looked at Marian feeling stunned and off-balance. "This is real. I'm not dreaming. I truly am the new master of Blacklea?"

She nodded. "Indeed you are, good sir. May God have mercy on your soul." Offering him yet another impertinent wink, she marched her children from the hall.

Chapter Four

"Sir Faucon? Hsst. Sir?"

Faucon blinked awake and squinted. By that reaction alone could he tell he'd slept longer than he'd intended.

The bedchamber had three arrow slits in the east wall that served as windows. Even though the shutters were closed over them, bright fingers of light, evidence that the rain had not returned, streamed between the slats and cracks to reach the center of the bed.

With a sigh, he rolled onto his back then smiled. His bed. Not the cot in the corner of the hall he slept on at home, but his own bed in his own private room. It was more luxury than he'd ever expected to possess, and it would remain his rent-free for a whole year.

A nice bed it was, too. It had a feather mattress and posts at each corner of the frame that held aloft a wooden ceiling. Thick blue drapes trimmed in red hung on three of its sides. When closed, they trapped heat within the confines of the interior. And, if he hadn't grown too warm last night and pushed them back against their posts, they would also have kept out the light.

Stretching, his muscles popping, he sat up and looked toward the door. It was barely ajar and he could see no figure in the opening.

"Who is it?" he called, rubbing his eyes.

"It's me, Robert." Marian's son pushed his head between door and frame to look into the chamber. "Maman sends me to tell you that a man has come from the priory to lead you to Priors Holston. The brother who was here yesterday sends word that you must go there as soon as you can, because a man in that village has been killed."

The messenger from St. Radegund's was a scrawny young man with a thatch of red hair and a badly mended tunic worn over bright blue chausses. Faucon let him ride on Legate's rump for their four-mile journey to Priors Holston.

They looked a pair, the two of them, both ragamuffins. Because Faucon hadn't wanted to either don his armor or ruin his most expensive clothing with horse sweat, he wore only his under-armor. The thick woolen chausses that protected his skin from his chain mail leggings served as stockings, while atop his shirt he wore his knee-length padded gambeson as a tunic. His sword belt, to which he'd tied his purse, held the gambeson closed around his waist.

Priors Holston proved to be almost three times the size of Blacklea, but it looked much the same. There was a similar patchwork of fields and orchards and the usual whitewashed cottages topped with thatch. Woven withe fences enclosed each home's toft, the area around the house itself, and croft, the back garden that every peasant family counted on to supply provender. The only difference was that Priors Holston was empty of men.

In the smithy, the bellows were silent, the coals slowly cooling. Two women, their sleeves rolled up above their elbows, used large wooden paddles to shift baking bread in the village's domed-shaped ovens. In front of another cottage, a woman sat on a stool using a wicked-looking awl to lace sole to upper as she assembled a boot. As they passed a carpenter's work shed, its door standing wide, Faucon saw a rasp laid across the top of a half-built chest. It was as if the man had ceased his labors mid-stroke.

"This is so strange," his guide said from behind Faucon, his voice alive with surprise. "Do you suppose the villagers and hundred have already been called for the inquest jury?"

That was exactly Faucon's thought. Was Brother Edmund's arrogance great enough that he'd dare convene the jury before his employer's arrival? The possibility was enough to make Faucon's breakfast–a tasteless dry oatcake and a cup of hastily gulped sheep's milk–burn in his gullet.

"We'll soon know," he replied.

"Soon indeed, as we're close now," the messenger agreed from behind him. As Faucon urged Legate back into a trot, the man pointed to a turn in the grassy, rutted track that led through more cottages. "Follow this, then ride straight on to reach the mill." It was Priors Holston's miller who had died.

A few moments later, his horse splashed through a small stream. It wasn't much of a brook, not even knee-deep to Legate. On the opposite bank they skirted a line of coppiced alder trees and ended up on a narrow lane, where they stopped abruptly. They had no choice.

The inquest jury had indeed been called. From boys of twelve to tottering ancients, there were more men here than Faucon had seen in one place since King Richard's army. They filled the lane and packed into the front garden of a nearby cottage, then spilled through the passage between cottage and fence to cram its expansive back garden.

So many rural commoners in one place made for a colorful crowd, what with their homespun tunics and stockings dyed every hue that could be wrung from woodland or field: the brown of walnut shells, the blue of woad, elderberry red, and the green of wood sorrel.

It was a quiet gathering in spite of its size. Most of

the men stared at the mill, the two-story wooden building next to the cottage. From atop Legate, Faucon could see the front half of the tall waterwheel pinned to its side.

"Let us pass," he called to those in the lane as he urged Legate forward.

Although men shifted and stepped this way and that, trying to move out of his way, they couldn't make enough space for the comfort of his horse. Legate began to sidle nervously. Calm for his breed he was, but he was still battle-trained and that made him more than capable of killing with his hooves. Faucon turned his horse back to the copse of alder trees at the head of the lane.

"Stay here with him," he told the priory's messenger after they dismounted. "Let him graze as he will, but keep him well away from the crowd. Whatever you do, do not leave him."

This time when Faucon reached the back of the crowd, he caught the attention of the closest man, a doddering ancient with sparse white hair. "Where is the dead miller?"

The man grinned at him. Not a tooth remained in his mouth. "Halbert's been et by his wheel."

"Aye, drowned, he was. And no better fate could have befallen him," added another man at least a score of years younger than the first. This one's lips curled in satisfaction. "A vicious and uncivil man, Halbert Miller was," he said, "though no one dared say such things to his face, him having been a soldier in his youth and as good with his fists as he was."

As more than a few of those around the speaker nodded their agreement, Faucon began threading his way through the crowd. There was an advantage to being both armed and unknown. Every man he touched either stepped back in instinctive reaction to Faucon's sword or to get a better look at the newcomer. He made his way past the surprisingly large cottage and through the opening in the low wall that surrounded the mill.

More men filled the mill courtyard. Faucon started through their midst only to catch sight of a single small woman standing beside the stone steps that led to the mill's raised doorway. At that same instant, Brother Edmund's voice rang out from around the corner and the millwheel.

"Once again I protest, my lord sheriff! By the order of the Archbishop of Canterbury, only this shire's new coronarius has the right to move this body. You must desist. As God is my witness, you are no longer authorized to examine the bodies of the dead." The monk's cry was fraught with indignation.

"I know nothing of any new royal servant being named in my shire," another man replied. Although his words were measured and calm, tones of threat filled his gruff voice. "Therefore, I cede nothing of my right to uphold the law, certainly not to you. What sort of monk are you that you dare say me 'nay?' If you think your Church can protect you from me when you so usurp your position, you are wrong."

Faucon put his shoulder to all who yet stood between him and his new clerk. As he rounded the building, he came up short at the edge of the mill channel. Here, the stream Legate had crossed only moments ago was no burbling brook. Instead, the miller had dammed it behind his mill, creating a pond, then funneled it into a stone channel. The mill race was deep enough that the water became a rushing cataract beneath the wheel.

The wheel wasn't turning at the moment, not with the miller's body trapped beneath it. But if it had been moving, Edmund would have been riding it. The monk had his arms wrapped around the rim closest to him and a foot hooked around one of the slick, moss-dabbled paddles—the short lengths of wood placed between the rims to catch the water and turn the wheel.

Edmund's attention was focused on the three men across the race from him, where a sturdy wall supported the end of the great timber axle on which the wheel rotated. All three wore hardened leather hauberks over their tunics, and swords belted to their sides. One squatted at the edge of the race, his wet sleeves clinging to his arms. Another sought to use his dagger as a tool to loosen the brake, the massive wooden clamp that kept both axle and wheel from turning.

The third man stood with his arms crossed over his chest and his back to the support wall. Although his clothing beneath his hauberk appeared travel-stained and worn, this one's sword belt was chased with silver. Of medium height, he was barrel-chested, with sandy hair shot with gray; his face, all sharp lines and weathered creases, was framed by a grizzled reddish beard, worn heavier than was the fashion.

But it was the flatness of his expression that held Faucon's eye. He'd seen that same look on the faces of old warriors, soldiers who'd dealt out so much hurt in their lives that their hearts had turned to stone. By his expression alone would Faucon have known this was the sheriff, the man Marian thought could suck the marrow from a younger man's bones.

"I am here, Brother Edmund," Faucon announced, then offered the sheriff a brief bow. "I am Sir Faucon de Ramis, the newly-elected Keeper of the Pleas in this shire."

Although he spoke in his native French, his announcement stirred life in the watching commoners. Those who understood him passed his name among the others. It moved from man to boy, lip to lip, until the echoing syllables took on the sound of a surprised question.

Across the race, the crouching soldier eased back on his haunches to better see the newcomer; the other man

41

paused in his efforts to look over his shoulder. The sheriff's gaze shifted to Faucon. Nothing changed in his flat expression.

"Sir Faucon," Brother Edmund said, offering his better a nod of greeting without giving up his precarious position on the wheel, "this is Sir Alain, lord sheriff of this shire. Sir Alain, I say again. From the moment of Sir Faucon's election yesterday, he was charged with the examination of all unnatural deaths in your shire. It is now his exclusive right."

Sir Alain's arms opened, his right hand coming to rest upon his sword hilt. "I do not know you," he said to Faucon.

"You would not," Faucon replied evenly. "I have spent little time in this shire."

"Then how came you to be coronarius?" the sheriff asked. "I was yet at court when the announcement was read. Keepers of the Pleas are to be of their shire."

"The lands that are my inheritance through my lady mother lie at the edge of the Forest of Arden," Faucon replied. "As of last night, I also took possession of Blacklea Village, along with all its rights and rents, and was elected as Keeper. If you wish to know of my election, it might be best if you ask after it of Lord Graistan and my lord uncle, Bishop William of Hereford."

That information set a muscle to twitching along Sir Alain's jaw line. Otherwise, he stood as a statue, his hand yet resting on his sword hilt. The quiet stretched.

From the reeds along the brook bank below the mill a small bird warbled. The water danced and played in the day's bright sun, tumbling merrily over the back of the dead man. The dark-haired miller seemed to be sleeping chest-down in the race, one cheek pillowed on the stony bottom. His right arm was caught beneath the right rim of the wheel while his shoulder was pressed to the floor of the channel, held down by one of the paddles. He wore only his shirt and a dark blue tunic with no chausses to cover his legs or shoes upon his feet. It was the manner in which about half the men in the yard were dressed.

At last the sheriff gave a single brusque nod, then pivoted. "Leave it," he told the soldier who was working at the screws that closed the brake. "We have other matters to attend."

With that, the three men made their way along the far edge of the race channel to where it ended in front of a fuller's property, or so Faucon assumed. Nowhere else would lengths of cloth be held taut on tenterhooks in large stretching frames. The men and boys gathered among the drying fabric swiftly parted to allow their lord sheriff and his soldiers to pass.

The instant the three could be seen no more, a collective sigh left the gathering. Men began to shuffle and shift. Low conversations broke out among the crowd. So many muttering men had a sound like distant thunder.

At the wheel, Edmund freed his own long slow breath and released his grip. He stepped carefully onto the edge of the race, his back against the wall of the mill behind him.

"Sir Faucon, that is Halbert the Miller," he pointed to the man caught beneath the wheel. "According to the fuller, who was the first finder and who most properly raised the hue and cry with his neighbors, it seems Halbert fell into the race last night and drowned when he was drawn beneath the wheel and could not win free."

Edmund curled a proprietary hand around the wheel. "You must claim this wheel as *deodand*. It must be dedicated to the Church to cleanse it of the sin of murder."

Chapter Five

"**N**ay, you cannot take my wheel!" came a man's pained cry.

Faucon looked over his shoulder. The one who spoke was tall and auburn-haired, a young man no older than he.

"I am Stephen, only son of Halbert. Now that my father is dead the mill belongs to me, and it is my family's livelihood," this Stephen said, not the slightest sign of grief for his deceased sire in his hazel eyes. "Without the wheel, we will starve."

His protest teased a muted rumble of laughter out of the ranks of waiting men. The sound seemed to echo Faucon's thought that the miller's son didn't look like a man in danger of starving soon. If Stephen's powerful form was a testimony to the physical requirements of turning grain into flour, his attire was hardly that of a working man. His ankle-length tunic was made of fine wool, trimmed with braid shot with glinting, golden threads, although smut dulled the gleam of the expensive trim at its hem. Then again, millers were famous for their wealth, which some said was ill-gotten, stolen *koren* by *koren* from the bags of wheat, rye, barley and oats entrusted to them to grind.

Faucon shook his head. "Livelihood or not, if the wheel killed your sire, I must take it into custody. You know as well as I that it must be given to the Church so the sin of murder can be rinsed from it. That is the law."

"My wheel didn't kill him. I'll show you the one who did," the son snapped.

He turned and stepped around the corner. There was a female shriek. When Stephen reappeared, he held the arm of the petite woman Faucon had noticed in the courtyard. She wore a worn red undergown beneath an undyed linen over-gown. A clean white head cloth covered her brown hair. Although middle-aged, he didn't gauge her old enough to be Stephen's dam. Her left eye was blackened and her expression was twisted with tears.

"This is the one who murdered my sire. If my father is in the race, it's because she pushed him, as sure as I live and breathe, doing so because he had finally proved that she made a cuckold of him." His accusation set the crowd to muttering louder this time.

The woman hardly looked the part of either murderess or harlot. If she'd ever been pretty, her beauty had faded long before someone had taken his fists to her.

"I didn't kill my husband, and it's not true that I betrayed my marriage vows," she protested softly, speaking the tongue of the commoners as she scrubbed the tears from her face with the backs of her hands. "If only I had known Halbert was so jealous before we wed. He saw my betrayal in every man's innocent glance, and no word I spoke could change his mind.

"As for last night, after he gave me this," she gently touched her fingertips to the bruise on her eye, "I ran from him, going to Susanna the Alewife's house, as I have done all too often of late. When I left Halbert he was standing right there," she pointed to the spot on the edge of the race. "So Simon Fuller can attest."

"Indeed I can," called a man from those gathered in the fulling grounds across the race.

The fuller came forward to stand in the same space the sheriff had occupied, just below the wheel. Short and stout, he wore a thick fabric apron over a sturdy brown tunic, its sleeves rolled up above his elbows. Like Halbert Miller, the fuller's feet and legs were bare. The day's warm sun gleamed on the pale hair covering his shins and made his balding pate glow.

He offered Faucon a bow. "I am Simon, Fuller of Priors Holston, the first finder," he said, shifting into Faucon's native French, then returned to his own tongue to continue. "I was outside yesterevening when the shouting began between Halbert and Agnes. It was the same argument they ever had, Halbert accusing his wife of making him a cuckold. And I did last night as I have done far too often since they wed two months past. I crossed the race to separate them."

Simon turned to cast a stern glance at the miller's son. "But your father wouldn't be calmed last night, Stephen," he said, "not even after Agnes left. With you and 'Wina away for the night, he'd dived both sooner and deeper into his cups than usual. God be praised that he had, else he might have landed a few of the blows he aimed at me and done to me what he did to Agnes." He pointed from Agnes' bruised eye to his own, then continued.

"When I left him, he was standing right there," he pointed to the same spot Agnes had indicated at the edge of the channel. Then the fuller lowered his hand to the miller in the race. "And when I arose this morn, he was where he is now."

"Does that make it any less this outsider's fault for my father's death, Simon Fuller?" Stephen demanded. "You know he's been a changed man since he married again. Because of his new wife, he's taken to drink, and because of drink, he's been destroying our trade, and because of drink, he went into the race."

The fuller made a scornful sound. "You can blame Agnes if you want, but we all know your father was losing his mind to drink before they wed. All their marriage did was make sure my children and I lost our peace at night."

Stephen's mouth narrowed to a thin line. He looked at Faucon. "What say you to that, sir? You heard Simon Fuller. It wasn't the wheel that killed my sire, but his cup. You," he gave Agnes a shove that propelled her back toward the corner of the building, "go collect all the cups from the house and bring them to these men so they can be made deodand and dedicated to the Church. After that, pack your belongings. I won't tolerate you in my home any longer."

Burying her face in her hands, the woman turned and made her way toward the corner of the mill, her shoulders shaking in quiet sobs. The men in her path shifted aside to let her pass, a few offering quiet words of sympathy.

"No cups!" Brother Edmund shouted after her, once more speaking when he had no right. "If the wheel held Halbert under the water until he breathed no more, then it and only it must be removed and cleansed."

At the opposite side of the race, Simon Fuller crossed his arms over his chest and glared at Stephen. "Mayhap the wheel did kill him. After I left him, he started shouting. He went on for some time. I didn't need to hear what he was saying to know he was once again cursing your precious wheel."

Here the fuller paused to scan the watching men, gathering their attention before he continued his tale. "It's what he always did every time he got that besotted. He'd stand out here and shout his curses, then he'd start blaming the profits he'd earned from milling for attracting Agnes and saddling him with one he deemed a whore. When he was done, he'd fall into drunken slumber right on the edge of the race," he told them, then looked back at Stephen.

"Last night, after he finally fell silent, I thought I'd have some peace. I found the comfort of my bed, then of a sudden the wheel began again to turn, making all its usual racket. I was about to come out and confront your father, thinking he'd released the brake to spite me, when it stopped All remained blessedly quiet after that. That must have been when it happened. I suspect your father misjudged how besotted he was, having been almost knee-walking when I'd last seen him. In that state, opening the brake would have been too much for him. I'm guessing that when he yanked on the handle of his tool, it overbalanced him. As he fell into the race, his tool went flying to where we found it this morning."

He pointed to a spot a little way from the axle, then sneered at Stephen as he moved his hand to indicate the millwheel. "Or mayhap yon wheel reached out and grabbed him. Mayhap it dragged him into the water so it could eat him. Mayhap your wheel was as tired as Agnes at being held responsible for all the wrong your father found in what seems to me a blessed life. After all, Halbert didn't come by his trade through the sweat of his brow like some of us do. He got his wealth and comfort by marrying your mother and letting her teach him how to turn grain into flour." The fuller ladled scorn into his words. All who heard him called out their agreement.

"Mayhap you all should keep your opinions to yourselves." Stephen mocked, sending a scathing glance across the men nearest to him.

When the miller's son once more looked at Faucon, it was to plead again. "You cannot take my wheel. Without it, the village and the priory cannot grind their grain."

Faucon held up his hands. "Why don't we leave the matter of deodand until after we've extracted your sire and viewed his injuries as you know we must." He raised his voice so his words could be heard by as many as possible. "I'm sure you all would like to be back at your daily doings. The sooner the miller is viewed and the cause of his death is confirmed, the sooner you all may leave."

"But, Sir Faucon," Edmund started.

Faucon shook his head in warning, lowering his voice and shifting back to French to keep his words private between him and the monk. "Not now, Brother. No matter what protocol is expected, I'm not leaving that man under the wheel a moment longer. It is not meet."

Edmund's eyes widened. The look on his face said he did not approve, but he held his tongue.

"So how do we retrieve your father from the race?" Faucon asked of Stephen.

Rather than answer the question, Stephen turned toward the front of the mill. "Alf, the sheriff has gone," he shouted in the tongue of the commoners. "Come out and help me free your master from the wheel."

Faucon blinked in surprise. How had Stephen refused to aid to his lord sheriff when Sir Alain had wanted to extract the miller, and why? Somehow, Faucon doubted Edmund's protests—that the sheriff had no right to move Halbert—could have been that persuasive.

A moment later, a tall fair-haired man appeared. This man's worn leather apron covered a dusty green tunic, while the fabric of his shoes was so completely permeated with flour that there was no telling their original color. Tucked into the cord that tied his apron around his waist was a long-handled tool Faucon didn't recognize. As powerfully built as the new miller and no more than a dozen years Faucon's senior, there was something about the way this man moved that reminded Faucon of Stephen. Then this Alf nodded to the new miller; the movement of his head identified him as a servant rather than kin.

After Alf offered a show of respect to Brother Edmund and Faucon, he looked at his employer. "Master, we cannot divert the water," he told his better in the commoner's tongue. "Remember, your sire took apart the sluice gate the other day. He never got to rebuilding it."

Stephen gave an irritable groan at that news. "Well

then, we'll have to bring him out with the water still flowing, won't we?"

"So *we* shall," Alf replied with a grunt of amusement.

He stepped across the race and went to the brake on the axle. Faucon watched as the servant placed the tool from his apron over one of the two great screws that made a clamp of the twin blocks of wood. Alf yanked once, twice then a third time. The screw released. The wheel groaned as if alive, the axle straining to turn.

Ducking under the shaft, the workman put his tool to the second screw in the brake, then looked over his shoulder at Stephen. "Master, I'll need someone in the water to hold onto the old master when I free the wheel, else he'll just be drawn deeper."

"I cannot, not in this," Stephen said, the sweep of a hand indicating his fine attire.

"Not I," the fuller said, almost speaking over Stephen in his hurry to refuse. "I'll not risk Halbert's fate." There were many men within hearing who agreed with him.

Faucon shook his head in his own refusal. He'd never been comfortable in the water, and he certainly wasn't going in while wearing his heavy gambeson. He'd once seen a knight nearly drown in waist-deep water because the weight of his armor held him pinned to the bottom after he'd fallen.

"I can do it," a man called from the pond bank at the head of the race.

It was a monk wearing the same black habit as Edmund, although this brother's attire was already well wetted. On his head was a broad-brimmed hat that concealed most of his face, while on his back was a large leather pack, the feathery green fronds of Mare's Tail making a huge spray above the top of the pack. Stepping over the dam at the head of the race, the brother half-swam, half-slid down the channel in the waist-deep water until he neared the wheel. After laying his pack and his hat upon the edge near Alf's feet, revealing a face as wrinkled as a dried apple and a thick head of pure white hair, he reached into the water for Halbert's feet.

"Should I pull or push?" he asked Alf.

"Pull, Brother. Know that both wheel and water will be against you, so you'll have to pull with all your might just to hold him in place," the servant told him, then pointed to his deceased master. "Look how his shoulder is trapped beneath the paddle? Perhaps if you shift toward me and pull in this direction? If he's not caught too deeply, his shoulder and arm may slide out from underneath what pins it. Whatever you do, don't let him be dragged any farther under the wheel when it begins to move else he'll be jammed even tighter than before. I'll join you in the water the very instant I release this last screw. Are you ready?"

"I am," the monk replied.

With that, Alf pulled hard on the handle of his tool. The wheel gave another shuddering groan. It stuttered and strained, trying to rotate, but unable to do so as long as flesh and bone remained trapped beneath it. The monk shouted wordlessly as he pulled with all he had.

There was a subtle crack from beneath the water, and the paddle that trapped Halbert's shoulder broke. With the snap of bone as the rim rode over the dead man's arm, the wheel squealed and began to turn. The miller floated free.

Shouting out a surprised cry, the monk stumbled backwards in the water and lost his hold on Halbert's feet. Even as the current again took the dead man toward the wheel, Alf was there. Grabbing up his deceased master, he easily lifted Halbert out of the water and laid him on the ground beneath the turning axle. Then, hoisting himself out of the race, he returned to the brake and used his tool to secure it once more. When the screws were tight and the leather-lined wooden clamp once again snug around the axle, the wheel shuddered to a halt.

As it stopped, Faucon stepped to the other side of the channel, followed by Edmund and Halbert's son. The fuller came to stand with them. Not being as tall as Alf, the monk in the water found he couldn't lift himself up over the edge, so he splashed back up the race to find an easier spot to clamber out.

The miller had already grown stiff in death. This meant his head remained turned to the side, making it seem as though he rested his cheek on an unseen pillow. His arms were bent at the elbows as they had been in the race, which meant his hands now thrust awkwardly out to the sides. Beneath half-closed lids, his eyes were cloudy, but Faucon could still see that his irises were the same greenish color as his son's.

"So now that he's free," Edmund said, turning a shoulder to Priors Holston's new miller as he addressed Faucon in French, "we must do what we should always do first, and ask for proof of the man's ancestry. We must ascertain if he is English or Norman."

"Proof of Englishry is not required when the death is accidental, is it?" Faucon asked, frowning at Edmund as he followed him into the same tongue.

All men in England knew that a murdered man was considered to be from England's Norman ruling class until proved otherwise. But Halbert hadn't been murdered, not if the fuller was speaking the truth. The miller's drowning had been nothing but a drunken accident.

"It is required for all unnatural deaths and must be included in my record for this death. As you would have commanded of me if you'd been here when I arrived, I've already scribed the fuller's name as first finder, as well as recorded the names of the four neighbors he recruited to stand surety for his appearance at court, when the time comes for him to testify that he did raise this day's hue and cry," Edmund told him.

Stephen made an angry sound deep in his throat. "First, you want to steal my wheel, now you wish to extract a *murdrum* fine from me and my community?" the miller's son cried in outrage. "Well, you won't get it. My father was English through and through, and so will I swear, as will my wife and my aunt." He glared at the two officials of the royal court who faced him, his look daring them to say otherwise.

The wave of Edmund's hand swatted away the young miller's oath as if it were a pesky fly. "You can swear, you are his son. But no women can offer up an oath to prove Englishry."

"Alf can swear." Stephen drew his servant closer, his arm over the man's shoulder.

"I can and do," Alf agreed, his French so accented that Faucon could barely understand them. "Halbert was as English as I am."

"You offer up a servant?" Edmund shot back. "What proof is that?"

Faucon pressed his fingers to his throbbing temples as his far-too-empty stomach groaned. Twenty pounds a year wasn't nearly enough compensation for keeping Edmund as his clerk, and so he would tell his uncle at the first opportunity.

"Halbert came out of Essex and has only relatives by marriage in Priors Holston," someone shouted from the crowd in English. "How do we swear when we don't know how he was born?"

Stephen glared in the direction from which the voice had arisen, shifting back into English. "Do you want to pay that fine, Jos?"

Shifting back to French, he told Faucon, "My father may not have lived here all his life, but I can supply as many witnesses as there are men here, all of them willing to swear to his English lineage. What say you, Simon Fuller? Will you swear on my father's behalf?" Stephen demanded of his neighbor.

He offered the man a sly grin. "Perhaps I should mention that my sire told me he saw the mill you described, the one being used to full cloth, when last he was in Coventry."

The fuller's arms opened. His gaze clung to Stephen, the expression in his eyes wary. "Did he now? And what think you of such a use for your mill? Are you of a similar mind as your sire, that building such a machine on my side of the race would be a waste of time?"

"On the contrary, I think anything that brings you more prosperity will also benefit me," Stephen replied.

All the hostility drained from the fuller. He smiled, the movement of his mouth slow and pleased. "Then I have no doubt we'll be able to find all the witnesses this good knight needs from among this crowd."

Stephen shot a smug look at Edmund. "This chore is better done at the front of the mill, where more can see and hear us. Come, Alf. Simon."

As they crossed the race and made their way around the corner of the mill, the older monk who'd helped free Halbert from the wheel came to kneel at the dead man's side. With the water draining from his habit adding to the already substantial puddle forming beneath the miller, the brother pushed up one of Halbert's eyelids. As it rose a distinct edge to the cloudiness in Halbert's eye was revealed. The monk made a satisfied sound, then, as Faucon watched in surprise, put his face close to Halbert's and pried open the man's lips as if he meant to count the miller's teeth, then turned one of the miller's palms upward to look at it.

"Brother Herbalist!" Edmund protested. "What are you doing? Move back from the corpse. When I agreed to let you accompany me to Priors Holston this morning, it was only to share our devotions while we traveled in the same direction. It was not an invitation for you to intrude in the matters of your betters."

Faucon touched his clerk's arm. Edmund shot him a startled look, snatching his arm close to his side as if the touch pained him in some way.

"Brother Edmund, the miller's son will soon be collecting those who can swear to his father's ancestry," Faucon said. "Where are your quills and ink, your parchment and knife? I thought your purpose was to record all the details of these events. How can you do that without your accoutrements?"

Edmund expression shifted until he looked honestly stricken. "Fie on me! When the sheriff arrived, I left all inside the mill in my haste to stop him from treading where he is no longer allowed to go."

Then he glanced around the small space between the millwheel and the axle wall. "Impossible! I cannot write here, nor can the jury of the inquest witness the miller's body at this place. The space is too small. He'll have to be brought into the mill courtyard. Come with me so you can instruct the miller's servant to fetch his master's body for us," this servant commanded of his own master.

"In a moment," Faucon replied, but Edmund was already across the race and rounding the corner of the mill, all else forgotten save his own errand.

Faucon lowered himself onto one knee into the wet beside the monk and watched the herbalist run his hands over the front of Halbert's tunic. "What are you looking for, Brother Herbalist?"

"Colin," the monk said, sitting back on his heels to eye Faucon from under thick snowy brows. "I am Brother Colin to men who can stomach a lay brother and former tradesman who dares speak as an equal to those of better blood. Am I wrong to suspect you are such a man?" His dark eyes sparked with vibrant, intelligent life.

That made Faucon smile. "Brother Colin it is then," he replied. "In case you did not hear, I am Sir Faucon de Ramis, the newly-elected Keeper of the Pleas for this shire."

"Keeper of the Pleas?" the monk repeated in confusion.

"Brother Edmund might have used 'coronarius' to describe my new position," Faucon replied.

"Crowner, is it?" Brother Colin offered, his easy translation of the Latin word suggesting that he was fluent in both the Church's and his king's tongue as well as his own. "And what is it that a keeper or crowner does?"

"I'm not wholly certain as of yet, having only been elected a few hours ago," Faucon admitted. "I take it I will mostly be counting and recording the fees owed to king and court. This, I am told, is to prevent the sheriff from slipping a penny here and a penny there into his own purse. However, amongst all my counting duties is also the right to hold inquests over the bodies of those who die unnatural deaths."

"Huh. I expect our lord sheriff cannot have been too pleased to hear of your appointment, Sir Crowner," the monk said as he eyed Faucon much as Marian had the previous day. He looked back at Halbert and continued. "As for what I'm doing, I am confirming what I thought I saw when Halbert was lifted from the race–that the miller did not drown, but was dead when the one who killed him put him into the water."

His words took Faucon aback. He studied the miller. No matter how he looked, he saw nothing but a wet dead man.

"How can you tell that from a glance?"

"Hardly a glance," Brother Colin replied. "Let me show you what I see when I look at our miller. We'll start here." He once again maneuvered the miller's left hand so it was displayed palm up.

Faucon shrugged. "I see a hand as empty and as wrinkled as I would expect of one who'd been a night in the water."

"But what is it that you are not seeing?" Brother Colin asked. "Let us say it was you who'd fallen in the race. The water is pushing you toward the turning wheel. What would you be doing to prevent yourself from being dragged to your death?"

At the thought of being trapped under the water, Faucon's stomach turned and his throat closed. Even imagined it stirred panic. "I would grab whatever I could to save myself," he replied.

"So would I," the monk agreed. "Now, look at the wheel."

Faucon did as instructed. The miller had not been rigorous about cleaning his wheel. The paddles and rims were splotched with green moss and slick algae. He took Halbert's sinister hand from the monk to better examine it. It was clean.

"Do you mean that we should see marks on his hand when there are none? But that cannot be so strange. Wouldn't the water have washed all away?" Faucon asked.

As he spoke his gaze returned to the wheel, his thoughts turning as if driven by the water in the race. With Halbert's right shoulder trapped under the paddle, he had only his left hand to use. The most sensible place for him to grab would have been the left side of the wheel's wooden rim. Not that he could have saved himself by doing so. Once his shoulder was between the paddle and the stones, he was doomed. Still, in the desperation of drowning he would surely have torn at the wood with all his might as he fought for his life.

By the same token, the rim of the wheel was the only sensible place for him to have grabbed if he'd tried to save himself before the wheel had caught him. Again, he wouldn't have been able to stop the wheel, not with the greater power of the water turning it and pushing him toward death. Instead, as the miller clutched the wheel rim, it would have torn through his grasp, mostly likely tearing his flesh as well, as it moved.

In either event, if Halbert had battled to save himself, that fight should have left some sort of mark upon his skin. There was nothing on Halbert's palm, no cuts, stains, splinters or blisters, not even smut beneath his fingernails.

"He didn't claw at the wheel. He didn't try to save himself," he said. "Then again, the fuller says he was besotted. In that state he might not have been alert enough to try."

Brother Colin nodded in agreement. "True enough. What we see on the miller's hand doesn't prove he was dead when he went under the wheel. All it tells us is that he was either senseless when he entered the race or gave up to death without a fight. If either is true, then Brother Edmund will still have his deodand. However, this is not the only sign that dooms my brother to disappointment."

"If Brother Edmund is doomed to anything, it is that someday someone will murder him because he speaks with an 'honest' tongue," Faucon retorted quietly. "And the someone who does it might well be me."

The monk choked on a laugh, then cleared the humor from his throat. "I beg your pardon and our Lord's. It's not meet that I find amusement at my brother's expense.

"Now, look," he said and opened the miller's mouth.

Faucon did as commanded and looked. All he saw was a man's mouth filled with a tongue and a surprising number of fine, strong teeth, although they were a little snaggled in their arrangement. "What should I see?" he asked.

"A bit of foam. Those who drown often have a bit of

58

foam in their mouths or noses, even after being in the water far longer than Halbert was."

Closing the miller's mouth, Colin placed his hands at the center of Halbert's chest and pushed gently, then opened the man's mouth again. "Sometimes doing this will bring up more foam," he said in explanation, "but as you can see, there is nothing. That leaves us one step closer to satisfying the notion that our miller did not drown. Now, we must examine his eyes. What do you see?"

Again Faucon shrugged, this time feeling a little at odds because he had no idea what the monk wished him to see. "That they are half-open, and even though they are cloudy in death, I can see they are the same green color as his son's?"

Brother Colin once more pried up one of Halbert's eyelids. "Now what do you see?"

Once again Faucon noticed the edge to the milkiness that affected the lower portion of Halbert's eye. "The cloudiness ends where the lid was. Why is it like that?"

"When a man ceases to blink, his eyes dry where they are not covered by their lids. That is what happened here. Halbert's eyes began to dry the moment he ceased to breathe and blink. It's this more than anything else that convinces me he could not have drowned. You see, eyes cannot dry while under the water," he finished in satisfaction.

"How can you know all this?" Faucon demanded quietly. "Do men drown so often at your priory that you've learned these signs and can pronounce this without doubt? Perhaps I am wrong, but I somehow took the impression that St. Radegund's is a small place. I cannot think it sees tragedy of just one sort on so regular a basis."

Colin grinned. "For shame, you assuming such about me. Although you're right about St. Radegund's. It is small, with but a dozen men in residence. But neither is it my home," he said. "I work under the infirmarer at St. Michael's Abbey in Stanrudde. During the growing season, I visit all of our daughter and brother houses, helping them to collect and store the herbs needed to heal their sick."

Here, he paused to run his fingers through the feathery fronds that extended out of the top of the pack he'd laid upon the race edge. "There is never enough Mare's Tail, an herb good for treating any ailment, and no place better to find it than along the water's edge.

"As for my lack of doubt over how Halbert died, before I came to the Church, I was Stanrudde's apothecary. So aye, from the time I became a journeyman at eight-and-ten, I have dealt with death and dying, seeing folk move from this vale to the next in more variations than most can imagine. As the years went by, I could not help but notice that each sort of passing has its own distinct pattern. What my experience tells me today is that either Halbert is unique in the way he drowned or he did not drown at all."

Here, Brother Colin paused to cock his head and aim his lively gaze at Faucon. "So, if Halbert did not drown, then the wheel could not have killed him, therefore it cannot be deodand. Now, Sir Crowner, you tell me what follows that, other than Brother Edmund's disappointment."

The monk's expectant question transported Faucon to the abbey school of his childhood and the scholarly monks who had done their best to pound knowledge into his hard head. Only, unlike Brother Colin, there had never been a glimmer of kindness in those men's eyes as they prayed their reluctant student might guess correctly this time. Perhaps if there had been, Faucon wouldn't have been so grateful to become a knight instead of the priest or prebendary his mother intended.

"If the water and the wheel did not kill him, something or someone else did, because he is most definitely dead," Faucon replied like a dutiful student.

But as he gave the monk his expected answer, the thrill of the hunt overtook Faucon for the second time in as many days. The clean mouth, the half-milky eyes, these were spoor, tracks left by Halbert's killer. Just as when Faucon chased game animals, he would read these signs and track down the one who had ended the miller's life.

Now here was something that caught and held his interest. And here was the compensation he needed to make this crowner's job, Edmund included, tolerable. God willing, there would be as much sport in this sort of hunting as there was when he tracked the wily fox.

He grinned. "Brother Colin, if you can discern the means of Halbert's death, I will discover the man."

Chapter Six

"**W**ell said," Colin replied, offering the shire's new coronarius a nod of approval. "So now that we know Halbert did not drown, how else could his life have been ended? I am certain in my soul that he didn't die as some men of his age and mine do, simply dropping where they stand. Dead men don't move of their own volition and we know the miller lay out of the water long enough for his eyes to dry. Nor was he throttled or garroted since nothing marks his throat.

"And, unless he was poisoned, it doesn't seem that he was killed in this tunic." Colin once more ran his hands over the front of Halbert's garment. "I can find no blood stain or sign of damage that a weapon capable of dealing out death would make."

"Then we must remove his clothing as the law requires to find what hides beneath it," Faucon replied swiftly. "I need to confirm for myself and Brother Edmund's record that someone truly did murder to him."

"If you can lift him, perhaps I can remove his clothing," Colin replied.

Faucon slid his arms beneath the big man only to discover how heavy and unwieldy the dead Halbert was. That made the ease with which Alf had raised him out of the race a feat indeed. When Brother Colin's second attempt to pull up the man's sodden, knee-length tunic failed, Faucon put the corpse back on the ground and scanned those men and boys standing closest to the race.

Between the sheriff's departure and Stephen's absence, all interest in the death of Halbert the Miller had ended. On both sides of the race men had relaxed into small groups, all of them laughing and talking until the noise level challenged the ears. A few among those waiting had stretched full out on the ground to nap in the sun despite the noise. On the fuller's property, a group of boys now dashed between the large frames, tossing a stick between them and shouting joyously as they indulged in an unexpected holiday.

Faucon came to his feet, catching the attention of those just across the race from him. "Come help us," he commanded them in their own tongue.

Most held back, shaking their heads and making the sign of the cross. Only two, a man and a boy who looked younger than the twelve years he must be to participate in the jury, crossed the race. These two wore well-tended, if worn, yellow tunics over expertly patched red chausses. As the boy gaped at the dead miller, his elder, a thick-bearded man at least twice Faucon's age, first offered a respectful nod to Colin, then bowed to Faucon.

"I think you speak our tongue well, sir," the slight man said to Faucon. "That's a blessing as I fear I do not speak yours at all."

"So I am vain enough to believe," Faucon replied to the man in English. "You can understand me?"

"Well indeed, sir." The man smiled, his tone pleased. "I am Drue, son of Nicole. How may my apprentice and I assist you?"

"We must expose the miller's body so his injuries can be viewed," Brother Colin replied, "and to do so, we need to remove his clothing. I think we'll require more than just you two to do that. He's a heavy man."

"I think you're wrong," Drue replied with a cocky smile. "And I also think you'll be glad 'twas we two who came to help."

He patted the leather purse that hung from his belt. Three needles had been threaded through its front. "It's much easier to take apart Halbert's garments than to try to remove them. I remake and sell used clothing here in Priors Holston, when not tending my fields. Opening seams is just what this lad and I might be doing today, if not for the call to attend the jury," he said.

"Aye, that will suffice," Faucon replied in surprise and satisfaction.

"Then I will do it for you, but only if you let Stephen Miller know that it was done at your command. I dare say Stephen is his father's son, and anger can often get the better of him. This tunic must be new, for I've not seen it on Halbert before this day. Although he didn't purchase it from me, I suspect it was meant to replace one he'd torn so badly I couldn't mend it so that the repair didn't show."

Here, the commoner grinned. "What I lost by not selling him this new tunic, I made up when Halbert sold me the ruined one. He's a big man. I got his torn garment for next to nothing, and sold it three times over, after turning it into garments for boys."

Such a profit was no surprise. Garments and the fabric from which they were made were worth their weight in gold. In the de Ramis household, Faucon's mother stored even their oldest and most worn garments in locked chests.

"I hereby command you to do as you must to bare the miller's corpse," Faucon told the tailor.

The tailor nodded, then drew from his purse a scissor no larger than his hand. Carefully crafted, its looped handles fit neatly into his palm. "Step aside and let me at my work," Drue commanded of his betters.

Colin came to his feet, joining Faucon as they backed away from Halbert. The tailor swatted his apprentice across the top of his head. The boy squeaked more in surprise than pain, and looked up at his master.

"Stop gawking, lad, and hold the garment taut as I've shown you, so we can open it here," he said, pointing to the left side of Halbert's tunic.

Once the two had stretched the fabric between their hands, the tailor slid his shears up the length of the seam that joined front to back. Threads popped and snapped as he did the same to the joining between sleeve and tunic. When both were open, the lad pulled the left front of the tunic up and over Halbert's crushed right shoulder. The hem of the garment slid over the edge of the race to once more enter the water.

Beneath his tunic Halbert wore an undyed linen shirt. This the tailor also opened along the seam line, and the boy folded back the pieces to reveal Halbert's torso. The miller's chest was covered in thick coarse hair from the base of his throat until it disappeared beneath the voluminous folds of his braies, the undergarment that all men wore beneath their clothing.

Over the course of his life, Faucon had seen a great many wounds, of late most of them the gaping holes left by war, including a lance thrust that had torn a man in twain, spilling his entrails as the parts of him dropped in opposite directions. He'd even seen his cousin Gilliam gored so badly by a boar that it had been a wonder he had survived.

Save for Halbert's crushed right shoulder and arm, the miller's chest wore only two obvious signs of injury. Both were old and well-healed. Just below his left shoulder was the almost star-shaped mark where an arrow had penetrated his flesh, then been pulled out again. Judging by the shape of the scar, the journey out had done more damage than the journey in. The second was the mark of a sword that ran across his chest from his collarbone to the base of his ribs. It was easy to see, because Halbert's chest hair had never grown back along it. More than the arrow mark, this scar confirmed the miller's previous life as a soldier.

Colin returned to Halbert's side to run his hands over the man's chest. "You must be here. Where are you hiding?" he asked of the wound he sought.

A moment later, his fingers circled over the center of Halbert's chest, where his heart nestled beneath flesh and bone. "Here is something."

Brushing aside what concealed it, Colin revealed a puncture wound just to the left of the miller's breastbone. "The placement could mean a heart wound. What say you? Do you know what could have made this hole, and could it have ended the miller's life?" he asked of Faucon.

It was a fair question, directed at a man who'd happily spent almost half his life training with every sort of lethal weapon, so he might use them on the battlefield to kill other men in every possible way a life could be ended.

Faucon examined the wound. It was round and seemed too small to be deadly until he probed it with the tip of his little finger. The wound was larger than it first looked, having closed in on itself after the weapon exited. No blood crusted around it, but that was no surprise, not with Halbert in the water so long.

At last, he sat back on his heels. "The blade of whatever made this left a hole no larger than the tip of my smallest finger. And as you say, Brother Colin, the wound is in the right place and at the correct angle to do damage to Halbert's vital organs, whether heart or lung. Because there is only one wound and it is neither torn nor distended, as might happen if the blade had been repeatedly thrust into him along that same path, I believe Halbert's death came with a single thrust of this weapon. That is certainly not improbable, not if that thrust penetrated his heart on the first blow. I once saw a man drop dead within the space of a few breaths when an arrow pierced his chest and lodged in his heart."

Now Faucon used his forefinger to trace a circle around the hole. "I see no bruising on his chest, when I think I should," he said. "To kill with but one blow demands a certain amount of force. In my mind, the thrust should have been powerful enough that the hilt of the weapon would have marked him. That is, if the hilt made contact with his flesh. Because there is no bruise, I can only guess that this weapon is either long enough that the hilt didn't touch him when the blade entered, or it has no hilt."

He shook his head, finding it hard to imagine either case. "But what a strange weapon that would be. Not to mention one with a very odd shape. Nothing I've wielded has a blade this round, much less a long round blade with no hilt. That leaves me thinking what killed Halbert must be a tool of some sort."

As Faucon said this, one bit of knowledge knit to a piece he hadn't realized he already had in store. The woman he'd ridden past on the way to the mill this morning, the one sewing together a boot. She had been using an awl, a tool about the length of his hand and with a shank that must have been at least half as thick as his little finger.

"A tool, indeed," he said and smiled at Colin. "It's the damage done by an awl we're looking at here. And since the handle didn't bruise his chest, I'm thinking it was an awl with a long shank. Now there's an awkward weapon for sure."

Faucon extended his hands over Halbert's chest as if he held the tool he imagined. With his right hand cupped about the non-existent handle of a workman's tool, he put his left at the opening of the puncture wound. "Remember, it can enter Halbert once and only once, and the handle will leave no bruise upon his flesh. See how with such a long shank I must keep a steady slow hand to guide it into him?"

When his right hand, the one gripping the invisible handle, was an inch or two short of Halbert's chest, he paused. "But could such a gentle stroke actually pierce his heart and cause his death? I cannot say for certain, but I doubt it."

Then he shifted his pretended grip on his imaginary tool until his pinched fingers seemed to hold something slender and handleless. "But if the awl has no handle, which would mean it is more needle-like, it becomes much easier to guide."

Again, he pushed the non-existent tool into Halbert until his pinched fingers almost rested on the man's skin. "But here I am again, with no way to drive my weapon into the man with the force I believe necessary for a lethal blow. Worse, how do I remove it from him without tearing or disfiguring the wound, for that is what happened. Moreover, if his heart is pierced, he will bleed. Now I must not only remove my tool, I must do it while both the awl and my hands are slick with blood."

Colin held up a forestalling hand. "Never mind all that. The better question is how you get Halbert to stand still while such a weapon is pushed so exactly into him? I say that is the greatest trick," he finished in wonder.

"Easier than you think in all instances," Drue the Old Clothes Seller replied with confidence. "I have no need of a handle, not when I have this."

He pulled one of the needles from the front of his purse and held it up so Faucon could see the loop of thread through its eye. Holding out his opposite arm, Drue pushed the needle into the fabric of his sleeve but didn't draw it all the way through. "In it goes," he said, then took hold of the thread loop and pulled the needle out again, "and out it comes.

"As for adding power to my thrust." Drue brought out a tiny metal cup from his purse and placed it on top of his middle finger, the one on the hand in which he held the needle. Smiling, he tapped this cup's metal base against the end of the needle he held. "With the eye end of my needle braced on this, I can drive its tip through the thickest of fabric with ease, and it goes exactly where

68

I will it every time."

"Aye, that would work," Faucon replied in new excitement. "With the awl's butt braced on something, say the flat of a dagger's blade, and its tip properly placed against Halbert's chest, a sharp thrust would send it deep into the miller's heart with all the power necessary to kill him. Once the damage is done, a quick yank on the cord, if it has no handle, and out it comes."

His excitement dissolved with his next breath. "Nay, none of this can be. Brother Colin is right. The only way Halbert could have been killed was if he lay still and allowed those bent on doing their worst to murder him."

"And so Halbert would have done, if he was as besotted as Simon Fuller says," Drue retorted. "Once Halbert had enough ale in him, he'd fall into a slumber so deep that no amount of prodding or shouting stirred him. At the last two village feasts, Alf and Stephen have had to carry him home because he was senseless. If Halbert was like that last night, he'd have been a lamb at the slaughter."

Faucon almost gaped. Could there be a better opportunity for stealthy murder than while a man was dead drunk? "So he would be," he agreed.

With that, the bits and pieces in his mind began to assemble and the trail he followed shifted, curving unexpectedly. He leaned forward to examine Halbert's undergarment, which was held closed about his waist by a simple knotted cord. Faucon examined the voluminous folds, shifting makeshift pleats this way and that. No obvious blood stains marred the creamy undyed linen.

"Tailor, tell me. Do you see any sign of damage to Halbert's garments? Was an awl like the one I've described thrust through them?" Faucon asked, certain he already knew the answer but wanting confirmation.

Drue pulled the pieces of Halbert's tunic and shirt back over the man who'd owned them, then ran his fingers across the breast of the tunic. "There's nothing," he reported. "The awl that made that wound would have punched the same size hole through the fabric as it did his chest. It wouldn't necessarily have torn or gashed the cloth, but the weave would surely have parted, stretching around the shank to let it pass. Even after the awl was removed, and even after his garments spent hours soaking in the water, I think I would still find a gap or edge where it entered and exited the cloth. All I feel on the front of this tunic is unblemished woolen fabric, far finer than any Simon Fuller has ever produced," he added snidely.

Faucon offered Colin a grim and knowing smile. "Since there's no blood on his shirt or tunic, I think our miller was unclothed when he took the wound that killed him," he said. "What we see here is no accidental killing, nor a murder driven by passion that is later regretted. This is a death well-planned. Not only did the one who ended Halbert's life choose a weapon that would leave an insignificant wound, he stripped the senseless man of his garments before he delivered the killing blow, so they would not be stained as Halbert bled his last. This was done to conceal the true cause of his death and befuddle us all."

"Ah, so that is why I found nothing upon his garments to guide me to the death wound," Colin said with a nod.

"And that is also why you'll find no trace of blood here." The sweep of Faucon's hand indicated the clean stretch of hard-beaten earth around the wheel. "Not all heart wounds spurt blood, but they most definitely can. I wager our senseless miller was undressed here, then carried to some hidden place where any blood he might shed wouldn't be noticed. In that hidden place, the one who delivered the blow that ended his life let him lie there until he bled his last." He looked at Colin. "That is when his eyes dried."

Brother Colin nodded. "Aye, and since they did dry, we can assume his wound oozed for some time. This one had no choice but to wait until it ceased. If he didn't wish the means of Halbert's death to be discovered, then he couldn't risk the wound leaving a telling bloodstain on Halbert's shirt or tunic."

"Just so," Faucon said, then pointed to the race. "After Halbert's wound ceased oozing, he was carried back here, washed clean by the race and redressed. The brake was released, Halbert was lowered into the water and swept under the wheel. Once he was lodged, the brake was reset. Then Halbert's killer retired, going to his nightly rest, convinced he had misled us all. He expected today's inquest to render only one verdict—that the besotted miller had fallen into his race and been drowned under his own wheel."

With that, Faucon offered Colin a respectful bend of his head. "And that is what would have happened here today, if not for you, Brother. I would never have recognized the meaning of the miller's cloudy eyes, and would have done Halbert and his family an unwitting injustice. I am most grateful for your aid."

The monk smiled. "Then I give thanks that our Lord sent me your way this day. I'm glad I could assist you, and even more pleased to have met you, Sir Crowner. I don't doubt you'll find the man who did this to the miller."

Then the monk paused and cocked his head to the side. "I do have one thought, though. As much trouble as we had trying to undress the miller when he was dead, could all this have been accomplished by one man alone?"

Faucon's gaze flew to what he could see of the miller's cottage. In that oversized house lived the wife Halbert had abused and a son who did not grieve for him. Who else had cause to wish Halbert dead? Who else had the tool that opened the brake on the wheel so it could be used to conceal what had really happened here?

Almost as swiftly, certainty faded. That made no sense. If Halbert were declared drowned by his millwheel, the wheel would be named deodand and confiscated. As Stephen had said, the cost of replacing the millwheel might well drive him to the brink of poverty, if not completely ruin him.

As for Agnes, while her bruises certainly gave her cause to wish her husband dead, it was clear her new freedom had come at a price. By Stephen's words, she was now without hearth and home. Faucon doubted her stepson would let her leave Priors Holston with a farthing more than she'd brought with her into her marriage, no matter what dower Halbert might have endowed upon her in their marriage contract. Indeed, he suspected she'd have to bring a plea for her dower to the royal court before Stephen gave it to her.

But most importantly, according to the fuller, neither Agnes nor Stephen had been at the mill last night to do the deed.

If not the miller's family, then who? Whoever it was must hate the miller and his kin with all his heart, for he'd concocted an elaborate scheme calculated to not only kill Halbert but destroy his family's livelihood.

"I need to find the place where Halbert bled his last," Faucon said, the huntsman in him demanding it. "I think it must be close by, but I guarantee it won't seem instantly obvious that a man died there." The care taken by the one who killed Halbert assured Faucon of that.

As he spoke, Alf and three others walked around the corner of the mill to stop across the race from them. The miller's servant looked at Brother Colin. "Will you speak for me, Brother? Please tell the knight that his clerk sends us to bring my master's body to the courtyard so the viewing may begin."

Chapter Seven

Faucon clenched his teeth, biting off the urge to shout in rage. Once more, Edmund trod where he had no right to step. This had to stop.

"Go as you must," Drue said to him, "leaving your search to me and my apprentice. We've already viewed Halbert and give our oaths that, before God, we hereby render the verdict of murder, with you as our witness. Oh, and if Stephen complains about his father's tunic, pay him no heed. Don't tell him, but I've a mind to repair it at no charge, given the importance of what lay hidden beneath the cloth. Perhaps with a little haggling, I can convince him my work is worth his grinding at least half of my grain at no cost," he added with a wink.

Faucon offered the tailor his thanks, then turned to Brother Colin. "Will you come with the miller's body for the viewing, to offer your explanations if required?"

"I will," the monk replied.

With that, Faucon looked at Alf, a man strong enough to lift Halbert without the aid of those he'd brought to help him this time. It remained to be seen if Alf was a man capable of carrying the besotted miller to the place of his death, then putting a dead Halbert into the race.

"Take up your master and bring him to the mill yard," Faucon commanded the workman.

Then, stepping across the race to make room for Alf and the others to do what they must, Faucon turned his back to the wheel and entered the mill's courtyard.

A makeshift catafalque, nothing more than a few planks of wood atop four barrels, now stood at the center of the yard near the entry gate. The mill towered over it, built as it was on a stone foundation half as tall as Faucon. Perhaps the additional height was needed to protect the building and its precious machinery from flood. Whatever the reason, the result was that the door to the mill stood high enough over the yard that three steps were needed to reach it. The top step widened into a spacious wooden porch before the door. It was here that Edmund sat, having claimed this space as his temporary scriptorium. His flask of ink, his knife and the container for his quills, as well as a bound roll of parchment, were all neatly arranged along the porch edge.

Faucon came to a stop at the base of the steps. His clerk set aside the short length of wood that presently served as his desk, then descended to join his new master in the yard.

"The time has come to begin the viewing," Edmund announced to his better.

"Is that so?" Faucon retorted, his voice low. "I don't recall commanding that."

His clerk blinked in surprise. "You haven't yet, but now you will. You must. This is how all inquests must be. Once we have recorded the oaths of those who swear to the miller's Englishry, as I have just finished doing, the time arrives for jury to view the body of the deceased. Until each man has seen the corpse and confirmed the manner of Halbert Miller's death, none may leave."

"*I* have not commanded the viewing to begin because *I* am not yet ready to do so," Faucon retorted, his eyes narrowed and his voice hard. As he spoke, he leaned even closer to the monk, his hand resting on his sword hilt.

A startled Edmund took a backward step, his gaze darting between Faucon's face and his weapon. "But you must begin now," the monk cried, almost pleading. "I vow if we don't, we'll be here all night waiting for so many to do as the law requires."

The logic in his words punctured Faucon's outraged pride. Edmund was right. It was almost midday and there were so many men waiting here. Who knew how long it might be before the place where Halbert bled his last was found? If Faucon delayed the viewing until then, it was entirely possible night could fall before the jurors were released.

Faucon eyed his clerk, pride battling common sense. "Brother Edmund, I concede your point," he said at last, his words stiff. "I also concede that I have much to learn from you. But it will not serve either of us if you persist in your present manner. Take caution to do no more than remind me of what is mine to do. Know that you command me at your peril."

Edmund made a sound that suggested ancient frustration, then pressed a fist against his temple as if his head ached. "But remind you is what I did," he protested, honest confusion filling his dark eyes. "Did I not send Alf to you so you could command him to bring the miller's body for the viewing?"

Irritation hissed from Faucon on a sigh as his pride admitted defeat. His hand opened over his hilt. Once again, he surveyed Edmund's writing tools on the porch. This time, his eye told him they weren't just neatly arranged. Nay, each piece stood precisely a hand's breadth from the next. In that precision, Faucon thought he understood Edmund's honest tongue and rigid world. Edmund found comfort and certainty in the exactitude of laws and rules. It was this certainty that gave a simple monk the courage to confront a baron, a bishop and a lord high sheriff, using nothing more than words as his sword and shield.

But like any weapon, Edmund's inflexibility cut both ways. Faucon would have wagered all he owned that his new clerk had once too often insisted that others apply the same rigor to their lives. That was likely how Edmund ended up without a house and trapped in his new position, one he considered a penance.

"I accept your explanation," Faucon said, turning what had not been a plea for pardon into an apology, "and agree that we must now begin the viewing."

Edmund's sigh was heartfelt. His face relaxed. "Now remember, all must pass by the dead miller. That doesn't mean they can mob the body, shoot a glance at Halbert and hurry on. Each man is required by law to look, and this should be done in an orderly fashion. That said, neither can any man linger for an unseemly time, else all the others will be delayed."

Apparently, Edmund meant to pretend as if nothing had gone awry between them. Faucon wondered if the monk expected that to serve as his apology. Although hardly polite, it was reasonable. Considering that attention to their duty was of prime importance at the moment, Faucon could tolerate reasonable, as long as Edmund neither gloated nor sulked. Such were the emotions not-Will ever aimed at Faucon, that was, when his brother wasn't swimming in his usual sea of sullen resentment.

"Good advice," Faucon said, then returned his attention to the mill yard as the men within it suddenly quieted.

Alf and his aides passed through their midst, carrying Halbert to the catafalque. Once the dead miller lay atop the planks, the crowd pulled back, men and boys arranging themselves in a cautious circle around their deceased neighbor. Brother Colin came to stand near Halbert's head. Stephen trailed after the smaller monk, stopping a short distance from the foot of his father's bier. Faucon kept his gaze on Halbert's son. If the mill's new master had any reaction to the wound that had ended his father's life, Faucon wanted to note it.

"Tell me this," he asked of Edmund without looking at his clerk. "As these men view the body, is it the law that we must point out to them the wound that caused the miller's death?"

"There is no need to show a wound unless it is clear that this was the injury that did cause death. Since Halbert's crushed shoulder and now-broken arm did not kill him, it isn't worthy of note," Edmund replied, his pedantic tone another reminder of the tutors Faucon had so despised in his youth. "You must only tell your witnesses to confirm the cause of the miller's death. You must say that he was drowned under his wheel, as I have already noted in our record."

Faucon shot the clerk a swift sidelong look. "You have already written that he drowned? Then ply your knife and scrape off those words, for they are mistaken."

Edmund's eyes flew wide. "I will not!" he protested, his voice rising in complaint. "I cannot. I am required to note the truth, and we all saw that Halbert had drowned."

"Did we?" Faucon asked with a quiet laugh, then crossed the yard to stand at the left side of Halbert's bier.

He scanned the ranks of the waiting men and boys, thinking to gather their attention. It wasn't necessary. To a one they already watched him.

"Come all, and view your deceased neighbor, Halbert the Miller," he called out in their tongue, his voice lifted to a shout so as many as possible could hear him.

"Wait!" Edmund called. "Don't forget to tell them they must swear before God that they will speak the truth if they give any information about the death, and do the same if asked to give any appraisals or assessments regarding the miller's property and the deodand."

Faucon looked at his clerk with a frown. "I think they cannot all hear me. If they cannot hear me, how will they all know to swear?"

That made Edmund blink in surprise. His mouth opened, but there seemed to be no answer on his tongue.

"We know what must be done," Alf said. "Ask for the oath. As those too far back to hear your voice catch the sound of the oaths being given, they will add their own vow to those that already ring out from in here."

"So it must be," Faucon replied, uncomfortable with this. How could an oath be true if the one demanding the oath couldn't hear the response of those who swore? Then again, who was he to question? Perhaps it was up to God to punish the foresworn.

"Swear before God that any assessments and information regarding Halbert Miller's death or his property you give will be honest and true," he demanded at the top of his lungs.

"I so swear!" The words rolled like distant thunder across the mill yard, then echoed out into the miller's croft and over the race into the fuller's yard. A final and faint retort came from the lane that ran before the miller's cottage.

Faucon nodded. "Then come all you jurors and view Halbert the Miller. You must look upon the wound that killed him, then confirm my verdict that he was murdered by persons yet unknown."

"What?!" Stephen shouted, his voice rising to an almost girlish squeal, his face twisted in abject surprise.

As he fell silent, his brows remained high on his forehead, his mouth yet agape. In the next instant, the miller's son bent at the waist, grabbing the edge of the board beneath his father's feet, as if he feared he would fall. Yet bent in twain, Stephen clung to the wood, panting and trembling. The sound of his gasping breath echoed in the quiet courtyard.

Faucon wasn't the only man in the crowd left a little startled by the depths of Stephen's reaction. Alf shot a frowning glance at the dead man's son, then stepped to

Stephen's side. He rested his hand on his new master's back as if to comfort. That brought Halbert's son upright with a start. Keeping his head turned away from his father, Stephen shook off his servant's touch and took a backward step from the bier, still gasping.

"Murdered?" Simon Fuller called out as a new muttering filled the yard. Men whispered to each other, spreading the startling news about Halbert's death back and beyond, to those who couldn't hear what happened in the mill yard.

The fuller pushed past all the others to make his way to Stephen. "What cause have you to say such a thing?" he demanded of Faucon, his tone and stance saying he spoke for all the men of this inquest, demanding the proof that was their right. "Did I not find Halbert beneath the wheel this morn, with the wrench that opens the brake right on the edge of the race this morn? Did we all not see our miller removed from that channel only moments ago? How can you say that he did not fall in and drown by accident?"

As Simon spoke, he offered his neighbor a quick pat on the back. Although Stephen accepted this touch without reaction, he didn't look in the shorter man's direction.

"Aye, what you describe is indeed what we saw," Faucon agreed, "but it was not the truth. Halbert's presence in the race was a ruse, one arranged to convince us that he had drowned. The one who killed him took great pains to hide the true manner of the miller's death. Unfortunately for Halbert's killer," Faucon again scanned the faces in the yard, meeting the gazes of the watching men eye-to-eye as he continued, "he did not know that a drowned man has foam in his mouth, and that his eyes will never be cloudy. Those are the signs that set me to seeking the true cause of Halbert's death. Now, look for yourselves and see that I am right."

Faucon lifted the fronts of Halbert's garments, pulling them back until the miller's face was covered and all of his torso, including his crushed left shoulder, was revealed. Even with his gaze aimed away from the bier, that caught Stephen's attention. He yelped, his distress giving way to dismay as he stared at his father's opened garments.

"You've ruined my father's clothing!"

"Not ruined. What was done was necessary and it can be repaired. We were looking for this," Faucon finished as he used his finger to trace a circle around the otherwise insignificant puncture wound in Halbert's chest.

"Here is the cause of your neighbor's death," he told the watching men. "I believe the one who killed the miller used an awl, or something like an awl, to do his worst to Halbert. This tool would be long and slender, for it slipped easily between his ribs to deal out death to him. Given Simon Fuller's tale of drunkenness, I believe Halbert Miller was senseless when it happened."

Faucon did not add that he suspected Halbert had not been killed beside the millwheel. There was no need.

"Nay, it cannot be," Stephen whispered.

His face had paled to a pasty white and he once again shook on unsteady feet. Then, even though he was too far from the bier to do it, he extended his hand as he meant to touch his father's wound. The next instant, he snatched back his fingers and crossed his arms tightly around his middle.

"Do you think as I do, Master, that our awl was used on him?" Alf asked him, his voice gentle, nothing but concern showing on his face.

The miller's son nodded, the movement of his head swift and jerky.

"Shall I examine the wound for you?" the workman asked.

Again the miller's son nodded. Alf stepped close to Halbert and laid his hand on the dead man's torso. Stephen turned his face to the side as if he could not bear to watch. As the workman moved his fingers around the wound, Alf's fair brows rose high on his forehead.

"Mother of God, there it is, just as Sir Crowner says. If the knight is right in his description of the weapon, then I fear this hole has a size I know all too well," he announced quietly. There was no need for him to speak any louder. The only other sound in the courtyard was the steady drone of bees.

Alf looked at Faucon. "There's a special awl we use to sew drawstrings into hempen bags when we use such bags. It's almost as long as my forearm, but as slender as my finger."

"I would like to see it," Faucon replied.

"Master?" Alf asked of Stephen.

One more time Stephen nodded mutely.

It wasn't until Alf had walked back through the crowd, heading toward the three-sided shed that filled one corner of the yard, that the miller's son found his voice. "Papa," he said to the dead man, "I shouldn't have left you alone. I shouldn't have gone."

With that, Stephen buried his head into his hands and sobbed.

Chapter Eight

"Cloudy eyes and no foam in his mouth, indeed. Who has ever heard of such things? And, hole in his chest or no, I still think that wheel killed him," Edmund muttered, and not for the first time since reclaiming his seat on the porch.

He'd returned the plank to his lap and once more had the parchment sheet stretched across it. With his nose aimed at the skin, he plied his knife, scraping off the words that had wrongly identified the cause of Halbert's death.

"Tsk! Look at the mess I'm making. I'm going to scratch right through the skin."

Faucon hid his smile. He gave his new clerk credit for doing no more than muttering his complaints. Nor did Edmund aim his dismay at his employer. In fact, had Faucon not stood near the stairs as he awaited Alf's return with the awl, he wouldn't even have heard the man. It almost felt like a victory.

A moment later, Alf pushed his way through the crowd once more. As he rejoined the shire's new coronarius, he set a long needle-like tool into Faucon's hands. "Here it is, Sir Crowner."

His use of the title for the second time made Faucon laugh. "You're not the only one this day to name me Crowner, but how came you to use that word for my name?"

Alf gave a small shrug. "I heard Drue Tailor use it. Have I offended?"

"Not at all," Faucon said, still smiling as he turned his attention to the awl.

As Alf had said, it was long, almost the length of his

forearm, and exactly the size Faucon expected given the hole carved into Halbert's chest. Unlike some awls, such as the one the cobbler's woman had been using to sew the boot, this one didn't have its eye in its point. Instead, it resembled Drue's much smaller sewing needles, with the eye and point opposite each other.

Nor did it have a handle. Instead, a loop of twisted hemp cording ran through its eye. No doubt this was how it was stored, by hanging the loop over a peg in a wall.

The cording looked new and no sign of blood showed on the iron needle. Faucon would have been surprised, and not a little disappointed, in the one he hunted if he'd found such stains. The man who'd killed Halbert had expended far too much effort hiding the means of the miller's death to be so careless.

Nay, as near as Faucon could tell thus far, Halbert's killer had made only one misstep.

He turned the awl in his hands, this time noting that the eye end seemed a little off. He looked at the damage from every angle. Not only was that end a little flattened, it was ever so slightly bent to one side.

He almost smiled, so great was his satisfaction. It was just the sort of bend he might expect to see had the flat of a dagger blade been used to drive such an awl into a man. Why the awl would deform under such pressure lay upon the anvil of the smith who'd made it. No doubt its metal hadn't been as well-tempered as that of the dagger.

"Has it always been bent like this?" Faucon asked Alf, pointing out the end of the awl.

The workman shook his head as he looked at it. "I can't say I've ever noticed that before today. Then again, I can't say I've ever looked at it that closely before now. All I can tell you about the awl is that it's old, so much so that Master Halbert had started threatening to replace it, and he's not a man who easily parts with coins." He offered the breath of a smile at that, then all humor left him.

"So was this tool used to kill my master?" There was nothing to hear in the servant's question save concerned interest.

"I cannot say that it was this particular awl, but I'm certain it was a tool very much like this one," Faucon replied. "Take it to Brother Colin and have him lay it beside the miller, so those who view him can witness the sort of weapon used by the one who killed him."

As Faucon laid the awl in the servant's hand, he asked, "Do you make your bed in the mill?" It was a legitimate question. Many tradesmen's servants took their nightly rest in their masters' shops, doing so to protect goods and supplies from thieves and vandals.

"I do," Alf said as he examined the damaged awl, turning it in his hands much as Faucon had done. Then he dropped his hand to his side and looked at his new coronarius. Nothing in the workman's mien suggested he was at all distraught, or even nervous at handling the suspect awl. Then again, to have killed Halbert in stealth and whilst the besotted man was unconscious in drunken slumber was cold-blooded, indeed. Someone capable of that was hardly the sort of man to flinch after the fact.

"Then tell me something," Faucon continued. "The fuller says he heard the wheel begin to turn late last night only to stop abruptly a little while thereafter. Did you hear the same?"

Alf's eyes narrowed and his mouth tightened until it was a hard line. He shook his head. "I fear not, although it shames me to admit it. Such was the day we had yesterday, Master Halbert and I doing our own work and sharing Master Stephen's portion, that, when I retired, I heard nothing at all from the mill or the wheel."

There was something in the way he parsed his words

that caught and held Faucon's attention. "'Struth? You heard nothing when the fuller, whose house is at least a furlong from the race, was awakened by the millwheel turning?"

Alf gave a stiff shrug. His expression was shuttered, leaving nothing for Faucon to see but the blank look worn by all servants when they interacted with their betters. "What can I say? I heard nothing from where I slept."

Faucon kept his gaze on Alf. He'd heard it said some men could pick out the truth by studying just a man's eyes. If that were true, either he lacked the talent or Alf was innocent of Halbert's murder. No trace of guilt lurked anywhere in the workman's expression.

"A shame that, certainly for Halbert's sake," Faucon said. "Although we now know your master was already beyond rescue when that wheel began again to turn last night, if you had come out, you might have seen or apprehended the murderer. Perhaps you can tell me this, then. When I arrived this morning, the brake on the wheel was set. Since it's a sure thing Halbert didn't rise out of the race to set it, there's only one man who could have done it: the man who put Halbert into the water after he was dead."

Alf still stood easily, no tension affecting the line of his shoulders. His hands, including his right in which he held the awl, were loose at his sides. He continued to meet his better's gaze without flinching. It was uncommon boldness for one so humble.

"But why set the brake at all?" Faucon continued, using his words the way beaters used sticks, to drive their prey out into the open so the hunters could make a kill. "After all, the wheel had already stopped turning once Halbert was lodged beneath it. That had me pondering for a bit until I realized it was set because of long habit, because setting the brake is what this man always did.

"This morning," Faucon went on, "the sheriff's man couldn't move those screws with his dagger as he tried to open them. After the sheriff left, I watched how much effort it took for you to release the brake even using the proper tool. No easy feat, it seemed. Tell me, are you the only one strong enough to open and close that brake?"

It was an accusation framed as a question and aimed at one who had no right to refuse to answer. Nonetheless, Faucon expected Alf to say nothing. The workman surprised him.

"Nay, not at all," Alf replied with a shake of his head, his voice quiet and as flat as his expression. "Opening the brake is no one man's chore here, and you're wrong to think it difficult. It's just a matter of setting the wrench rightly on the screw. That is the purpose of the wrench, to make the screws turn with ease. Not only does Master Stephen do it, as did Master Halbert, but even the young mistress wields the wrench when we need a hand. It was only difficult this morning because of how my master was trapped beneath the wheel. That put pressure on the axle and thus on the screws. If you doubt me, I'm sure Master Stephen would be happy to let you try opening and closing the brake for yourself."

Although Alf continued to meet his gaze, the expression in his eyes was as impenetrable as the stones that enclosed the courtyard. With every breath, Faucon grew ever more convinced the man was hiding something.

"Perhaps I shall try it," he replied. "There is one more thing that puzzles me. Why did Stephen not release the wheel for the sheriff? It wasn't until Sir Alain departed that your master called you to come from the mill with your wrench and release that brake."

"It is not my wrench and I but do as I'm told," Alf replied, countering another oblique accusation with ease. "As the sheriff was arriving this morning, Master

86

Stephen commanded me to wait in the mill with the wrench until he called for me. As that was his command, that is what I did. If you wish to know why he might command that of me, you'll have to ask him."

Faucon nodded, the movement of his head acknowledging that they were at an impasse. Alf chose to interpret the gesture as dismissal. As the servant carried the awl to the bier, Faucon surveyed the courtyard, seeking Stephen.

Enclosed by the low stone wall, the yard was a pretty place, or it would have been if not for the many men packed within it. The big square was neatly kept with clumps of late-blooming wildflowers lending their oranges and purples to the gray of the wall. Stephen had retreated to the same shed from which Alf had retrieved the awl. Housed within its three walls were a few barrels, a pile of the hempen sacks that Alf had mentioned, planks of wood stored upright, and the miller's larger tools-both those belonging to any farmstead and some that must be particular to a mill, since Faucon didn't recognize them.

Stephen sat upon the forwardmost of the barrels in the shed. His shoulders were slumped and his head bowed over his folded hands. A group of men and boys, those who had already completed their tour past Halbert to confirm Faucon's verdict and were thus free to do as they pleased, were gathering around the new miller. Simon Fuller stood at Stephen's side. The promise of a fulling mill had transformed this morning's irritable neighbor into the new miller's greatest ally.

As Faucon joined them, Stephen released a shuddering sigh and rubbed his hands over his face before looking up. The grief that had been so noticeably absent this morning now left wet streaks on his cheeks.

"Ah, I'm sorry that you must grieve," Faucon said, his tone neutral, "but I am glad to see that you do at last. This morn when you first addressed me to protest the

87

deodand, I suspected you had yet to grasp your father's passing, for it seemed you did not mourn him at all."

"Did it?" Stephen replied, bracing his forearms on his thighs. His gaze drifted back to his clasped hands. "I'm not surprised that it might have seemed that way. God knows I was furious at my father when I arrived home this morning. I hated him for shaming us and our name yet one more time."

He glanced sidelong at Faucon. "To fall into his own race and die because of drink! You don't know what it's like living with someone like him. Clear-headed one minute, with great plans for the future. A few hours later, he's besotted and raging, saying things to folk or about folk that make them hate him, me and our trade."

That made Faucon's lips twist into a tight smile. If only he didn't know a man of that sort. "Do you think your sire is the only one in the world who behaves this way?"

Stephen offered him a wry and ragged grin, then released another slow breath. "I suppose not. Now that I know my father's death came at the hands of another and not because of his love for ale, a hole has opened in my heart just as was done to him. I am missing him already."

"Can you think of anyone who might want to kill your sire?" Faucon asked.

"Better to ask me who didn't wish to kill him," the new miller retorted with a scornful snort. "I doubt there's a man here today who would say he liked my father." That teased nods and mutters of agreement out of some of the men standing near him.

"My father was not a pleasant man. He was quick to anger and brutal with his fists. And as fast as he was to strike out, he was just as slow to forgive."

Stephen shot Faucon another look, this one sharp and swift. "Because of that, there'll be those who'll say Halbert Miller was a thief. Don't believe them. I vow to you, my father never took so much as a single corn that belonged to another. He didn't need to cheat to make a profit here, not as hard as he worked. Although it's true he wasn't born to milling, instead came to it through marriage to my mother, he loved this mill, every bit of it, from the constant rumble of the turning stone to sweeping up the last of the grain dust at the end of a day."

With that, Stephen straightened on the barrel and raised his gaze to meet Faucon's. "But none of that answers your question. If I can imagine many men who might have wished my father dead, I can think of no man who would have been moved to actually end his life."

"What of a woman? What of Agnes, his wife? You have accused her of his death once today," Faucon reminded gently.

Stephen's eyes narrowed and his jaw tightened. "All I can say about her is that she'd best be gone from my home before I have to go within doors. I don't care what it takes to be rid of her, she had just better be gone." As hard as his expression was, his voice lacked any of the bluster Faucon had heard when he first arrived at the mill.

"Do you rescind your charge of murder against your stepmother, then?" Faucon persisted. "If so, why did you accuse her at all?"

"Because I would have killed him if he treated me the way he treated her," Stephen said simply. "As hard as my father was on me, he was harder still on Alf, and hardest yet on that woman. I don't understand why she married him in the first place. Mary save me, but I don't even know why he took another wife. After my mother died, my father was content to let 'Wina, my wife," Stephen offered in explanation, "care for us and our home. Then, of a sudden two months ago, he travels to Stanrudde and comes back with that woman, returning already wedded and bedded without me knowing a thing of it beforehand. He didn't even tell me he intended to marry." The pain of his father's betrayal filled Stephen's voice and gaze.

Faucon shrugged. "Perhaps he missed having a woman in his bed?"

"Him?" Stephen said in scorn. "There hasn't been a time when he didn't have access to a woman when he wanted one, even when my mother was alive. He's always had Greta. Keeps her well enough, he does. Did. Well, he and half these men here today keep her." The sweep of Stephen's hand indicated the inquest jury, while his words set a good number of the listening men to laughing under their breaths.

As their amusement died away, Stephen shook his head. "Nay, I cannot accept that sating his desires is why he married Agnes," he said, using his stepmother's name for the first time in Faucon's hearing. "I don't think he even liked her, not from the very first. If I were to count nights after her first week here, I think she spent more of them sleeping at Susanna's than in my father's bed."

Stephen's gaze shifted to the mill door. "Now he's gone, and he's left me with no idea what sort of dower he promised her."

That took Faucon aback. "There was no contract between them?"

Only two sorts of marital unions didn't have witnessed contracts stating dowry and dower: those handfasts made between paupers with no wealth to their names, and the secret unions sealed under the stars with only the Lord God to witness. If Halbert was too wealthy for the first sort of union, the second sort was always a bond of the heart, hardly a fitting description for the miller's marriage to Agnes.

Stephen shrugged helplessly. "I don't know. My father never showed me a contract. Or rather he refused to show it to me," he continued, correcting himself with considerable bitterness.

"When I asked to see it, wanting to know what piece of my inheritance he'd promised her, my father accused me of prying into what was none of my business. Then he told me that the mill was his to do with as he pleased, and he'd disown me if I ever spoke to him of it again. Until that moment, I thought he considered me his partner and equal in running the mill, not some greedy heir, waiting to gobble up another man's lifetime of hard work. I cannot bear that he might have given someone else, a strange woman no less, a piece of what is mine without even speaking to me of his plans."

"An odd marriage, indeed," Faucon agreed. "Was your father given to impetuous acts such as marrying Agnes?"

Stephen gave a sharp shake of his head. "Never. Until he married her, I'd never seen my father do anything that cost him more than he gained from it. And their marriage cost him dearly, stripping him of his peace of mind. The moment Agnes walked through our door was the moment my father lost all patience with the world, or what little patience he'd ever had. From then on, nothing Alf and I did, even if we did exactly what he asked, could please him. I vow he woke in the morning screaming and went to bed at night still shouting at me.

"At least Alf didn't have to listen to him after our workday was done. Every evening, there I was, trapped in the house," he pointed to what Faucon could see of the large and well-kept cottage that stood outside the mill wall, "unable to stop my father as he drained cup after cup of ale, watching him grow ever more resentful as each drop slid down his throat, his rage and voice rising steadily as he recounted my many faults.

"Meanwhile, here Alf was," this time the lift of Stephen's hand indicated the mill, "enjoying the peace of his quiet bed."

Faucon nodded at that. "The fuller mentioned earlier that you weren't home last night."

"I was not," Stephen agreed. "My wife's mother passed three nights ago. Yestermorn, my wife, my daughter and I left Priors Holston to bide for a sennight at her family's farmstead. I didn't want to be away for a full week. But 'Wina insisted, even though I cannot see why she needs me at her side to settle matters with her sisters. Theirs is a close and agreeable family."

"You know that isn't her real reason for wanting you with her for the whole while," Simon Fuller interjected, his voice gentle.

Stephen shifted on the barrel to send a frowning look at his neighbor. "What other reason could there be? When her father passed, we stayed only for the wake and the funeral before returning home."

Simon put his hand on the younger man's shoulder. "'Wina saw her father just before he passed. Not so her mother, and now she's grieving mightily. Last she spoke to me, the day before her mother died, she was saying that the illness was nothing, and all would soon be right again. I think she blames herself for not visiting her mother before death came to take her."

"I hadn't thought of that," Stephen said, his voice trailing off into another sigh.

Try as he might, Faucon could see nothing contrived about Stephen's grief. "Tell me something, for I'm curious. This morning when I arrived, the sheriff's man was trying to release the wheel with no success. Why did you not help him open the brake?"

"Why do you ask me that?" Stephen frowned up at him. "Was it not at your command that I did so?"

"My command?" Faucon repeated in surprise. "How could it be? I hadn't yet arrived."

"You weren't here but your clerk most definitely was. He arrived before our lord sheriff and spoke most forcefully in your name."

Faucon blinked at that, not surprised by Stephen's description of Edmund's manner, but by the fact that the monk had been in Priors Holston to spew commands at all. "How did Brother Edmund even know to come here?" The question was out before Faucon realized he should be asking this of Edmund, not the son of the murdered man.

Stephen only shrugged. "Through our bailiff I expect," he said. "It's on our bailiff to report to the sheriff any felony that occurs within our boundaries. Simon, you called for the bailiff after you raised the hue and cry, didn't you?"

"I did," Simon agreed. "He came, saw your father in the race then left for the priory to send his message."

Faucon glanced between the men, still confused. "Then your village name tells the truth? The Priory of St. Radegund holds Priors Holston?" It wasn't uncommon for whole villages and hundreds to be bound to monasteries, the same way that serfs and bondsmen owed the bounty of their strength and their fields to a nobleman.

"Not for much longer. There are but a few of us yet bound in servitude to the priory," Stephen replied. "A good number of my neighbors have bought their freedom from the Benedictines the way my father did a few years past, when he purchased the right to operate the mill and take its profits from the prior. As freeholders, we now owe the monks only a token rent. But that's not why our bailiff went to the priory. The monks always have messengers going hither and yon. They don't mind adding our words to a pouch that's on its way to the sheriff's clerks, whether at he's at Kineton or Killingworth. I've no doubt it was through our bailiff that your clerk knew to come to the mill. I'm sure all the brothers were aflutter at the news of my father's death."

Simon nodded at that, then glanced around the

courtyard. "I haven't seen Gilbert since he left this morning."

"That's because he had to continue on to Stanrudde to catch the man carrying the pouch," one of the other men said.

"A fool's errand," another man laughed, "since the sheriff's already been and gone this morn."

Faucon frowned at that. "How far is the sheriff's seat from here?"

"Across the shire," a man replied.

"Then how did Sir Alain arrive before me?"

"Now, that's a different tale and much of it depends on our Bertie, here," Stephen said.

As he spoke, he reached out to pat the arm of a beardless youth of no more than ten-and-four. At the same time, Simon put his arm around the boy's shoulders. That was all Faucon needed to confirm the lad's parentage. If the son was taller and more slender than the father, he had the fuller's round face and fair hair, and his brown tunic exactly matched the color of Simon's attire.

"Simon sent Bertie running to my wife's family home to bring me the news of my father's death. Once I heard the tale I sent Bertie running once again, this time going another mile farther to the west to fetch the sheriff." Stephen offered a weak smile. "You see, Gilbert is traveling in the wrong direction although he doesn't know it. The sheriff is staying at Aldersby, a manor that belongs to his wife. That's where I sent Bertie. Aldersby is closer to us than Blacklea by a mile or so.

"I only knew to send Bertie there because three weeks ago my father and I milled the first of the grain from Aldersby. When Sir Alain's steward came to collect his flour, the man mentioned the sheriff would be stopping at the manor for a time upon his return from the royal court. The only reason I remembered any of that this morning was because it had surprised me so. I can't recall when Sir Alain last stayed at Aldersby, if he ever has. As I said, it belongs to his wife.

"So you see, even though your clerk flew to Priors Holston to tell me that you were this new servant of the crown and that only you had the right to view my father, he was already too late. Bertie was already on his way to fetch Sir Alain. That's what I told your clerk, saying it was a sure thing Sir Alain would arrive before you could. I also told the brother that I doubted our sheriff would wait for you before calling the inquest, royal edict or no. Well, your clerk grew frantic at that."

"I can imagine," Faucon murmured.

"He kept insisting I would be a law-breaker if I let anyone but you examine my father's body. At last, knowing you were coming from only as far as Blacklea, I told him I'd do what I could to stall. I sent Alf to hide in the mill with the wrench, then told Sir Alain that the wrench had gone missing from in here," Stephen pointed to where the wrench hung on the wall beside a spot that showed the dark outline of what looked to be the shadow of the awl, "and Alf was searching along the race for it."

"So it *was* the sheriff who called the hundred to the inquest," Faucon muttered to himself in relief. Edmund hadn't overstepped his authority, at least not as far as the inquest jury was concerned.

"Of course it was the sheriff," Stephen replied harshly. "I'm certain Sir Alain sent his men to raise the jury from town and hundred even before he exited Aldersby's gates. Our sheriff isn't one to spend any attention on matters that annoy him, and my father's death could have been no more than an annoyance. He wouldn't have cared about foamy mouths or cloudy eyes. He would simply have said my father drowned and told us to shout our 'ayes.'"

"So he would have done," Simon agreed, "and so we

would have done as well, even if half of us didn't know what we were confirming when we called out our agreement, or that we were wrong to confirm that verdict. We'd have done what he told us and been glad to be released so we could be on about our day."

That set the men gathered around them to muttering. "Do you know that I can't recall a time when we've ever had a viewing as you've asked of us here today, sir," one said.

"Aye, and that makes me wonder how many other deaths we've confirmed that were mistaken," another added.

Simon offered Faucon a nod. "I give thanks to you for the care and concern you spent on one of our own, Sir Crowner."

"I give thanks to his clerk," Stephen shot back then looked at Faucon. "Because of that monk's courage in defying Sir Alain, my father will surely rest more easily in his grave. If only I'd thought to change my gown before I raced for home this morning. We were leaving for the parish church for the funeral when Bertie arrived with the news."

Stephen made an impatient sound. "Look at the mess I've made of my finest." Indeed, his shoes were thick with dust, which had transferred to the expensive trim that decorated the hem of his long tunic. He bent forward and slapped at the bottom edge, trying to beat out some of the heavy smudges.

Faucon drew a swift breath as one thought connected to another. Stephen hadn't want to ruin his best any more than Faucon had wanted to stain his richest attire with horse sweat as he rode to Priors Holston. He shot a frowning glance over his shoulder at Halbert's body, at the tunic that had been taken apart and was now pulled over the dead man's face. Halbert had done the work of two men yesterday, what with his son away for the day.

"Did your father usually wear his finest or newest on a work day?" Faucon asked.

That brought Stephen upright with a start. "Of course not. Who can afford that?" the new miller retorted, his tone suggesting the question was foolish.

"But he's wearing a tunic I don't recognize, Stephen," a man said to him. "It must be new."

Stephen's expression flattened in surprise. He shifted on the barrel until he could look at his father's corpse, then looked back at Faucon. "I didn't even notice he was wearing that tunic this morning when I saw him in the race. All I saw was my father under the wheel. That isn't what he was wearing when I last saw him yesterday, and I have no idea why he would have donned this tunic between then and now."

Then he sighed. "Not that it matters. He's dead and the garment's ruined. I might as well bury him in it."

As Stephen fell silent, Simon Fuller removed his arm from his son's shoulders. The movement caught Faucon's eye. As his gaze met the fuller's, Simon offered a lift of his chin, the gesture suggesting he had something to share.

Content with what he'd garnered from his conversation with Stephen, Faucon laid his hand on the new miller's shoulder. "My condolences on the loss of your father. I can see you will greatly miss him."

"That I shall, sir," Stephen whispered, his eyes closing.

Chapter Nine

Side-by-side, Faucon and the fuller walked back to the edge of the courtyard, stopping near the millwheel. The last of the men and boys who had occupied the tenting grounds were now stepping over the race to file into the yard. It was an orderly migration, so much so that Faucon was certain Edmund must be grinning in pleasure from his perch on the porch. As the jurymen shuffled past, more than a few of the commoners shot curious glances at their new crowner.

Simon leaned his head close to Faucon, seeking to keep his words private between them. "My pardon for interrupting, but you were asking Stephen about his father's tunic. It was that garment that had Halbert seeking to beat Agnes last night. He was screaming at her, accusing her of having whored to purchase it for him."

A jealous man, Agnes had said. Then again, perhaps Halbert had reason for his jealousy. "Do you know if Agnes did in fact give him that garment, and if futtering was how she acquired the tunic for him?" Faucon asked.

Shock dashed across the fuller's face. "I have no idea how he came by that tunic, and of course she didn't spread her legs for it," Simon spat back in sharp disgust. "Don't you think she'd need to be a far comelier woman to use bed play to earn as much as that tunic is worth?"

His words stirred thoughts of the whores Faucon had used on those instances when he had both the opportunity and the coin. Appearance was never as important to him as availability and price. Besides, comely whores tended to think themselves worth more than those who were less attractive, when both sorts rode the same as far as he could tell.

"I also know that Halbert would have beaten Aggie for bidding him 'good morrow,'" the fuller was saying. "She could do no right by him no matter how she tried."

Here Simon paused, and looked in the direction of the miller's cottage, then sighed. "I don't understand why she stayed with him after he showed her who he truly was, or why she kept trying to win him. She's too sweet by half, that woman. She's never once raised her voice to him, save to plead that he strike her no more.

"As for the tunic," Simon continued, "Halbert wore it the day he came home from Stanrudde with Aggie. Before he'd even wiped the road dust from his shoes, he started strutting up and down here," he pointed to the raceway that separated their properties. "He kept it up until he was sure I'd noticed he was wearing a garment that hadn't been made with my fabric. As far as I saw, he never again wore it after that day."

He leaned forward once more, new excitement in his face. "But that's not what's important. It's that Halbert wasn't wearing any tunic when I stepped between him and Aggie last night. That's what matters. All he had on was his shirt and braies, just as he would have done at the end of any other day on which the stones turned.

"Or rather, at the end of any day the stones turned since 'Wina married Stephen," Simon added with a laugh. "Poor 'Wina. She married into the wrong trade, she did. She can't tolerate her menfolk shedding flour all over yon fine house of theirs. That can't be an easy trait for a miller's wife to tolerate in herself, I think. At the end of each milling day, after they brake the wheel, 'Wina insists they all leave their dusty garments on the wall. Then, as her menfolk finish their chores, sweeping up or whatnot, she brushes their outer garments clean.

"Yestereven, as my family and I were stretching the last of our fabric, I saw both Alf and Halbert strip off their tunics and hang them where they always do." He pointed to a spot along the enclosing wall near the gate.

"With 'Wina gone, Aggie came out to do the brushing. When she finished, she put their tunics back on the wall and returned through their croft to the house, no doubt off to prepare supper. That's when it started. Of a sudden, there's Halbert, standing in the middle of the yard, holding his workaday tunic and shouting that Aggie hadn't gotten it clean enough.

"This from a man who three years ago never brushed so much as a mote off his garments," Simon offered with scorn before continuing.

"When Aggie came back into the mill yard, he threw his tunic onto the ground and trampled it into the dirt, then told her to clean it once again. While she did so, crying and trembling as she worked, Halbert left the mill and went toward the house." Simon rolled his eyes in disgust. "Off to start drinking as usual.

"I didn't see Aggie finish cleaning his tunic, because it was time for me to go within doors for my own meal. Still, it didn't surprise me when the shouting started anew after dinner was done. I came back out here to the race to find Halbert and Aggie in the courtyard. He was stalking after her, his every move meant to intimidate as he drove her around the yard. He was still in his shirt and braies, holding his fine tunic–the one that's on him now–in one hand and his cup in the other. From the way he was stumbling, I'm guessing he'd wasted no time filling and draining that cup far more than a few times. He was shouting that she'd made a beautiful thing foul by spreading her legs for it, and because she had, he could never again bear to feel it against his skin.

"He finally trapped her back here," Simon pointed to the outside of the courtyard wall between the mill and the miller's cottage, "against the race. Even as she begged him not to hurt her, he held her pinned in place with his words as he named her 'whore' and 'harlot.' Although they were only words, I could see that she felt them like blows by the way she cowered and covered her ears. Because she had her head bowed, she didn't see his fist coming. He caught her in the eye.

"That's when I crossed the race to separate them, sending Aggie to the alewife's house. Once Aggie was gone, Halbert tossed aside the tunic with no care for its expense. It fell there." Simon pointed to a spot not far from them, then shot a hard look at Faucon.

"And before you go thinking he might have come back later and donned it, trust me. By that time, he was already too deep in his cups to so much as find the tunic again, much less get it over his head on his own. That didn't mean he was too far gone to start swinging at me, calling me foul names for interfering, something he's done far too often these past two months.

"I let him do his worst, knowing that after a few minutes of futile exertion, he'd be ready to drop. That's when Alf came out of the mill. I think he intended to see to Halbert, mayhap take him back into the mill with him or perhaps to the house to put him to bed. I wouldn't have it. The mood Halbert was in last night, he'd have sent Alf packing for no more reason than that the poor man breathed. Or done even worse to him.

"Since Stephen wasn't here to distract his father, I told Alf to leave his master where he was." Simon sighed and shook his head. "Now, in the light of what you've revealed this day, I know how wrong my decision was. If I'd let Alf do as he wished, perhaps Halbert would yet be alive. But how could I have known last night wouldn't be like all the other nights these past two months? I expected only that Halbert would spend an hour or so cursing the wheel then fall asleep on the race." He fell silent, shaking his head as he stared at the wheel.

"What happened after that?" Faucon prodded.

Simon looked up, blinking as if startled. "Where was I? Oh aye, Alf. Well, Alf argued with me, insisting he had to take his master within doors. Stephen had told me perhaps two weeks ago that his father had started venting his wrath on Alf as well as him. I couldn't bear the thought of Alf enduring a beating last night for no reason. I commanded him to join Aggie at Susanna's. I told him to stay there for a few hours, saying Halbert would be safe enough where he was until then, and if Alf wished it, I'd help him take his master into the house once Halbert was senseless."

Faucon caught a stunned breath as the trail that had been so clear only a moment before disappeared before his eyes. Why had Alf not told him this when it excused him of all blame? "Alf and Agnes were both at your alewife's house last night?"

Simon offered a sharp lift of his brows as a vindictive grin twisted his lips. "So they were. There's no better place to be in Priors Holston if you want to avoid Halbert Miller. Susanna is Stephen's aunt. Susanna despises—despised," he corrected himself, "Halbert. That's why Aggie can sleep there night after night. Aye, Susanna's hated Halbert from the day he married her sister, although that never stopped her from selling him as much ale as he could drink. Or maybe she sold it to him, hoping he'd drink himself to death." The fuller loosed a harsh but pleased laugh. "Ha! I never thought of that before today."

"Did Alf return last night?" Faucon asked, hoping he didn't sound as if he were pleading.

"I don't know," Simon replied, then shrugged, "but I assume not. If he had, Alf would have either found Halbert under the wheel or moved him into the house and saved his life. I wouldn't have heard Alf if he had returned, not unless he came to my door. I was tired from my day and angry at Halbert. After Alf left, I went to claim my own bed, glad for what calm I could find there.

"Although I'm surprised Susanna managed to keep

Alf from returning. He doesn't much care to keep company with others. Even at our village ales and festivals, he maintains his solitude, much to the dismay of more than a few of the lasses."

The fuller's smile at his own jest dimmed into new shock. "Nay! You're thinking it was Alf who did this to Halbert!"

He shook his head, rejecting the notion with all his will. "Nay, you're wrong. I won't—I don't believe it. Everything about Alf, his manners and habits, suggests he's a year-and-a-day man. Such a man doesn't risk the freedom he's striven so hard to win by doing murder to his employer, especially when I can count a dozen men in Priors Holston who would have happily hired Alf away from Halbert. And this Alf knew."

Faucon drew an astonished breath. Alf was a runaway serf?! He immediately rejected the idea. The workman was far too bold in manner to be some backward rural bondsman.

Simon growled in frustration as he realized what he'd revealed to his better. He shook a finger at Faucon. "Now, don't you go thinking you heard me offer any certain truth about Alf, Sir Crowner. I know nothing of his history. I'm just spinning out the yarns tangled in my head. All that's in here," he tapped his temple with his forefinger, "is how Alf has acted since he arrived in Priors Holston—like a man who at any moment expects to find hounds nipping at his heels.

"And even if it's true that he ran from his rightful lord and master, you're too late to return him. Last month, he was a full year in Priors Holston. That makes him a free man. May God bless him and grant good fortune to every soul who helped him make his escape I say, and I don't care if you hear me." As he finished, Simon drew himself up, squaring his shoulders and thrusting out his chest as if in challenge.

"Nor do I care what I heard you say," Faucon

replied, offering the man a crooked smile and a conciliatory lift of his hands. "As far as I can tell, having held my position for but one day, my purview seems to be limited to dead men, assessments of estates and royal revenue."

Simon relaxed in relief. "Good. If you can forget that much, then you should also forget any ideas I might have wrongly given you about Alf killing Halbert. He didn't do it. I know it, aye."

"If not him, then who?" Faucon asked.

Simon blew out a long breath at the question and again stared at the millwheel. The quiet between them stretched.

"I don't know," he said at last, "and I'm not even certain that I care. Good riddance. All I am certain of is that Halbert wasn't wearing that tunic when last I saw him alive and sitting right here."

Simon again pointed to that spot on the edge of the race, the same spot he'd indicated for the tunic. Then he looked at Faucon. "So, who put that tunic on Halbert? That's what I want to know, sir. Because after listening to the vehemence of Halbert's curses over that garment, I don't believe he would ever have donned it on his own accord, sober or besotted."

Faucon nodded, deep in thought. Putting Halbert into that expensive tunic before the dead man went into the race seemed almost an act of vengeance. But vengeance for what? Mistreating Agnes? The only one who seemed to care about Halbert's wife was Simon, and as open as Simon was, Faucon doubted even the fuller would offer up the very bit of information that damned him.

"A strange marriage, theirs, Agnes and Halbert," Faucon said, still chewing on what he'd learned.

"For sure," Simon agreed. "None of us could understand why Halbert wed her. After Cissy, Stephen's mother, died, Halbert made it clear to all the village that he had no desire to marry again."

"And yet, wed again he did," Faucon said. "Tell me, if you can. Do you have any idea what the hour was when you heard the wheel begin to turn once more?"

That made Simon think. "Perhaps after Matins?" he offered with no confidence, then took back his words. "Nay, I cannot be certain of the hour, save that it was still full dark, and that's the best I can tell you."

"Papa! You must come!"

The call came from a lad of no more than eight, wearing a too-large brown tunic. The child came dashing toward them through the tenting frames, something much easier to do now that all the men of the inquest had passed onto the miller's property. The boy's hair was yet sleep-knotted, its wayward spikes framing a face that named him another of Simon's progeny.

"Come where, son?" Simon asked as the lad came to a dancing stop across the race from them.

"Into the croft, Papa! You must come and you must bring that knight, too!" He pointed at Faucon. "Master Drue says he thinks he may have found the place the knight seeks, the place with hidden blood. It's where we do our slaughtering. Emmie says if there's something hiding there, it isn't from that pig we killed yesterday!" The lad whirled and started back through the frames as fast as he had come.

Simon drew a sharp breath. "Nay, Drue's wrong," he said, his voice so low that Faucon wondered if he'd meant to speak the words aloud.

The fuller looked at Faucon. His expression was flat, his skin had lost its color. "It's mad to think anyone would carry Halbert all the way into my croft to do his evil." Strong words, but Simon's voice broke as he spoke, and he crossed his fingers to ward off that evil and the devil who created it.

"You're likely right," Faucon replied as he stepped over the race, following the boy. His movement stirred

Simon into following.

"You slaughtered a pig yesterday? Is that the way here? Where I'm from, we don't usually cull our swine until well into November, after they've eaten their fill of fallen nuts." Faucon asked, intending more to steady the man than to inquire after Priors Holston's slaughtering practices. Although, he was curious. To slaughter before the pigs had added the flavor of acorns and hazelnuts to their flesh was a waste of ham, at least in Faucon's estimation.

"Nay, it's no different here," Simon replied, still working to shake off his reaction to his son's announcement. "This was a little gilt that had broken her leg, poor thing. I bought and slaughtered her–" He yelped, then hopped on one foot away from the corner of a frame.

Cursing beneath his breath, Simon stumbled a bit before catching his balance, then sent Faucon a rueful grin. "Bless me if, after living here for all of my life, I still don't run into one of these things at least every other week."

"Hurry, Papa!" The lad had reached the gate in the enclosure that surrounded the fuller's croft. Simon had made his fence from wooden frames into which whip-thin branches had been woven until it looked as much like a basket as a wall. Each panel was pegged in place and fastened to the next with leather bindings. Pausing in the opening, the child sent an impatient wave in the direction of his elders–the motion suggesting they were moving far too slow to suit him–then disappeared.

They followed him into the croft. The space that provided Simon's family with their vegetables measured at least a furlong by four rods, which made it about the same size as any other croft Faucon had ever seen, around seven hundred feet in length and forty in width. The fuller's family had divided the space into a series of small rectangular plots separated by a grid of well-worn paths. Each plot included a fruit tree beneath which grew neat rows of cabbages, parsnips, herbs or beans drying with the season. Just now, two of these plots were piled high with recently-harvested garlic. The heads had been left upon the earth to cure in the warmth of autumn's waning days.

At the far end was the fuller's cottage, a dwelling that appeared to be about half the size of the miller's home. Just behind the house stood the wide vats in which the fuller and his family walked newly-woven woolen cloth into fabric worthy of a garment. At this end of the croft, as far from the house as possible within the enclosure, grew a massive chestnut tree, its low-hanging branches heavy with sweet nuts dressed in their spiny coats.

The tailor stood with his back to the chestnut's burly trunk, one hand on the end of the fuller's pole axe. The tool, nothing more than a great knob of wood with a handle almost as long as Simon was tall, had but one purpose–to deal a stunning blow to an animal prior to slaughter.

Dashing and darting in noisy play was a veritable mob of children. Save for Drue's apprentice and the lad who had come to fetch Simon, the rest were girls. To a one, these lasses wore garments dyed the same shade of brown as the fuller's tunic. Only two of the girls didn't participate in the play: the eldest, a sad and sober lass of no more than ten-and-six with a housewife's apron atop her gown, and the youngest, the toddler she balanced on her hip.

"These are all your children?" Faucon asked Simon.

The fuller sighed as if beleaguered, but there was pride in his voice when he spoke. "They are indeed, every last one. I have two more lads. You met Bertie, but didn't see Willie, who was yet waiting to view Halbert."

"Your wife is young to mother such a brood," Faucon

said, indicating the girl as they crossed the garden to join the tailor. If she was without doubt too young to be the mother of any save the child she held, that didn't mean she was too young to be married to the fuller.

"Nay, that's my eldest daughter. My wife is gone. We lost her last year," Simon said softly. "She just wanted one more babe. She always liked the little ones best of all."

Before Faucon had a chance to offer his condolences, the fuller lifted his voice and called, "You're mad if you think Halbert died here, Drue. If there's anything to find in my croft, it can only be a bit of offal that my sons missed yesterday after we'd finished that gilt."

"You are most likely right," Drue called in return. "That's why I wanted the knight to come and see this for himself, him being wise in the ways of death." As he spoke, Drue pointed to a stump not far from him.

Although now only knee-high, the width of the former tree suggested it had originally rivaled the chestnut that had replaced it. The stump's face was scarred and long since stained to a rusty brown. That said it was being used for slaughtering fowl and smaller animals.

Uneven drifts of wood ash blanketed the ground between the stump and the chestnut. The spilled lines of charred wood led back to a fire pit. Faucon was certain yesterday had seen that pit filled with burning coals as the fuller heated a great pot of water. A pig's carcass was always dipped after slaughter; the hot water made scraping off the animal's bristly hair so much easier.

Both Faucon and the fuller coughed as they joined Drue in the shade of the chestnut, doing so in instinctive reaction to a smell that would soon be the stench of rotting blood. Flies buzzed and circled around the base of the stump.

"Have you been slaughtering chickens?" Faucon asked the fuller.

Simon shook his head. "Not this time of year," he said. "Emmie, I swear we didn't spill anything yesterday. Did you and I accidentally leave something out here to rot?" The sweep of his hand indicated the ashy expanse. "And if we did, how did the boys miss it when they cleaned up? They know better."

The fuller's eldest daughter must have resembled her mother, for she was a sweet-faced girl with dark hair and pale eyes. She shot her father an amused look, then set down the child she held. The fuller's littlest lass trundled off after the other children, crying for them to wait for her.

"You know better than that, Papa. How could we have spilled blood when we put the gilt's head in the pot before we cut her throat? Come now, you're too fond of blood sausage to let me waste so much as a drop." There was both irritation and affection in her tone. Her manner suggested she had stepped comfortably into the hole her mother's death had left in their family.

"Nor did the boys miss anything," she continued. "I'm certain that what Master Drue believes he has discovered wasn't here yesterday when the ash was spread. Neither Bertie nor Willie would have spread ash the way this has been done."

Here, the fuller's girl shifted to look at Faucon. "See how it's piled so it crawls up our stump? My brothers wouldn't do that. If they left warm ash like that, it might set the stump on fire. And we only ever use a thin layer to cover the ground after we've finished slaughtering. It's really all that's needed to keep down both the smell and the flies. Anything more means trouble. It's too tempting for the little ones, isn't it, sweetling?" she asked of the toddler.

The littlest girl had been unable to keep up in the game of tag presently being played and had returned to cling to her sister's skirts. Lifting the child to once more balance her on a hip, Emmie caught the wee one's chin in her hand and turned her face toward Faucon. Although it had been only a moment, grimy streaks already crisscrossed the child's rosy cheeks and darkened her wispy brows.

"See? I'll be scrubbing faces all evening, won't I just?" the elder girl said.

The child chortled at that, then buried her head into the curve of her sister's shoulder. Faucon laughed with her and Emmie shot him another glance. Their gazes met. The girl gasped, her fair skin taking fire until her blush burned almost scarlet. She dropped her gaze to the ground and bobbed a quick curtsy.

"Pardon, sir," she offered at a whisper, mortified by her forward behavior.

"Emmie said the same to me about the ashes when I first asked," Drue said, speaking over her. "That's when we started searching and I found this. I didn't look any further, sir," he said to Faucon, "wanting to wait until you were here to see."

The tailor dropped to one knee on the ashy ground, while Faucon knelt at the other. Waving off the flies, the tailor pointed to an area on the front of the stump.

Faucon had to lean close before he saw what Drue indicated. Small dark splotches looked as if they'd been sprayed up and down the side of the stump. He brushed his fingers over the spots. As he found and read the spaces in those lines of gore, he closed his eyes and followed the trail they made. It led him to an image of Halbert, stripped of all clothing so his shirt and braies wouldn't be marked with blood and ashes, slumped against the slaughtering stump. The awl was driven into him. Too drunk to react to the lethal blow, the miller had slipped to the side as his life's blood spurted from him. As he came to a rest on the ground, the final beats of his heart spattered blood against the stump.

"Brush aside this ash. Let's see what hides beneath it," he commanded.

As Faucon returned to his feet, slapping smut off the knee of his chausses, Emmie set her young charges to clearing away the piles of ash. This they did with a shovel and broom, arguing over who was to use which implement. A few moments later and all of them, young and old alike, looked upon an uneven circle of stained earth that was already attracting more insects than just the flies. Not realizing its import, the little ones made play out of gagging over the sight and smell.

Drue shook his head. "You were right, sir," he told Faucon. "Here is the spot where Halbert died. They carried him into Simon's croft, did their worst, then waited until he bled his last. When he was in God's hands, they removed him to the race then added more ash from the pit to cover this area, thinking no one would notice, not even Simon. Even if he caught the smell, why would he think anything amiss? He wouldn't, not when he'd slaughtered here earlier the same day."

Drue looked at the fuller. "If not for Sir Crowner, we would never have found it, would we have, Simon? Even you thought it must be just a bit of offal that your lads had missed, didn't you?"

At his words, Emmie once more lowered the child she held to the ground. Then, turning to the side, she lifted the hem of her apron until she could bury her face into it. After a moment of dry retching, she began to cry, her face still covered by the fabric.

Simon fell to his knees on the ash-covered ground, then slid to the side to sit. His face was as gray as what coated his bare legs and feet. His eyes were wide in terror.

"God save me, call Father Walter to come here for me, Drue. He must bless this ground else Halbert will haunt me for certain."

Chapter Ten

"**N**ay," Edmund said in stern reply and frowned at his new employer.

Upon Faucon's return to the mill from Simon's croft, he'd called Edmund down from his perch on the porch. They stood near Halbert's corpse. There was no longer a crowd in the courtyard, now that so many had viewed Halbert and confirmed the verdict, then returned to what remained of their day. The only men yet waiting to make their way past Halbert were those whom Faucon had first encountered, the ones who had the misfortune to approach the mill from the lane beyond the wall.

"You don't have the right to say me 'nay,'" Faucon warned the monk.

It was a toothless reply. Although he was looking at his clerk, he was giving him only half an ear. The remainder of his attention lingered on that bloody spot in Simon's croft. He'd missed something beneath that chestnut tree. Try as he might, he couldn't identify what it was.

He breathed out in frustration. Or, perhaps he hadn't missed anything and this was just his reaction to watching the fuller tremble in fear of Halbert's ghost. For sure, the depth of Simon's distress left Faucon regretting he'd ever sought out the site of the murder. This was especially so since locating the spot hadn't added anything to what he already knew of Halbert's death.

Or had it? Faucon huffed again in frustration. What had he missed?

"Sir Faucon?" Edmund asked.

Faucon blinked, pulling his thoughts back to his

clerk. Edmund was watching him. When the monk realized he had his employer's attention again, he launched into speech without preamble.

"Indeed, as your clerk, I have no right to deny you. However, Bishop William wished me to guide you. I would be remiss if I didn't warn you against a misstep," Edmund offered, no hint in his voice that he intended to be disrespectful even as every word he spoke betrayed his arrogance.

"I do not think it can be your duty to seek out the man who committed the miller's murder." The monk offered a firm shake of his head to emphasize just how strongly he believed what he said. "I think our only duty is to reveal and note the details of an unnatural death. If murder has been done, as it was here, I think it is still the sheriff's right to pursue and capture the one who committed the act."

Faucon eyed him in surprise. "You only *think* it isn't our duty? Yesterday you were far more certain of what is and is not ours to do. You recited a great list, doing so with complete certainty."

As he spoke Faucon realized all he knew of his position was what Edmund had told him. The monk was hardly objective, not when he classified his service to Faucon as a despised penance.

"Tell me exactly what the archbishop said about the Keepers of the Pleas and their duties. What was said when this new office was announced? When you've told me that, I can determine for myself what is mine to do."

The monk crossed his arms, tucking his hands into the wide sleeves of his habit. His expression flattened until it was as shielded as his body. "I don't think it matters what was said at court."

"Perhaps not, but I would know," Faucon pressed.

"It wasn't much," Edmund replied, his lips barely moving as he spoke.

"Tell me what was said," Faucon commanded

without anger. He didn't begrudge this argument. So it would be between them until they learned to trust each other.

"Well, if you must know," Edmund said almost irritably, then closed his eyes to better draw the words from memory. "'In every county of the king's realm shall be elected three knights and one clerk to keep the pleas of the crown.'"

Faucon waited. Edmund uncrossed his arms and opened his eyes. He looked at Faucon, his expression still shuttered.

Faucon blinked as he realized the recitation was finished. "That's it? There's nothing more? What of all those duties yesterday? Where did they come from?"

"You speak as if I created them out of clear air," the monk protested. "I didn't. Most of them already existed, being part of what the sheriffs did when keeping the pleas was their duty. The others are those Bishop William told me would soon be added to the duties of all the coronarii."

Faucon freed a surprised breath. "Well, answer me this then. What sense is there in only recording the manner and means of a murder, and not taking the next step to discover the man who committed the act? We're at hand, viewing what happened and how it was done. The sheriff is not. Think on it, Brother Edmund. Do not those who commit murder forfeit all to the king?"

"Not all their property is forfeited," the clerk replied in what Faucon was beginning to recognize as his rote reaction to an error. Edmund had to correct, the way a fish needed to swim.

"Murderers forfeit the profit they would accrue in a year and a day, along with all waste land and all their chattels," the clerk said.

"Well, then it must be we who seek out and arrest the one who killed the miller. That revenue is exactly what Archbishop Hubert Walter wishes to collect for our king and the reason for the creation of my new position. If we do not prove the murderer guilty and deliver him to the sheriff, how can we collect what he owes?"

Edmund's eyes widened in pleased surprise at this. "I never considered that!"

"Apparently not. I hereby state it is my duty to find the man who ended Halbert Miller's life, and with all my heart I shall do my duty to my king," Faucon told him. "Feel free to scribe that I spoke these words in that record of yours. Put it right below the description of Halbert's death wound." Offering Edmund a nod and wondering if the monk would discern the sarcasm, Faucon started across the courtyard, walking toward the gate that led to the miller's croft.

"Where are you going?" his clerk cried out.

"To speak to Halbert's widow. Talking with her is my next step as I seek the man who killed her husband," he threw back over his shoulder.

"Wait for me!"

From the corner of his eye Faucon watched Edmund dodge and dart through the last of the commoners. The monk twisted this way and that, as if he wished to avoid making physical contact with any of the men and boys. He came abreast of his employer just as Faucon entered the miller's garden.

"Of course you are right, sir," Edmund said, new enthusiasm in his dark eyes. "We must identify and pursue those who do murder, so they might be brought before the justices and right be done. This is sure to please Bishop William well indeed." The clerk nigh on glowed at that thought.

Faucon almost grinned. 'We,' was it now? He wondered if Edmund realized he'd again revealed that it wasn't the shire's new crowner he intended to serve.

The miller's croft was no different in size than Simon's. But where the fuller grew his crops in small plots, Halbert's family opted to raise their vegetables in long rows that ran the length and half the width of the croft. The other half was a grassy swath that hosted a number of sheds and small barns. A ewe and her half-grown lamb grazed near one such structure, while nearby a young pig lifted its head and grunted a greeting to them.

Waist-high hurdles, double-sided braces made from thick branches, separated the back of the miller's whitewashed cottage from the croft. Agnes, or maybe Stephen's wife, had used them to dry the household laundry. Three shirts, two tunics, two pairs of chausses, a child's tiny blue gown and four aprons, two of them so ancient and well-used that they were now a mottled brown, had been left to air on them. Faucon and Edmund made their way through the braces and started toward the rear entry of the cottage.

"So now that we are agreed you must seek out the one who killed Halbert," Edmund said, his previous excitement dimming into new worry, "how will you do that? How can you know who committed the act?"

"By following the trail that began with the lack of foam in Halbert's mouth and his cloudy eyes," Faucon replied, shooting a laughing, sidelong look at his clerk.

The creases on Edmund's forehead deepened into crevices. "I don't understand how those things can lead us anywhere."

This time Faucon did laugh aloud. "Neither did I until I arrived at Priors Holston this morning. Yet here I am, learning to read this trail just as I was taught to track game animals by reading their spoor."

Their voices were enough to announce their arrival. Even before they reached the cottage, the top half of the back door opened. If no more wet streaks marked Agnes' face, her nose remained reddened from her earlier upset. As she recognized who waited outside, she opened the lower half of the door and stepped into the portal.

"Have you come to remove me from this house, sir?" she asked quietly, speaking Faucon's native French with more fluency than he expected.

"Nay, that is not my purpose nor my intent," Faucon replied in the same tongue. "However, I fear that moment is coming for you all too soon, goodwife. Might we enter and share a word or two?"

She offered him a tiny smile. "Thank you for asking and not commanding." Her words were little more than a whisper. Then she drew herself up to her tallest and squared her shoulders. "Since the moment of my removal has not yet arrived, I still have the right to offer you welcome in my stepson's home. Please come within and take your ease."

As she shifted to the side so her guests could enter, Edmund breathed out a quiet "Oh." The only thing this cottage shared in common with other peasant abodes was a floor made from bare earth, which generations of feet had walked into rock hardness.

Hidden within these walls was all the opulence Faucon expected of a miller, and that meant chattels aplenty to assess for levying the death tax. Decorating the plastered wall across from them were two tapestries. If their colors were dissimilar, their designs reminded Faucon of the Holy Lands. Two brass-bound chests stood against the wall beneath the tapestries. The smaller of the two was open and items of clothing were draped over its raised lid and sides.

Three well-made chairs, their tall backs looking like half-barrels, were arranged around the hearthstone near the right end of the room. There were no cooking implements near the hearth. That suggested the miller's meals were prepared in one of the outbuildings and carried within doors, just as was done in much grander households.

A yellow and red cupboard, as tall as the wall and finer than anything Faucon's mother owned, was placed where it would be the first thing visitors saw when they entered through the front door. Items crowded its shelves: green ceramic serving platters and bowls, cups made of horn as well as several carved from wood, a large mazer and a number of wooden serving utensils.

The miller slept at the end of the room farthest from the hearth. The curtain that divided the sleeping area from the living area was open. Faucon could see a bed that rivaled the one he now used as his own. A second bed of equal richness stood in the open loft that stretched overhead, the loft's floor reaching about halfway across the main chamber. A ladder, sanded until it gleamed like silk, offered access to this upper sleeping chamber. Judging by the cloth poppet that dangled its arm over the edge of the loft, this was where Stephen and his family found their nightly rest.

The wooden table at the center of the room was sturdy enough to suggest it was left assembled at all times, and not dismantled when it wasn't in use as was done in many other households. The two long benches pushed beneath it offered seating. Various items cluttered the table's surface: a few prettily carved cups, a small trinket box, a pair of shoes, bits of ribbon and head scarves. Agnes was packing.

"Where will you go when you leave here?" Faucon asked.

"I haven't yet decided," Halbert's widow replied quietly.

She picked up the trinket box and carried it to the open chest, turning her back on her guests.

Not waiting for an invitation, Faucon drew out the nearest bench so he and Edmund could sit. They watched their hostess fold the box into a gown, then set it carefully into the chest.

"Perhaps back to Stanrudde," she said at last, her back still to them, "even though I can no longer claim any place there as my own. My mother passed some six months ago, and when I left the city to come to Priors Holston, I sold her home. Perhaps some of her neighbors will remember me kindly and find space for me. Or perhaps I'll travel to Banbury where my sister and her family lives." She sighed. "Although I think I cannot count on a well come from her. We were never close."

"You don't need to leave Priors Holston, you know," Faucon replied. "You could stay if you wished."

Looking over her shoulder at him, she eyed him in sharp surprise. "How can you say that? Only a little while ago Stephen told the whole village that I am no longer welcome in his home. So, go I must. Not that I would stay here with him if he offered. For all he played the obedient child to Halbert, Stephen's ambition eats at him the way Halbert's need for drink consumed him."

"Nay, not Stephen. Simon. If you wished to stay, the fuller would have you," Faucon told her.

That made her smile. Her fondness for her neighbor glowed in her eyes. "So he would," she agreed. "But I won't have him, not when such a match would only be to his detriment. Besides, there's not room for one more body in that house of his," she laughed, then turned back to the chest and began to rearrange the items within it.

The quiet stretched. Edmund shifted uneasily on the bench, seeking the best position from which to study the widow. Faucon sat as he did when he was tracking: still and silent as he waited for the creature he followed to make its next move.

Agnes paused to again look over her shoulder at them. "Do you know how long it will be before Stephen comes to remove me?"

"He told me he expected you gone by day's end," Faucon said. Her stricken look teased him into adding, "But perhaps that's his grief speaking."

"Grief?" she repeated with a harsh laugh. "Greed,

more like. Stephen quakes in terror over what piece of his property I might have the right to claim."

Faucon hurried to exploit the opening she'd just offered, daring to ask a question he had no right to pose. "What dower did Halbert promise you?"

Agnes' lips pinched into a tight smile and her brows rose until her expression was the picture of wicked amusement at Stephen's expense. "Absolutely nothing," she said. "I leave here with no more than I brought with me into this marriage."

"Are you saying there was no contract between you and Halbert?" Faucon demanded, no less shocked at hearing Agnes seem to suggest this than he'd been when Stephen had said much of the same.

"Oh aye, we had a contract, albeit not scribed but spoken before a priest." Agnes told him. "In it, Halbert agreed to feed and clothe me, honoring me as his wife. He promised that I would enjoy the comfort of his home, which is indeed comfortable although I cannot precisely say I have enjoyed it. On my part, I gave Halbert a fine tunic as his wedding present, along with my vow to care for him as if we were heart companions, doing so until the end of my days. Or his," she added, then made an irritable sound and shook her head.

"All of this I would have told Stephen, if he'd ever once spoken to me of it. But he preferred to pretend I didn't exist, all the while whining and complaining about how his father refused to discuss our contract with him. I vow I've never seen a pair of more stubborn, hateful men than the two who live here."

Once again, Faucon dared to tread where he had no right to step. "Begging pardon, goodwife, but judging from that eye of yours, as well as the tales Simon relates, you and Halbert were hardly suited. Why did you marry him at all?"

All the animation drained from her face. She returned to the table to claim one of the wooden cups.

It was a worthy piece, its narrow stem carved with such skill that it looked as if it were made from living ivy. Bits of shell had been inset along its lip until the rim gleamed iridescent white. She curled her hands around the stem of the cup, her fingers working as if she expected to wring liquid from it.

"It was arranged for us. Halbert and I did not meet until the day of our wedding," she finally said, her voice low and flat. "I place no blame on Halbert for the failure of our union. Nay, that all rests on my shoulders. When my mother passed, I mourned her, but I also looked forward to what I expected would be new freedom after so many years spent caring for others. Imagine my shock when instead of freedom, I discovered only lack of purpose, and rather than pleasant solitude, there was nothing but long lonely hours. That's when I realized caring for others had been the one thing, the only thing that gave my life meaning."

She sighed. "I can look back now and see how the emptiness of my life at that moment left me panicked. My fear was so great that it drove me to react too quickly and without consideration. In an instant, I had concocted the idea that if I could find an older man, one who needed someone to make his waning years comfortable, I would again be safe..." her voice trailed off into another sigh and it was a moment before she continued.

"I was told that Halbert was just the sort of man I sought, one who would care for me if I cared for him," she said. "In my desperation and loneliness, I trusted too deeply and believed too swiftly. Shame on me. Needless to say, I now know that even an arranged relationship must be created from something more than a few words spoken before a priest. Its success depends on either previous affection or long familiarity. Or amazing tolerance. All of that was lacking in my union."

She took up the mate to the cup she held and carried

the pair back to the chest. Then, removing the smaller of the two tapestries from the wall, she rolled the cups in it and placed the bundle into the chest. After that, she gathered up all the garments cluttering the sides of the chest and tossed them carelessly within it so she could close the lid and use it as a bench.

Once she sat, she continued her tale, brushing her fingertips over the bruised skin around her eye as she spoke. "Before the first week of my marriage to Halbert played out, I knew how great my mistake had been. But by then it was too late. We were wed, and I was trapped."

"What of an annulment?" Faucon asked.

"She's a woman. She can't petition for an annulment," Edmund told him, his harsh voice quiet.

Agnes nodded in agreement. "Your clerk is right. Only a woman's male kinsmen can author such a petition. I have neither brothers nor uncles, and my father is long since gone to his heavenly reward. Even if I had been allowed to petition on my own behalf, I couldn't afford it. I am only a woodcarver's daughter."

"Did you consider seeking refuge in a nunnery?" the monk asked, the tiniest grain of sympathy softening his otherwise flat tone. "Although it would have taken seven years before your marriage was at last dissolved, you would have spent those years safe within God's walls."

She eyed Edmund for a moment, then her head tilted to the side. Her mouth twisted into a smile that was more grimace than grin. A tiny choked laugh escaped her.

"That did occur to me, Brother. Indeed, I spoke of the possibility with the prior at St. Radegund's. I fear Prior Lambertus did not find me to be of the right temperament to take up residence in a holy house. Nor would he allow me to plead barrenness as a way to escape my marriage. This, even though I am past five-

and-thirty and have never once felt the stirring of life within my womb."

Faucon's brows rose at that. A fruitless marriage could be dissolved without prejudice, since the production of children was the point of wedlock. "What reason did he give for refusing?"

"This is—was my first, my only marriage," she replied, stumbling over her words. "Because of that, the prior said I must wait. He said that old Queen Eleanor had brought forth a son at my same age. He felt there was still hope God might grant me children. Now, just how he thought that might happen is beyond me, since Halbert refused to do his marital duty. Such concourse had not been addressed in our contract." Agnes gave another sharp laugh, her amusement aimed at the impossibility of the trap that had held her so tightly until only a few hours ago.

Faucon heard the story she told them, but also heard the tale she wasn't telling. A whore, Halbert had accused. A woodcarver's aging and unwed daughter, a woman who had lived with her mother and had no apparent livelihood of her own.

Yet, if putting that tapestry into her chest hadn't been an act of theft, Agnes laid claim to an exotic piece from a distant land, an item with a value far beyond that most knights could afford. Also, she had not pleaded to the prior that she was virgin still, when protesting her childless state, or he would have had no choice but to dissolve the union. Lastly, someone had arranged for her to marry a wealthy miller, someone so powerful that the miller had accepted her even though he'd told others he never again intended to wed.

"Did he arrange the marriage for you?" Faucon dared to ask.

"Did who arrange her marriage?" Edmund glanced between his employer and Halbert's widow.

Agnes stared at her shire's new servant of the crown.

Gone was any pretense of feminine humility. Instead, she reminded Faucon of Alf, her expression bold and blank, and as hard as stone. In that instant she didn't look the beaten wife of Simon's tale, but a wise and willful woman, more than capable of caring for herself.

"I cannot see how the arrangement of my marriage matters to anyone, especially now that I am widowed," she finally said.

It was all Faucon needed to follow the trail left by the information she had unwittingly scattered about her as she spoke. Although unremarkable in personality and plain in feature, Agnes had once been a rich man's leman. That man, whoever he was, had kept his lover well, for as long as he had kept her. Then, when Agnes found herself in need of another man to support her, her former lover had found one for her, albeit much to her detriment.

"I suppose you're right," he offered with a smile, seeking to smooth the feathers he'd just ruffled. "Still, I think whoever brought you and Halbert together owes you at least an apology."

She said nothing, only kept her now-hard gaze fastened on Faucon. He read it in her eyes. If he pressed for any more information about the man who had aided her in forming her marriage, she would end their conversation. That wouldn't do, not when he had other questions begging for answers.

"Tell me about Alf," Faucon said. "Simon Fuller says he sent both you and Alf to Susanna the Alewife's house last night. Is that true? Were you there together?"

She blinked. She hadn't expected him to retreat. "We were."

"The whole night?" Faucon pressed.

A soft crease appeared between her brows. "I cannot speak for Alf's presence after I closed my eyes last night. All I can tell you is that he was yet seated at Susanna's table when I found my pallet near her hearth.

Although I cannot name the hour, it was full dark by then."

"What was his mood?"

That crease between her brows deepened until she eyed him in startled curiosity. "His mood? What does his mood matter?"

"Simon tells me that last night after you left for Susanna's, Alf joined him at the race, seeking to calm Halbert," Faucon said. "However, Simon wouldn't allow Alf to either take Halbert into the house or to the mill. The fuller said he feared Halbert might try to hurt Alf in some way. That's why he sent him after you to your alewife's establishment. I'm curious about Alf's thinking, why he resisted leaving Halbert alone at the mill when everyone, even Stephen, speaks of how violent the miller could be when he was besotted."

"Do you not think you should be asking this of Alf?" Her tone was guarded.

"I did," Faucon replied, with a shrug to suggest Alf had refused to speak with him. It wasn't precisely the truth, but it served.

"Ah," Agnes breathed in understanding, and her expression relaxed as she recognized safe ground. "Alf is not one for spilling more words than is necessary, as you have discovered. Nor can I give you any insight as to his thinking. What I can tell you is that Simon was right to make him leave. Halbert's purpose for drinking last night was to fuel his rage."

"Purpose?" Faucon asked in surprise. "Does a man need a purpose to drink?"

That teased a grim smile from her. "It may not be the same for other men, but Halbert was most definitely a purposeful sot. Until he put ale in his belly, he wasn't able to use more than words as his cudgel. The ale freed him to use his fists. Last night, the one Halbert really wanted to beat was Stephen. He was furious with his son for leaving him when there was so much work to be done. Before Stephen departed yestermorn, Halbert had all but come to blows with him as he tried to force his son to remain home rather than stay the week with 'Wina."

"Stephen told his father he wished to stay a week with his wife's people?" Faucon interrupted.

Agnes gave a shake of her head. "That I cannot say. All I heard was Halbert ranting over Stephen leaving for a sennight. More to the point, it was the first time since my arrival here that I'd seen Stephen stand his ground against his father's wishes. No brutal word Halbert threw at him, no threat of violence or disinheritance could shake him. I think this is something Stephen hasn't often done. For the remainder of the day after Stephen departed, I could see Halbert's disbelief in the way he kept watching the lane. It was as if he expected his son to return at any moment, simply because Halbert willed it to be so."

"Huh," Faucon said, considering. "Simon believes Halbert would have taken his fists to Alf last night. Would Halbert have done so to ease what boiled in him?" Then, before she had a chance to respond, he added, "From what I've seen of your workman, he hardly seems the type to bow his head and meekly allow even his master to beat him."

Agnes gave a scornful snort. "I am certain Halbert would have tried to beat Alf. And, although Simon had no way of knowing this, I'm equally certain Halbert would never have landed a blow, not unless Alf allowed it. Unlike Stephen and me, Alf had no reason to tolerate Halbert's abuse, since there was never a consequence for him if he resisted. Of all the folk in this household, Halbert likes–liked Alf best, as much as he could be fond of anyone. You see, Alf had been a soldier once, just as Halbert had been."

Faucon wasn't surprised by this revelation. "So Alf isn't a runaway serf?"

His question startled honest amusement out of her. Untainted by any other emotion, her laugh was merry, the sparkling sound suggesting a far more intriguing woman hid behind her plain features.

"Of all things! A serf? Who told you that?" she demanded, still smiling.

"Simon," Faucon replied with an answering smile and a shrug.

Again she laughed. "Well, at least I now understand why Simon insisted that Alf go to Susanna's. Simon has close experience of those who suffer under abusive and forced servitude. His wife nearly died at her former lord's hands before she escaped to find a new home here in Priors Holston. As soft-hearted as Simon is, I wager he couldn't bear to think of Halbert misusing Alf. I'd also wager that Simon isn't the only one in this village who's been conjuring up tales of Alf's past. Folk bend toward those sorts of ideas when a stranger arrives and is as secretive as Alf. I had my own ideas about him until I finally spoke to 'Wina," she added.

As he'd been busy concocting his own tale around Alf, Faucon couldn't resist asking. "Is that so? And what was it you were thinking of him?"

Agnes offered a quick lift of her brows and a thin smile. "That Alf was Halbert's bastard, come to steal Stephen's inheritance. The truth, according to 'Wina, is far less romantic. She says Alf came to the mill last year after parting ways with his mercenary troop once they returned to England from the Holy Land."

"A crusader?" Faucon replied in surprise.

That sent his thoughts flashing through the time he spent in the Levant, seeking some recollection of Alf's face, in case their paths had crossed. He quickly released the notion as impossible. Early on, King Richard had discovered that Faucon's cousin Gilliam was a gifted jouster. The result was that Faucon and Gilliam, along with their foster father who traveled with them, had been invited into the king's own retinue to battle at his side.

"Aye, and according to 'Wina, it was Alf's crusading past that caught Halbert's attention when he arrived in Priors Holston seeking work," Agnes replied. "Years ago, at the end of the time when he was a soldier, Halbert had also traveled to the Holy Land. Apparently, just as happened to Alf, Halbert also lost his taste for soldiering while in our Lord's homeland. It was on Halbert's return to England from that journey that he bought his release from his commander and troop, then came to settle here."

Agnes paused and glanced from Faucon to Edmund. "You have asked me many questions and I have answered them. Now, answer mine. What purpose have you for asking me of Alf and Halbert, or any questions at all for that matter? If your answer does not satisfy, I believe it may be time for you to depart. I have much to do if I'm to be prepared to leave before Stephen comes and forces me from his home."

"How dare you speak so boldly to my master!" Edmund retorted swiftly. He sounded as outraged as he had yesterday when he chastised Lord Rannulf, and looked as ready to do battle as when he'd argued with the sheriff about extracting Halbert's body from the race.

"Brother Edmund," Faucon warned, but Edmund had the bit between his teeth and was racing full tilt ahead.

"Sir Faucon is the king's servant. It is his purpose to find the man who killed your husband. As that is his duty, he may ask you what he will and you will answer him, else answer to the royal court."

Abject surprise flattened Agnes' expression. "Killed?! What nonsense is this? Halbert wasn't killed. He fell into the race because of drink and drowned beneath his wheel."

"Nay, your husband was already at Heaven's gate when his body was put into the water," Edmund informed her, bent on revealing what Faucon had hoped to conceal until he judged the moment appropriate.

"Enough, Brother Edmund!" Faucon cried in panicked command.

"There's a hole in his chest, put there by the one whose name Sir Faucon and I shall soon discover," the clerk trumpeted.

Faucon sighed in defeat. More fool he for not instructing his clerk prior to beginning this conversation with Agnes. There would be no regaining the advantage Edmund had just stolen from him.

Agnes gazed at him, a new hollowness in her expression. She looked as if she were starving and knew he had the food she craved. "Is this true?" she almost whispered.

"It is," he confirmed reluctantly.

Sudden color rushed up her neck to flood her face. She swallowed and released a breath. In that long slow sigh, Faucon recognized the sounds of relief and gratitude. Then she folded her hands in her lap and bowed her head.

A few hours ago, Faucon would have thought her reaction simply that of a modest woman. Now, having glimpsed her true nature, he recognized this sham of humility as her shield, one she plied to great effect.

"Do you know who killed your husband?" Faucon asked. It was a waste of his breath. She would tell him nothing more, no matter how he asked.

She didn't disappoint. "I do not," she said without raising her head. "Until this very moment I believed only that Halbert had drowned."

Faucon watched in frustrated silence as she returned to her feet and once more turned her back to them. Opening her chest, she pulled out the garments she'd moments before tossed into it and began to fold. He didn't expect her to offer another word, save a suggestion that they leave. She surprised him when she paused, the gown she held pressed to her chest.

"Murdered," she breathed in disbelief, then shifted until he could see the curve of her cheek and brow from over her shoulder. "Nay, you must be wrong. How can Halbert have been murdered when I saw nothing amiss anywhere near the wheel this morning, save that the wrench was beneath the brake when it should have been in the mill? If he was stabbed as your clerk suggests, shouldn't we have seen his blood upon the earth around the wheel?"

"Halbert didn't die near the wheel," Faucon said, praying that if he gave her the information she craved she might continue to satisfy his questions. "The one who stole his life waited until Halbert was deep in besotted slumber, then took him into Simon's croft to do the deed."

She gasped at that. "Where in Simon's croft did my husband breathe his last?" Her words remained hardly louder than a whisper.

"At the place where the fuller does his slaughtering," Faucon told her, wondering at her question. "Simon had butchered a pig. It seems the one who took Halbert's life knew this, for he used that same location to murder Halbert, burying his blood under the ashes spread about that area." If only Faucon could puzzle out why it had been necessary to hide the true cause of Halbert's death.

Agnes bent to store the garment she held, then retrieved another to fold. "Poor Simon," she said as she straightened. "And here I thought I was doing him a boon, what with that ever-hungry brood of his, when I sold my pig to him. It was my gilt he slaughtered. Yesterday, I awoke to discover one of my pigs had a broken leg. It had been done apurpose. Pigs don't just break their legs," she added as harsh aside. "I confronted Halbert, but he denied doing any harm to the animal. I didn't believe him. How could I? There is—was no one else in this house cruel enough to hurt an innocent creature for no reason."

Then she whispered, "But there was a reason."

Faucon's hands closed into fists. He heard it in Agnes' voice and in the careful way she strung together her words. She might not have witnessed her husband's death, but she was certain she knew who had killed him. Damn her, but she had taken his tidbits, sewn them to those she already had in store, and found the one who waited at the end of this trail, when he lagged miles behind her, looking at nothing but a jumble of footprints!

Faucon wanted to command her to turn and face him. He wanted to demand that she give him the name she was even now cherishing. To no avail. She would only plead ignorance, then once more apply that shield of hers when he had no weapon to pierce it.

It was time to end this.

He came to his feet. "Thank you, goodwife. I will wish you a good journey from Priors Holston, and pray you find far greater peace in your next home than you have had here."

She threw a startled look over her shoulder at him. Once again, she had expected him to press.

"You are kind to say so, sir. Thank you very much," she said, as softly and humbly as any man would expect of a well-behaved housewife. She made no move to see them to the door, only concentrated on her packing.

"So, tell me. What is the name of the man who killed Halbert?" Edmund asked as they left the miller's cottage.

"How should I know?" Faucon snapped. "You

cheated me of my chance to winnow what I needed out of Halbert's widow to help me as I track this one. Why did you speak so rudely to her?" he demanded, even though it was his own fault he'd lost the chance to put his questions to the widow. Edmund was under his command and he had failed to control him.

His clerk frowned back. "Me! I did no wrong. You must never allow commoners to be disrespectful. That woman had no right to question your purpose." What started as a vehement protest softened with every word Edmund spoke, until the last word almost whispered from his lips. Reflected in his dark gaze was the barest hint that he now recognized his misstep.

The silence stretched between them. Faucon waited, but once again Edmund offered no apology.

He shook off his irritation. Dwelling on his clerk's misbehavior was a distraction he couldn't afford. At least he had one new piece of information in store: the best way to find the man who had murdered Halbert was to discover the name of the man who had once kept Agnes.

It wasn't a name known here in Priors Holston, of that Faucon was certain. Had it been, he would have already heard it either from Stephen or one of the many men in the inquest jury. Nay, if Faucon wanted that name, it was the folk of his own class he needed to ask. That was, if he could discover the right person to ask. He was an outsider in this shire, with no idea who among the knights and nobles was the most informed gossip. Or, who would betray the misbehavior of one of their own to a stranger.

"Edmund, collect your writing implements. We need to have a bite to eat, then I must make my way to St. Radegund's. I need to present myself to the prior, as my lord uncle commanded of me yesterday, before I return to Blacklea."

Aye, first he'd speak with Susanna the Alewife, then

he'd be on to the monastery. It was as good a place to start asking after Agnes' lover as any other. Hadn't his father always said, although not in his mother's hearing, that there was no greater gossip than a churchman?

Chapter Eleven

As he and Edmund returned to the courtyard, the clerk went to gather his scribbling supplies while Faucon joined Brother Colin. The former apothecary yet stood beside Halbert's corpse, ready to offer his explanations if asked. Colin's job was almost at an end now. There were so few jurors left in the yard that the wrens living in the mill's eaves had returned to trilling out that complicated song of theirs.

"Have you seen Alf, the miller's servant?" Faucon asked of Colin. "I'd like to speak with him."

"I fear you'll have to wait to do that," Colin replied, then pointed to the shed where Halbert's son yet sat upon his barrel. The new miller was now attended only by Father Walter, the village priest. "Stephen called for him a few moments ago and, after they spoke, the workman left the yard. Where he went, I cannot say. How goes your hunting, sir?"

But of course Alf was gone. Faucon reluctantly set aside the questions he wanted to put to the man for some other time. That left him wondering how long he had before the matter of the miller's murder was required to have a final resolution. Then again, perhaps there was no need to hurry. Hadn't Edmund mentioned that many pleas for justice had languished for years prior to the last Eyre?

"Both better and worse than I expected," Faucon told the monk with a frustrated sigh. "I vow my thoughts are so tangled at the moment, I want to throw away the spindle and start anew."

"I can listen while you think aloud, if that might be of use to you," Colin offered.

"Well, it cannot make matters any worse," Faucon shot back, tempering the harshness of his words with a laugh.

He began counting out the bits of information he now held dear by touching the awl that lay beside Halbert on his bier, then brushing his fingers against the sleeve of the miller's blue tunic. "I'm content to claim this awl as deodand and say it was used to kill our miller, even if that may not be the truth. Also, I know that the miller despised the tunic he wears, and that he would never have donned it, given a choice. Someone else put it on him and did so for their own purposes. And I know where he died."

"Where?" Colin's gaze came to life with interest.

"In the fuller's croft, but don't let your thoughts run wild, expecting to find anything of import there. That path has lead me nowhere, and nowhere is where I've been since I discovered it."

Colin laughed and shook his head. "You don't believe there's nothing important there."

"You may be right," Faucon admitted with a grimace. "Lastly, I've made no progress in discovering the 'who' in all this, because the two I believe mostly likely to have killed the miller weren't at the mill when he died." It was enough to make his head throb. He pressed his fingers to his temples.

Again, the monk laughed. "Then someone isn't telling the truth, because Halbert is dead, rendered so by murder most foul. If you want to know who is telling you tales, you'll have to pick at their stories. A lie is always more complex than the truth, and the liar, no matter how accomplished, will always forget something as he crafts his falsehood. It's up to you to discover where he's erred.

"So tell me. Why do you believe the place of Halbert's death has no story to tell? Prove that to me. Start by telling me where in the fuller's croft he died."

"At the place where the family does its usual slaughtering. It just so happens that Simon slaughtered a young pig yesterday, a pig that had belonged to Agnes and whose leg..." Faucon's words trailed off.

Whose leg had been broken for a reason. That's what Agnes had whispered. He caught his breath, knowing what he'd missed when he stood beneath Simon's chestnut tree.

"What is it?" Colin prodded.

"It was no accident that Simon had a pig to slaughter the morning before Halbert died. That's why the gilt's leg had been broken, and not by Halbert, although that's what his wife originally believed," he said, no longer seeing the last of the commoners as they made their way past their murdered neighbor.

The man who murdered Halbert had broken the pig's leg, knowing Agnes would offer the injured creature to Simon and knowing Simon wouldn't wait to slaughter it, not when he had so many mouths to feed. All this had been done so there would be a hidden place to kill Halbert. It was the same reason the awl had been used, so there would be an insignificant wound in Halbert's chest.

"Ach!" Faucon cried out, as his thoughts once more stalled anew as they came up against the way Halbert's death had been disguised.

"I don't understand any of this," he complained to the monk. "Why does the one who killed Halbert go to such trouble to kill him? Carrying a big man here and there, undressing then dressing him, putting him into the race. It makes no sense! If Halbert was truly deep in besotted slumber, why not lower him into the race and let the wheel take him? Why is it important to make it appear that Halbert drowned by accident when he was in fact murdered by design?"

"Well, putting Halbert into the race might have been a simpler death, but it wasn't as certain," Colin offered.

"The race is only waist deep. What if Halbert had awakened? Would he have come to his feet and avoided the wheel, or perhaps roused enough to call for help?"

"All possible," Faucon agreed, but he still felt as if he chewed on something distasteful.

That made Colin laugh. "I can see my reasoning doesn't satisfy you."

The monk's words shot through Faucon, tearing a hole in the wall that trapped him. Faucon threw back his head and laughed. "That's it! You've hit the nail, Brother. There was no satisfaction in simply drowning Halbert." Nay indeed, not when Halbert had drawn blood from a woman whom another man—a knight or nobleman well-trained in the art of war—had cherished, and might yet cherish. "Vengeance required his blood be shed."

Colin grinned. "Once again I am glad to serve. Does this mean you know why Halbert died?"

"The why I already knew but failed to mention. He died to free his wife from their marriage," Faucon answered with more than a little satisfaction of his own.

"Bless me," Colin cried. "A woman alone did this to him? Are you certain there was no man to help her?"

"Nay, it wasn't she who killed Halbert," Faucon started.

"I am ready, Sir Faucon," Edmund interrupted as he joined them. A cloth sack was now tucked behind one arm, its strap over one shoulder. The bundle was awkward and the roll of parchment thrust out from behind his head much like an archer's quiver.

Edmund acknowledged the lay brother with a brusque nod. "Brother Herbalist, is that the last of the jurors?"

Faucon glanced around in surprise to find there were no men left in the yard now.

"It is, Brother," Colin replied, his tone modulated to the more subdued expression employed by men of the first estate.

"Then you are free to return to your own tasks. Take with you our gratitude for your help this day," Edmund said in dismissal, then looked at his employer. "Sir Faucon, the inquest is now complete. You may instruct me to inform the family that the corpse is theirs to tend to as they will, may the miller rest in peace."

God take Edmund! Faucon opened his mouth, ready to skewer the monk for his impertinence in commanding his better to heel like some dog, as well as for dismissing Colin. From behind his clerk, the older monk shook his head, his gaze filled with warning.

Faucon caught back his chide. "You are so instructed," he snapped, finding his patience with Edmund worn as thin as his uncle's seemed to have been yesterday when Bishop William had chided the man.

If Edmund recognized Faucon's reaction, he gave no sign of it. Instead, he turned and strode to the shed and Stephen.

Once his clerk was out of earshot, Faucon looked at Colin. "Why did you bid me hold my tongue? It is my right to chastise him as I will," he demanded of the monk.

"True enough, Sir Faucon. And if all you had intended was to scold him for how he spoke to you, I would not have interceded. But that was not your sole intent," the older man replied with an easy smile, seemingly untroubled by Edmund's harsh behavior toward him. "Although your urge to leap to my defense speaks well of the man you are, in all honesty, you have no right to speak on my behalf. I am but a lay brother. As such, Brother Edmund is well within his rights to command me to his purpose. If it helps, know that I chose this life of mine, and have never once had cause to regret that choice."

His was a gentle chide with a well-honed purpose,

and unlike Edmund, Faucon understood the lesson and took the point. He vented what stewed in him with a long breath, then shifted to watch Edmund as the monk spoke with Stephen. There was no humility in the clerk's stance and nothing but command in his gestures.

"At every turn your brother in Christ demands respect from others, while offering no grain of it to those who deserve to receive it from him," Faucon complained.

Colin laughed. "You are expecting a dog to fly. Brother Edmund hasn't the ability to respect, or, I think, even admire another. Such things are not in his nature. Now, I have more herbs to gather before my day is done, and you must be on with your hunt."

He offered Faucon his hand, the way warriors did when greeting each other. Then again, today they had been warriors, fighting a battle of a different sort as they sought out the cause of Halbert's death. "Come find me when you have solved the riddle of Halbert Miller's death, knowing that I shall wait breathlessly to hear the identity of the one who did this. And should you ever again come upon dead men who have signs on them you cannot read, don't forget that I am attached to Saint Michael's Abbey in Stanrudde."

Faucon laughed as he took the monk's hand, well pleased by the offer of aid and friendship. "I shall indeed call upon you, perhaps more often than you intend."

"I stand ready." Colin winked, then gathered up his pack. He crossed paths with a returning Edmund, then was gone around the corner of the mill in a trice.

Edmund joined Faucon. "Now where?" he demanded of his employer, his tone as brusque and flat as ever.

Chapter Twelve

"**O**f course, Alf stayed the night. Do you think I'd let him go back to the mill when I knew that ass meant to have at him? Not in my lifetime!"

Susanna the Alewife's voice was so deep she could have been mistaken for a man. She looked like a soldier, standing with her shoulders thrown back and her hands braced on her hips. A massive woman, she was taller than Faucon and as wide as she was tall. The sleeves of her dark green gown were rolled as far up her forearms as their meaty girth allowed. A pair of dark red braids streamed out from beneath the simple white cap she wore.

She looked skyward and shouted, "I'm warning you now, Lord. If You don't send Halbert Miller straight to hell, You and I are going to have words when I make my way to Your holy gates." Her rooster took umbrage to the shout and crowed from its perch atop her roof. From the cottage across the lane, a babe squalled as if the alewife's cry had startled it.

Offering a final scornful sniff at what she perceived as Faucon's foolish question, Susanna pivoted. Her braids snapped from side to side as she marched toward her cottage's open door. "Your inquest kept my trade away this morning, so I've plenty to offer. Sit anywhere you like." She threw the words over her shoulder as she stepped inside her home.

Faucon stared after her, startled by her and this whole encounter, as he tied Legate to the gate and retrieved his cup from his saddlebag. He'd reclaimed his mount from the servant watching him, then sent the man back to St. Radegund's with a message to Prior Lambertus, warning of his visit.

Hens worked diligently at the soil in what would have been Susanna's front garden, had she not filled it with a half-dozen makeshift tables—naught more than bare planks of wood set atop braces—and equally makeshift benches to accommodate her trade. He chose one close to her gate, sitting on the bench that faced the lane beyond Susanna's woven withe fence. That narrow path was no longer deserted as it had been upon Faucon's arrival this morning. Instead, folk moved this way and that along the lane, old men burdened with great bundles of branches collected against winter's coming, boys armed with slings racing toward the surrounding fields. A beyoked woman made careful headway over the ruts and stones, carrying her full buckets, while a tanner laden with his leather hurried past her. As he crossed the lane near Susanna's gate, the tanner glanced into the yard and nodded as he spied Faucon. Surprised and a little pleased at being recognized, Faucon returned the gesture.

As Edmund found his cup in his sack, Susanna threaded her way back through the empty tables at her same thundering pace. She carried with her a good-sized iron pot and a tray on which stood a clay pitcher and a bread trencher; it was a fasting day for Edmund, so he was only drinking. After emptying her pitcher into their waiting cups, she set it on a nearby table. Laying the bread in front of Faucon, she ladled stew into the center hollow of the crusty trencher. She dropped a wooden eating spoon next to his cup, then set aside her tray and pot with the pitcher.

"The stew's warm, and that's all I can say for it. I'm no cook. Now, the ale will be better than any you've ever before had," she promised with no show of humility as she dragged over a short bench. As she sat, she rested her elbows on their table top.

The planks shifted so forcefully that Faucon snatched for his cup, fearing it might topple. Once it was in hand, he put the cup to his lips, preparing the polite compliments her boast required. Her ale was thick, malty and sweet, all in one delicious instant. He swallowed deeply in pleasure, draining half his cup. No wonder Halbert had bought his drink from a woman who hated him.

"This is wonderful," Faucon told her, as he set the cup back on the table.

Edmund nodded in silent agreement as he sipped his own brew, his gaze shifting warily between his employer and the alewife.

Susanna accepted Faucon's praise with as much grace as Edmund might have done. "Everyone has a calling. Ale is mine, as it was my mother's before me." Then, rubbing her well-padded chin with her thumb, she studied him for a long moment. "Crowner. Is that what you're called?"

"Coronarius," Edmund corrected. "Sir Faucon is the newly-elected coronarius for this shire. He is the Keeper of the Pleas for the royal court."

Susanna turned her hard gaze on the clerk. "Then why did every man who stopped here to tell me what was afoot at the mill call him 'Sir Crowner?'"

Edmund's jaw squared. His brows lowered as he prepared for battle. His mouth opened.

Faucon held up a hand. "Coronarius or crowner, either describes me and my new duties to our king," he told Susanna. "All that matters is that I'm the one who must discover who killed Halbert Miller."

Susanna grinned at that. "Whoever the glorious bastard is who did-in Halbert has my everlasting gratitude. My brother-by-marriage was a cruel bitch's son who killed my sister in soul, if not in body. And you'll never convince me that he didn't seduce Cissy so he could get his greedy hands on that mill."

"If you hated him so, why didn't you refuse your sister when she wanted to marry him?" Faucon asked, surprised that a woman as forceful as Susanna might have so easily relinquished a piece of her inheritance. "It's your right to do so, when their marriage gave him part-ownership of the mill."

"How could I refuse her?" Susanna shot back. "Cissy ran the mill all on her own."

Faucon frowned. "Your parents didn't share the mill between their daughters?" Had Susanna and Cissy been born boys, the eldest of them would have taken all. But daughters usually split any inheritance left to them.

Susanna brayed a laugh at his question, then waved a hand toward the lane and the folk walking it. "They told me you were new to our vale. My parents were Priors Holston's brewers, not its millers. I took to malting almost before I could walk, so it was a given that I would follow my mother into brewing. Although twins we be, Cissy hated ale-making, so she married Jervis. He was just a cottar, with no land of his own, but he ran the mill. Of course, that was years ago, and in those days the mill belonged to the priory. Back then, even though old Jervis did all the work of milling, he kept only a little profit, and paid his fee to the monks when he ground his own grain just like the rest of us.

"As we wives so often do when our husband has a trade, Cissy became a miller alongside her man. She was my match in all ways," Susanna grinned at that and patted one burly arm. "There was nothing he did that she couldn't and didn't do. Turns out that was a good thing. Jervis died a few years after they were wed, having given Cissy no child, although he did leave her that cottage where Halbert and Stephen live now. Since there was no one else to run the mill, and even though the prior protested long and loud, Cissy became our miller. For a few years, she did the job well enough, all on her own."

As Susanna spoke, Faucon dipped his spoon into the stew, then rolled the soupy mixture around his mouth. She'd spoken true, she was no cook; it was meatless and flat. But it was edible, and he was hungry, what with having had only oatcakes to break his fast. He set to eating with relief, if not gusto.

"Then Halbert arrived," Susanna continued. "Aye, he was a handsome stinkard, but I think Cissy wanted him mostly because he was a stranger, someone she hadn't known for all her life. Someone who hadn't called her 'a cock-less man' from time to time, the way I once again hear these days, now that the sweet fool I married passed last year.

"There'll be some who'll tell you that Cissy made a good match when she wed Halbert, even though he had only a little wealth to his name. They always go on about how Halbert was able to buy Cissy's freedom from the priory, how he now collects all the profits from the mill and pays only a token rent to the monks. What they don't say is how he achieved all that. With sacks full of silver that he got by stealing grain from other folk, that's how!" She slammed a heavy fist on the plank in punctuation.

Edmund's cup bounced. The clerk caught it, then stared wide-eyed at the woman across the table from him.

"And then they'll go on about that home of theirs," Susanna continued, "how fine it is now, the beautiful things she had. To them, I say 'bah!' What good is luxury when Cissy was never happy? All she ever got from Halbert was that whining boy of hers, while each of the half-dozen babes who followed him died in her arms, taking a piece of her heart with them as they went, just as my babes did when I lost them.

"If you ask me, that son of hers is almost as bad as his sire. At least Stephen had the sense to marry 'Wina. Now there's a worthy woman. No fragile flower like

Aggie, that lass. Instead, she's one that even Halbert would never dare cross. At their wedding, I told 'Wina right there in Halbert's hearing that if her father-by-marriage ever raised a fist to her, she should wait until nightfall, then douse him with a pot of boiling water."

The memory of that moment made the alewife grin. For all her smile was broad and vicious, the movement of her mouth made her dark eyes sparkle and revealed a glimpse of the girl she had once been. "I said I'd stand in court and swear it was an accident, that she slipped and fell while carrying it.

"Thing is, Halbert knew 'Wina wouldn't have any trouble doing the like. For sure, he's never laid a hand on her. If he had, she would have told me, and I would have helped her empty that pot on him. Nay, I would have brought a bigger pot!" She shouted another laugh.

"A vicious man, indeed," Faucon said, swallowing more ale to wash down the last of the stew. "Agnes tells me she thinks he broke her pig's leg, for no other reason than cruelty."

Susanna made a feral sound deep in her throat. "Sounds like Halbert."

Faucon eyed her, then decided that with this woman, he might as well give up subtlety and simply ask. "Do you have any idea who might have killed Halbert?"

That made her grin again. "Me, most likely. At least, that's what I thought when I saw Halbert under his own wheel this morning. I was sure he'd finally gotten senseless drunk on my strongest ale–that's the weakest you're drinking now–and done himself in. Imagine my disappointment when friends and foes alike began to pass by my fence, all of them calling out to let me know that Halbert hadn't drowned but had been killed with his own awl, then put into the race. Not that I never considered killing him outright. I just never had the opportunity, more's the pity. I definitely didn't have the chance last night, not with both Alf and Aggie here as my companions."

"Both of them? All night?" Faucon asked.

She eyed him curiously. "All night long, until Simon awakened us with the hue and cry after he found Halbert in the water. That was just after dawn. Why?"

"There's no chance that Alf might have departed and returned in the middle of the night without your knowledge?" It was a desperate question, filled with hope's last gasp.

She cocked a russet brow at him, then jerked her thumb over her shoulder to indicate the entrance to her home. "There's only one door. At night, I lay my pallet against it and put my back to it. It serves me better than any bar. Do you think even Alf could move my bulk and not awaken me whilst he did so? And he'd have to have done that twice, going out, then coming in again. Nay, Alf was within my walls from the moment I found my rest until Simon's shouts awakened us."

Faucon grimaced in disappointment. Why had Alf lied about his whereabouts? Whatever his reasons, they were his alone. The truth was that Alf hadn't killed his master, no matter how badly Faucon wanted it to be otherwise.

Susanna leaned back on the bench so she could put her hands on her hips again. "If you want the name of the one who killed Halbert, I'd be looking at Stephen, were I you. Worm that he is, that boy's been panicking over his father's marriage since the day Aggie arrived here. Two weeks ago, he even came crying to me about how his father was giving away the mill. It was newest and loudest of his ongoing complaints about how his father had brought a stranger into their life that Stephen had to support on what he thought of as his profits."

She winked at Faucon. "Of course, then I had to prick him a little by saying Aggie was no stranger to me, seeing's how she and I were living here together, and if she asked it of me, I'd help her make a go of the mill after Halbert was gone." She laughed at her own jest, then shook her head.

"I don't know why Stephen bothered to fret. His father is—was such a churl. We all knew Halbert would never have given anyone so much as a straw, unless his hand was forced or he was well paid for his trouble. As for Aggie, he wouldn't even give her a smile. Why did Stephen think his father would give her the mill? That's the most curious thing of all in Aggie's coming to Priors Holston. Why did Halbert marry Aggie in the first place, because he surely didn't want to be married to her. Among my trade, we're most of us wagering there were coins involved. Some are laying odds on Halbert having been paid to marry her, but I'm putting my silver on the opposite. I think Halbert would have lost coins if he hadn't wed her."

Her words drove the breath from Faucon's lungs. He froze, his cup lifted halfway to his lips.

"You need more ale," she said, misreading his hesitation. "The pitcher's empty. I'll be right back with more."

She thrust to her feet. Once again, their makeshift table top shifted. Faucon barely felt the movement of the boards, as the tidbits of knowledge in his head jostled, settling into a new order in his thoughts. But no matter how they rearranged, they kept coming up against how the miller had been put into the race after he was dead. This time, Faucon sidestepped his frustration over the race and the wheel, and moved on. That left his thoughts once more circling around Alf.

Edmund tapped the tabletop with his fingers, his hand stretched out so it was almost next to Faucon's trencher. Faucon blinked, reclaiming his awareness of the world around him. Across the table his clerk watched him, his expression curious. As Edmund realized he had his employer's attention, he retracted his hand and put his elbows on the table.

"This is the second time you've done that today. The first was just before you asked me to tell you what our archbishop said about the Keepers. Now here you are looking at me when I don't think you see me. Have I again done something amiss?" Edmund's admission that he knew he'd done wrong this day was almost more startling than his question.

"Nay, you've done nothing. I am only thinking," Faucon explained, as Susanna returned with that heavy clay pitcher in her hand. She filled his cup, set the pitcher in the center of the table, and reclaimed her bench.

"You're not the first to tell me that Halbert had no desire to remarry after your sister passed," Faucon said. "In all the time you've spent with Agnes, did she never mention how Halbert came to take her as his wife?"

The alewife shook her head, her chins jiggling with the movement, then smiled. "Aggie is very good at saying nothing, while filling the air with words. Every time I tried to pry, she would change the subject and natter on, until I finally realized I was wasting my breath and ceased to try. All I'm sure of is that Aggie was as desperate to escape that marriage as Halbert was to have her gone, when they were well and truly trapped in holy wedlock.

"So was 'Wina, caught between them by no fault of her own, the peace of her home shattered. And although I know 'Wina wouldn't mind keeping Aggie at her side, now that Halbert's dead, I'm sure Stephen will soon have Aggie and her goods standing outside the door of his home. As much as I'll miss her companionship—I've had no one to share my empty hours with since that man of mine found his just reward, may the good Lord bless him—I think Aggie will be pleased to see no more of Priors Holston."

This time, when Susanna laughed the sound was

gentler, almost feminine. "'Wina has to be breathing in relief this morning, knowing Halbert has departed this earthly vale. I tell you, as distraught as she was over losing her dam, she was even more worried about leaving Aggie alone while she went to lay her mother to rest. It took quite a bit of talking before I convinced 'Wina it was safe for her to go spend time with her family."

Faucon looked at Susanna in surprise. "Stephen's wife didn't want to attend her mother's funeral?"

Susanna shook her head. "Oh, nay. She wanted to go more than she wanted to breathe."

Here she paused and stared out over the lane, as lost in thought as Faucon had been the previous moment. In the distance, a couple fought, their voices rising and falling in anger. That babe now wailed in true distress.

"What a wonder it must be to come from parents who have a care for you and from whom you've only ever known love," Susanna murmured, then brought her attention back to the knight and monk at her table.

"'Wina wanted to go, she just wasn't certain that Stephen should come with her. But there was Stephen, hounding her over how they had to go, not just for the burial, but also for the wake the night before. This, when it's usually he who frets over leaving his father unwatched in that house. Halbert's been known to break things when he's besotted, and God knows Stephen can't afford to lose a single thing," she added sarcastically.

"How far from Priors Holston is 'Wina's family home?" Faucon asked.

"Well, that's the thing, isn't it?" Susanna shot him a hard look. "There was no need for Stephen to stay the night if he wanted to go to either wake or funeral. The hamlet 'Wina's from is no more than a mile in that direction." She pointed to the west. "He could have worked the day, then gone to spend the evening hours with his in-laws, having missed nothing more than the first tear-filled moments of drinking at the wake. If he'd wanted, he could have returned to sleep in his own bed for a few hours, then walked back for the funeral in the morning, couldn't he have?"

Satisfaction tasted as sweet as Susanna's ale. Faucon raised his cup to his lips and drained it to the last tasty dregs. Taking coins from the purse at his belt, he offered the alewife the value of her brew, which was more than her stated price, then came to his feet and bowed.

"My thanks. You are indeed a master brewer, and I'm grateful I don't have to call you to stand before the justices for boiling the miller to death."

Susanna roared at that. She was still laughing as he mounted Legate and sent his horse down the lane, following the walking Edmund.

Chapter Thirteen

With Edmund leading the way to the priory, Faucon guided Legate for a half-mile along the bank of the miller's brook after it left Priors Holston. There was no exterior wall to separate the Priory of St. Radegund from the lands and folk it had once ruled. Instead, there was only a sloe hedge that grew along the front of the compound. Although pruned into a tall leafy wall, many of the plum bushes were so old they were either gnarled and barren or dead. At one time someone had cut away the bushes to create an opening along the path leading into the priory. There wasn't even the pretense of a gate to close out the world.

Faucon dismounted and walked Legate through the leafy gap. Just as there was no gate, there was no porter standing guard, waiting to challenge their entry. Then again, with but the prior and eleven monks–twelve now that Edmund had joined them–it wasn't likely they could afford to dedicate one man to do nothing more than watch an opening.

Beyond the bushes, the rectangular layout of the priory looked much the same as any other monastery Faucon had seen. The dorter, the two-storey residence where the brothers ate and slept, connected to the south transept of a small church. The monks' cloister, the walled garden with its arcaded walk that was meant to separate the world of the monks from the world of men, sprang from its nave. What looked like a barn of some sort had been built off the cloister's end and met with a long wooden kitchen shed that formed the last leg of the rectangle. The only construct Faucon expected but couldn't see was the chapter house, but experience told him it was most likely at the back of the dorter.

The priory church was ancient, or so walls of mossy reddish uncut stones and patched mortar proclaimed. However, its roof seemed new. Despite the dozens of doves, no doubt kept by the monks for their meat and eggs, perched atop its peak, Faucon could see no markers of time's passage on the dark gray slate tiles.

The dorter was also new, the hewn rectangular blocks of red stone in its walls typical of structures Faucon had seen raised over the course of his lifetime. So was the cloister, or at least its colonnaded walkway seemed to be. The arches cut into the roofed walk were low and narrow but outlined with costly carved stonework.

Without looking back to see if Faucon followed, Edmund started toward the dorter. At that same moment, the servant who'd ridden with Faucon to Priors Holston walked out from between the kitchen and cloister.

"Sir Crowner, Brother Edmund," he called to them with a smile of welcome. "Prior Lambertus sent me to greet you. You are to meet with him in the chapter house, sir. If you like, I'll see to your horse again," he offered. "We're becoming great friends, we two. If you say I may, I'll take him to an area where he can graze until you're ready for him. I'll keep watch for you here by the gateway," the servant finished with a jaunty salute.

"If you please," Faucon replied as he handed the man Legate's reins. Then he unbuckled his scabbard and sword from his belt and hung it from the pommel of his saddle. "My thanks indeed."

"This way, Sir Faucon," Brother Edmund said, once again turning his back on his master.

Faucon followed Edmund through the wide gap left between the kitchen shed and the dorter. Edmund opened the side door to the monks' living quarters. Faucon entered the refectory, the place where the monks took their meals, only to stop but a single step within the chamber, as awed by this room as Edmund had been of the miller's home.

Sunlight shot through the line of narrow, south-facing windows finding bright blues, greens and yellows in the patterned ceramic floor tiles and making the freshly plastered walls glow a pure white. A line of columns ran down the middle of the chamber to hold aloft the vaulted ceiling, or rather the floor of the monks' second-storey sleeping chamber. The same geometric pattern Faucon had noted carved onto the cloister was repeated here, decorating the stone window frames, the heads of the columns and the joints of the vaults. But in here, each line of the carved design had been painted a vibrant blue. That gave the upper reaches of the room an airy feeling, despite the clutter of the columns and low ceiling.

Two dining tables, one on either side of the central columns, stretched nearly the full length of the chamber. At the head of the room was a low dais on which stood a small table and single chair, no doubt for the prior's use. There was no pulpit; instead, a lectern stood to one side of the dais. This was surely where the designated monk would read the daily scripture as the rest of his brothers ate.

Edmund followed Faucon in through the door, then eased around his dumbfounded employer. As the monk stopped beside him, Faucon shot him a wondering look. "Everything in this chamber—tiles, tables and stonework—it all looks new," he said in surprise.

"I believe everything is new at the priory, all save for the old church," Edmund replied with a quick shrug, then started up the south side of the room.

Faucon followed. The sound of their footsteps echoed hollowly in the empty space. Now that he was closer to the wall, Faucon could see what he'd thought blank plaster wasn't blank at all. Faint drawings, outlines only, covered them. There were men and women, buildings and trees. He recognized the image of the Christ. It seemed the work in the refectory wasn't yet finished.

"Do you think the monks of St. Radegund allowed their former bondsmen to buy free of their ties so the priory could be rebuilt?" Faucon asked as they reached the far end of the room where there was another door, the one that should lead to the church.

Edmund opened it and stepped aside so Faucon could proceed. "I cannot know that answer, being so new here. But wouldn't that be a short-sighted policy?" His voice was as harsh as usual. "I cannot imagine that the rents these new freeholders pay are the equal in value to their previous tithes, tributes and days of labor. Once there is no more 'freedom' to peddle to the commoners and the coins have all been spent, what then? Will tithes alone be enough to supply my brothers sufficient bread and meat, ink and parchment?"

"Will they, indeed?" Faucon murmured.

What Faucon expected to be a narrow passageway leading from dorter to church was instead almost its own small room.

The floor within this space was covered with the same colorful ceramic tile as the refectory. A single column at the center held up a ceiling as tall as the two-storey dorter.

There was an opening in the nearest corner of the passageway; through that arched door-shaped gap Faucon could see the spiral stairway leading upward to the dormitory. Two other doors stood wide. One led to the cloister and its central garden, while the other offered access to the church.

The fourth door was barely ajar. It was toward this door that Edmund jerked his head. His movement indicated it was the entrance to the chapter house, the chamber where the monks wrangled over how to spend their new rents and less-than-sufficient tithes, and whether to continue to build, and where Prior Lambertus awaited.

When Faucon pushed it open, he once again drew a breath of appreciation. The monks might have spent coins on the refectory, but they had lavished treasure on this six-sided chamber. Anywhere stone could be decorated with carvings—on the columns holding up the vaulted ceiling, on the ribs of the arched vaults, around each of the five tall pointed windows—it had been, and then those carvings had been painted brilliant greens and golds. What with the yellow and brownish-red floor tiles, Faucon felt as if he stood in some forest glade.

Built out of the wall itself, the bench upon which the monks sat while discussing their business was a nearly knee-high stone shelf that ran unbroken around the chamber from one side of the door to the other. Unbroken, but not unaltered. Directly across from the doorway, the bench extended into a deeper seat, this extension framed by a pair of carved stone arms. The wall behind the seat had been painted to look like the back of a tall chair.

It was in this illusion of a chair that Prior Lambertus sat. With his narrow face, aquiline nose and straight brows over startlingly blue eyes, the leader of the Priory of St. Radegund looked every inch a sainted churchman. His black robe, no different from the one Edmund wore, was arranged so its wide sleeves draped his hands where they rested on the arms of his 'chair' until only his fingertips were exposed. His cowl lay in careful folds at the back of his neck. He offered Faucon a graceful nod of his head, then looked past the knight's shoulder.

"Thank you, Brother Edmund. You may close the door." His was a deep and musical voice.

"My lord prior," Edmund replied. The door creaked

a little as it shut.

"Sir Faucon de Ramis." The prior extended his beringed hand so Faucon might pay proper obeisance to him and his station. "Bishop William has informed me that for the time being you are to receive his portion of the income from our little house."

Faucon crossed the room, once again having cause to regret not wearing his best this day. After touching his lips to the prior's ring, he straightened and took a surprised backward step. There was nothing in Prior Lambertus's face or form to suggest it, but Faucon could feel deep anger wafting from the man.

"How fortunate you are to have an uncle who cares so for you," the prior said, punctuating his words with a what might have been a gracious bend of his head if not for that hidden rage.

"I am indeed," Faucon replied carefully as he sought to make sense of the contradiction between the man's inner and outer expressions. All that came to mind was that the prior didn't wish to give up his coins—the coins he was using to turn his priory into a treasure—to some inconsequential lay relative of his bishop, a man who had no right to live on Church income.

"I must admit I was taken aback by my lord uncle's gift, having had no idea of his intentions when I rode from my home yestermorn. Had I known, I would have come better prepared. I apologize for presenting myself to you in nothing but my under-armor." The sweep of Faucon's hand indicated his padded gambeson and chausses, which were now stained with sweat, water and the ashes from Simon's croft.

"I was even more surprised this morning when I found myself already putting my hand to my duties as a Keeper of the Pleas. Many thanks for sending a servant to me with the message of the miller's death."

"Ah, the matter of Halbert the Miller, may our Lord have mercy on his soul," the prior said with a slow lift of his brows. "It's fortunate that Brother Edmund had offered to read our scripture this morn when the village bailiff arrived. Since your clerk was already free to speak, he was the one who met with the bailiff, then convinced me that I must send a servant to call you to the village. Were you able to resolve the matter of the miller's death and release the man's earthly remains to his relatives?"

"I can report that the inquest is complete and Halbert's remains are in his son's hands. However, I cannot say I have yet resolved the matter of the miller's death," Faucon replied.

"How so? If you have completed the inquest, how can there have been no resolution?" A tiny crease appeared between the prior's brows, a bare suggestion of confusion. "The bailiff said that the miller had drowned."

"Therein lies the problem, for Halbert Miller did not drown," Faucon replied. "Instead, the jurors of the inquest did confirm my finding that the miller was murdered. The man who killed him used an awl to pierce his heart then, for reasons I yet seek to discern, dressed the miller in his best tunic and placed his body in his race so it would seem he'd fallen in and died beneath his own wheel."

Prior Lambertus blinked twice. That was the extent to which emotion played across his expression. Nonetheless, it was enough to convince Faucon that, like Agnes, the prior was privy to some piece of information he didn't have, and that the churchman had used that piece of information to identify the man who had killed Halbert.

Trapped so far behind that point, Faucon wanted to gnash his teeth in frustration. He wanted to shout at the churchman to spill what he knew. But as with Agnes, Faucon was utterly convinced that any demand he made for information would result in his expulsion from the chapter house, if not the priory. There had to be another way to winnow out what he wanted from the churchman.

"Why would the miller have been killed in such a strange fashion?" the prior asked as if he didn't already know the answer.

"That remains to be seen, as I have yet to identify the man who did the deed. Against that, the verdict of the inquest jury could only be that Halbert was killed by persons unknown," he replied, struggling to keep his frustration out of his voice.

"Unknown? Then the hue and cry was unsuccessful in apprehending the one who killed him?"

Again, the prior's words sounded calculated, his tone empty of any true curiosity. If Lambertus already knew the man, what profit could there be for him in playing this strange game of theirs?

"The hue and cry came hours too late," Faucon replied. "The miller was stabbed deep in the night while all in the village slept. There was no one abroad then to witness the act or chase the man who did this to him."

"How unfortunate," Lambertus said, his tone still without inflection or emotion. "Tell me, since I am unfamiliar with your new position. What part do you play in resolving such deaths in our shire? Are you the one who must seek out the murderer and accuse him, so he must stand before a justice or the royal court?"

"I am." Faucon filled these two words with more conviction than confidence. "As part of my duties, I am required to collect the king's portion from the estates of those who have committed murder. Thus, it is on me to discover whom to dispossess."

The corners of the churchman's mouth twitched, whether in amusement or something else entirely there was no knowing. "A welcome change, I think. Sir Alain has not always been so scrupulous. Many are the times I've suspected him of turning a blind eye to those who have done wrong, including murder, doing so for love or profit, or simply because our sheriff did not choose to seek them out."

"That seems to be the intent behind my new position, to prevent such occurrences," Faucon offered, the need to escape this ridiculous dance of words now goading him so deeply that it made him reckless. "I see you are a man who wishes justice to be done and one who feels its lack most deeply. Perhaps you can help me as I seek out the one who killed this man. I'm told you spoke recently with Halbert Miller's new wife."

Lambertus once more gave a graceful nod of his head. "That is certainly possible. Over the years I've spoken with a great number of the villagers from Priors Holston, offering my counsel where and when it's needed. That they seek me out to serve them in this way is a tradition between the village and our house. It rises from a past time when all the commoners in this vale owed the sweat of their brows and the fruits of their fields to my long dead brethren."

Faucon drew a slow breath, wondering how far the prior would allow him to go before he was stung enough to react. "You do not remember speaking with Agnes of Stanrudde? She mentioned she came to you only recently," he said, taking care to let no hint of emotion color his words. "It seems you instructed her to be patient with her husband, who was beating her out of anger and not in correction, and continue to pray that God might grant her a child from their union."

Something shifted in Lambertus' blue gaze. "Such a matter would not be one I would discuss with you, even if I did recall the event. Perhaps if I tell you what I know of Halbert Miller, you can find something of use in it.

"Five or so years ago, Halbert came to this house and offered my predecessor a substantial sum to sell to him the right to collect all the profit he earned from grinding grain at Priors Holston's mill. Along with that initial rich sum, he offered a yearly rent, and to grind our grain at no cost. I thought the rent he named a pittance, and, since we were already grinding our grain at no cost in our own mill, there was no gain to us in his offer to continue doing so. As this was the first such offer from a villager, much discussion ensued among my brothers and your lord uncle. There were some of us who held that the miller could not have accrued the sum he offered without borrowing from the Jews, and these brothers did not wish to take tainted coins. Most of the rest argued that he couldn't have borrowed from the Jews. That was the year so many of the Hebrews were slaughtered in this land. These brothers felt there could be no Jewish moneylenders left capable of lending so much. In my mind, that was even more damning. If the miller hadn't borrowed from a Jew, he must have borrowed from a Christian. If interest was being charged, that was the sin of usury.

"In the end, we could prove none of our suppositions, and agreed to sell the right to operate the mill with some restrictions. The deed was given in fee tail. None but the miller's legitimate heirs can claim the right to operate the mill, nor can the right we've given to Halbert and his line be sold or attached to another." The prior's tone was neutral, his words as careful and well-chosen as Faucon's had been.

"The only other thing I know of Halbert is that he returned to the priory for a second time only a few weeks past. On this visit he requested the aid of one of my brothers in Christ to act as a scribe."

Lambertus paused, his gaze catching and holding Faucon's. His brows rose. He offered a strangled smile. "It seems the miller wished to record his will." The barest hint of satisfaction colored his words.

It took every ounce of Faucon's discipline not to gape in astonishment as he deciphered the meaning behind the prior's strange tale. Someone held Lambertus in a grip that the prior found both repugnant and painful, a grip so tight that it tied the churchman's tongue, preventing him from revealing what he wished to share. Lambertus believed the key to releasing that grip was written into Halbert's new will, but he hadn't the freedom to make use of whatever was there. For that, he needed Faucon.

Having spoken his piece, Lambertus came to his feet in one graceful movement. "I can tell you nothing else, for I know nothing more to tell." That was a lie. The prior knew far more than he dared to share.

Faucon offered the expected response. "My thanks for the information you've offered. I'm certain I will find it helpful."

"Indeed," Lambertus replied. "Perhaps, once you have resolved the details of the miller's murder, you will return with the name of the man who did this foul deed. I am interested to know how this tale ends." However polite, it was a dismissal not to be brooked.

Faucon yet reeled at the oddness of this whole encounter. "But of course, my lord prior."

Once again, he bowed over Prior Lambertus' ringed hand, then started out of the room.

"There is one more thing," the prior called after him.

Faucon paused at the door, the latch in his hand. "Aye, my lord?"

Lambertus watched him the way a statuary angel might, his expression beautiful and remote. "About the business of your lord uncle's benefice. I'm sure you understand that we will have no payment for you until our Eastertide accounting. If our dear Bishop of Hereford wishes you to have our Michaelmas portion, he will have to disburse it to you from his own treasury as that is where it now resides."

"Of course, my lord prior. I completely understand," Faucon said.

"I thought that you did," the prior said. "Indeed, I was certain that you would understand all, from the description your lord uncle offered me of you," he added, then pulled his cowl up over his head and returned to sit in the place that demonstrated his authority over his house.

"Halbert came to the priory a few weeks ago and hired one of the monks to write a will for him," Faucon said to Edmund once he had closed the door behind him.

He hadn't expected Edmund to wait for him after the monk had closed the chapter house door, thinking their day's work had been at an end. Now he was thrilled to find his clerk in the passageway.

"If you wish to help me discover the name of the man who killed Halbert," Faucon continued, "you must seek out the monk who wrote that document and ask him what it contained. Or better yet, procure the copy if one was made."

Edmund sent him a strained look. "I can't ask after what is a private matter."

"Not even to discover the miller's murderer so we can place his estate into the king's hands?" Faucon used his words like a morningstar and Edmund flinched under the assault.

"Nay, you misunderstand. It's that I *cannot* ask. While it is true our order isn't completely silent, and that we do share speech for part of the day, when the time comes for that sharing it's considered poor taste to broach subjects that aren't in keeping with the Rule. The Rule suggests we limit our conversations to those that are profitable to our brotherhood or necessary to convey information about tasks and goals of the house."

"The issue of Halbert Miller's will is both profitable

and necessary, if we are to find the one who killed him," Faucon replied.

"To you and to me, that is true," Edmund agreed, nervously shifting the sack that contained his writing implements behind his arm again. Once more that parchment roll thrust up over his shoulder, quiver-like. "My brothers may not agree."

Faucon hid his surprise as he understood Edmund's hesitance. As brusque and outspoken as his clerk might be, Edmund was a newcomer here, and as such, feared making a misstep that might result in being shunned by his peers. Then again, Faucon well remembered the pain of being a newcomer, standing on the outside of the group until those at the center allowed him entry.

The urge to tell his clerk what the prior had shared caught Faucon by surprise. He swallowed it. However dearly Prior Lambertus wanted Halbert's will discovered, Faucon was absolutely certain the prior didn't wish anyone to know he was the one who had suggested it be sought out. It was a shame, but Edmund's 'honest' tongue made it impossible to entrust him with any confidence.

"I suspect this may be one time when you need not worry over a misstep," he said, trying to hint as best he could.

"I am not worried," Edmund shot back. "Nor can you assure me of what you cannot know."

"As you say, but what if you are wrong this time?" Faucon tried again. "What if a simple conversation between you and one of your brothers results in us acquiring the name of the man who killed the miller before day's end, and with no repercussions to you?"

Edmund's worry warred with his need to curry Bishop William's favor. As if he sought to hide his turmoil from Faucon, the monk whirled on his heel and started back through the refectory, head lowered and shoulders hunched. Faucon followed him to the exit, torn in twain between his desire to command his clerk to do what he was told and the equally pressing need to win Edmund's compliance, and his trust. One avenue promised a single success. The other might well guarantee a far easier time for them, as he and Edmund continued into their future.

It wasn't until they'd reached the door to the outside world that his clerk finally spoke. His words were grudging and low. "I will do what I can, but I make no promises."

Triumph and relief made Faucon smile. "I asked for none. Before I leave, tell me something else. How long do we have to identify the one who killed Halbert and confiscate his property?"

Edmund gave a tight shrug. There was a gentle clink from within his sack as one metal object touched another. "As long as it takes. If, when this man is discovered, he makes his confession, we can immediately claim his goods and property even though justice has not yet been meted out, although we cannot take his chattels or profits. All that remains in the custody of the bailiff or headman for the area until he is adjudged guilty. If he flees after he is confronted, he will be outlaw, and we can then claim his goods and property, holding them in trust until that time he is caught or abjures the realm."

"And if he is discovered but protests that he is innocent, refusing to confess? What then?" Faucon asked, more from curiosity than any need to know.

"We cannot take his property. Instead, he will sit in the sheriff's gaol at Killingworth until he stands before the Eyre and is judged accordingly. That is, unless he raises the funds required for his bail. Not an easy task that one, since he must also recruit neighbors to stand surety for him. They must agree to bring him to court when the time comes, or pay a fine if he flees before that day. But if he is able to pay his bail, he will remain free until he is called to court, and we must wait until he is adjudged guilty to take the king's portion. Why?" Edmund asked.

Faucon shrugged. "I once knew these things and have forgotten most of them, and I must know them again. I was concerned about needing to rush to resolve the murder of the miller, the way we had to rush to complete the inquest."

They exited from the dorter. Edmund stopped just outside the doorway, as Faucon started through the passageway that led out of the monks' rectangular world.

"God be praised! Sir Faucon!" The call came from a rider atop a dancing horse just inside the opening in the hedge. The man was dressed in mud-spattered hunting green. His horse whinnied in complaint and turned a nervous circle, harnesses rattling. The servant who had promised to care for Legate was racing away from horse and rider, running toward the field beyond the dovecote.

"Sir Faucon," the rider called again, "you must come at once. Lord Rannulf and Bishop William have found a murdered child."

Chapter Fourteen

As little as he liked it, Edmund bumped and jounced along behind Faucon on Legate's rump as they rode for more than an hour to reach the place where Bishop William and Lord Rannulf awaited them. It was an open spot, a great sweep of grassy hillside, undisturbed by homes or farms, trees or hedges, the drying vegetation rustling and shifting in a mid-afternoon breeze.

The hunting party had found their ease as they waited for their new crowner to appear. The horses grazed, while the hunting dogs dozed in a sleepy pile, ears occasionally flicking, a tail lifting now and then. The beaters and kennel master were just as relaxed in their own gathering, laughing and chatting as they reclined in the sun.

All that marred the idyllic atmosphere were the ravens. From high overhead, they threw down their raucous complaints as they circled. They had not appreciated being disturbed at their feasting.

Faucon looked from the carrion eaters to the valley that spread out below him. Although he did not yet know Blacklea's landmarks well enough to identify it from a distance, he could guess about where it must be. As near as he could tell, this was the same place he'd noticed yesterday when he'd seen the ravens from the road.

Once he and Edmund dismounted, Faucon left his clerk to fumble with his sack next to Legate as he joined Lord Rannulf and Bishop William. The stink of death reached out to assault them as they walked toward the girl's remains. Faucon raised a hand to cover his nose,

Susanna's stew stirring in his gullet.

Predators and putrefaction had left little to identify her as human, much less as the child she'd once been. The ravens and God only knew what else had made swift work consuming her face. Her eyes were gone, the meat stripped from her forehead down her cheeks and nose to her jaw. Her teeth and jawbone gleamed rusty-white in the sun.

Her simple shift, a long shirt no different from those all females wore beneath their gowns, had prevented the four-legged or winged flesh eaters from reaching all of her. It was here that the insects and the foul liquids of decay had done their work. As they had consumed her softer organs, the seeping liquid had stained what had once been white fabric until it looked mottled and rotten, and as filthy the ground beneath her.

Lord Rannulf crouched beside the girl. Dressed in the same leather hauberk over a huntsman's green tunic as yesterday, the nobleman looked less a baron than one of the beaters he employed. Faucon squatted next to him.

"Look here. I see a line too regular to be anything save the stroke of a well-honed knife." The baron extended a hand to point out what little flesh yet clung to the fragile bones of her neck. Whether moved by a carrion eater or because this was the way she'd been left, her head was twisted to one side, her chin lifted up out of the collar of her shirt. That had separated the cut meat of her neck, revealing its even edges.

"Aye, that seems the work of a blade," Faucon agreed.

"Pity the poor child," Lord Rannulf said softly. He lifted one of the girl's dark tresses. The movement dislodged the faded ring of blue flowers that, until that moment, had clung precariously to the top of her head.

"Would that we'd found her before the beasts and birds had their way with her," Bishop William added, yet standing behind the two warriors. As he had yesterday, he wore his gold-trimmed green gown over dark green chausses and brown boots cross-gartered to his legs. "We will never discover who she was, with nothing left of her face to see."

He continued, speaking this time to the remains of the child on the ground before him. "I pray our Lord accepts the blessings I laid upon you this day, even though you are already gone to Him."

"Who was the first finder?" Edmund asked, his voice as harsh and brusque as ever. "And did this one raise the hue and cry?"

Faucon drew a sharp and irritable breath, only to catch back his chide. Edmund was right. This child had been murdered, then left here without family or friend to see to her final rest. Only the shire's new crowner could help her now, by identifying her killer and bringing him to justice.

Beside him, Bishop William released an angry breath at Edmund's questions. Lord Rannulf shot Faucon a swift sidelong look, filled with impatience and the arrogance of his rank.

"It is the law that these questions must be asked and answered," Faucon told them both, coming to his feet. Lord Rannulf followed. When the three of them stepped back from the girl's body, all of them coughed a little to clear their lungs of the stench.

"So it is," Lord Rannulf replied, his brows rising slowly as subtle surprise filled his gray eyes. He glanced from Faucon to Bishop William, then called, "Hobbe."

A slight man in his middle years wearing the green garb of a forester rose from among the baron's waiting men. Faucon recognized him as a man he'd met time and again while hunting with Lord Rannulf and his brothers. As the forester joined them, he offered a brief bow.

"My lords," he said to the noblemen, then nodded to

Faucon. "Sir."

"Hobbe atte Lea was the first finder, Pery," Lord Rannulf said to Faucon, a half-smile clinging to his lips. "He was running with the beaters this day when he came upon her."

"Did you—" Edmund began.

Faucon spoke over him. "Did you raise the hue and cry, Hobbe?" he asked the smaller man.

"In as far as is possible here, sir, I did," Hobbe replied, speaking the nobles' tongue with a heavy accent. "Of course, we knew when we looked upon the poor babe that we were far too late. The one who had done this to her would not be found here. Still, I cried out for my fellow beaters to search the area, looking for anything that murderer might have forgotten or discarded that might identify him."

"And you found nothing?" Faucon asked.

"We found nothing," Hobbe confirmed.

"But Sir Faucon, the law requires—" Edmund began.

Faucon again interrupted him. "I believe I remember that the law requires these men to answer 'aye' or 'nay' to the question of hue and cry, doing so on pain of being fined for either not raising it when needed, or wrongly raising it.

"In all truth, there was no need to raise a hue and cry here." He lifted his hand to indicate the open hillside. "This is no town or village with nooks and crannies where felons might yet be hiding. Brother, you saw as I did that we passed no hamlet or even a farm house for the latter half of our journey. Instead, Hobbe and the others did right by searching the area just as their betters did right by calling for the Keeper of the Pleas to come. And, as their Keeper, I declare that all their actions satisfied the law, even if those actions weren't a perfect reflection of what is written."

"But sir," Edmund tried one last time.

"I assure you, Brother Edmund. You may safely

scribe on your parchment that Hobbe atte Lea was first finder and properly raised the hue and cry. Lord Rannulf, will you promise surety to see to it that Hobbe attends the Eyre when I bring the one who did this before the court to receive his earthly punishment?"

"It is the right question to ask of me, Pery, but unnecessary," Lord Rannulf replied with approval and none of his earlier impatience. "These are my lands, and I have a franchise to sit as justice over all issues that arise, including those felonies committed within my boundaries and those of my vassals."

"Thus, I do vow to present myself as first finder when called to testify before Lord Rannulf," Hobbe said, then retreated to join the others of his rank.

Edmund blinked rapidly in thought. His mouth tightened and his brow creased. At last he nodded.

"Aye, Sir Faucon. I can see how what you say about this place would make the hue and cry moot. I shall scribe that the first finder did all that was required and did it properly, and that Lord Graistan has promised to see justice done. What shall we do about proof of Englishry?"

"There is nothing that can be done about it at the moment," Faucon replied. "Since there is no family from whom to demand proof, we will have to levy the murdrum fine against this hundred. My pardon, Lord Rannulf," he said, offering the baron a swift bow.

That made the nobleman laugh. "It's not my fine, but this hundred's to bear. Collect it as best you can."

"As you say, so it will be," Edmund replied with a nod.

Then swinging his sack out from under his arm, he pivoted, scanning the grassy expanse around them. "Fie on me for not realizing I must always carry a traveling desk with me, rather than count on finding a place to write. Might I remove the bag from your horse's saddle, sir? It is about the size and firmness I believe I need."

As always, Edmund didn't wait for permission, merely started toward Legate.

"Can you not remember what is said here and scribe it later?" Faucon called after him.

"Memory is a risky business, sir. Only a fool relies upon it," Edmund threw back over his shoulder, already working to loosen the saddlebag that Faucon had left belted onto the side of Legate's saddle yesterday.

"You did well enough remembering what our archbishop said at court a week ago about the Keepers," Faucon reminded him.

"That was nothing that might need to be presented at an Eyre court," Edmund countered, taking a seat on the ground as he began pulling his scribbling supplies from his bag.

"What is this?" Bishop William whispered, a strange tone in his voice as he stared at the monk.

Faucon shot his uncle a quick look, suddenly uncertain about what he'd just said and done. "I know the law requires fines be levied on those who don't properly execute the hue and cry and that the archbishop seeks to collect all such revenue, but surely that can't be applied to such a discovery as this. As for the murdrum fine, I always believed that it was levied in every case where the one who died an unnatural death could not be proved English."

The bishop shifted to look at his nephew. His face was alive in astonishment. "Nay, you mistake me, Pery. You've more than satisfied the law. It's the miracle you've performed with Brother Edmund that has me stunned. He was almost civil! How did you win that from him and do it in so short a time?"

"Oh that," Faucon replied with a grin of relief, then continued, his voice lowered. "If anything is different with the brother, you cannot credit the change to me. Until a few hours ago, I was ready to beg you to release me from this new position so I could be free of him."

"And now you no longer wish to be free of him?" Lord Rannulf said.

"Not at this moment, although I will not vouch for the morrow," Faucon replied, still smiling. "I'm not certain how it happened, but he and I have begun to find our pace, doing so while we spent our day seeking out the one who murdered the miller at Priors Holston."

"You've already taken up your duties?" William's face again filled with surprise.

"Was I not expected to?" Faucon asked, as startled as his uncle.

"Of course you were, but–" the bishop paused, smiled a little then glanced at Lord Rannulf.

The baron laughed out loud. "Did I not tell you Pery was the perfect man for this position, William?"

"So you did, Rannulf. A murder is it, Pery? How did it happen, and will you be sending the one who did it to the gaol? I suppose I must also ask if there will be anything resulting from this action to add to the royal treasury. Commoners usually have so little," he added as an aside.

"I can only say that this whole day has been strange beyond all my previous experience," Faucon replied. "When I arrived at the village this morning, the miller was in his race. He had been besotted the night before, and all believed that he'd fallen into the water due to drink, then drowned, trapped beneath his wheel. But once we extracted him, I discovered he'd been murdered with an awl that pierced his heart. Not only that, the one who killed him took him away from his home to kill him, waited until he'd bled his last, then returned him to the race and the wheel."

"So what man pierced his heart, Sir Keeper of the Pleas?" Lord Rannulf asked.

"Sir Crowner," Faucon corrected, reveling in his conversation with these men. It felt both strange and right to be speaking to them as an equal rather than as a mere second son with no prospects. "That seems the name most folk feel comfortable calling me.

"As for who did this, and why the miller was made to look as if he drowned—" Faucon once again struggled to tame his frustration. "I don't yet know, but I am slowly following the trail left by the murderer, learning to read his tracks as I go. One thing I can tell you. If not for Brother Edmund's insistence on following the rule of law exactly, Sir Alain would have declared the miller drowned, and taken the millwheel as deodand before I arrived at Priors Holston this morning. Edmund kept the sheriff at bay until I came."

Bishop William frowned at that. "Sir Alain was at Priors Holston this morn? How in the world did the sheriff come halfway across the shire and arrive before you, when you were only at Blacklea?"

"Because the sheriff wasn't across the shire," Faucon said with the lift of his brows. "He was close at hand this morning, something the miller's son had discovered several weeks before. It seems Sir Alain has been residing at his wife's manor of Aldersby since returning from Rochester and court."

"What!?" Lord Rannulf retorted in harsh surprise. "Lady Joan finally let her husband cross the threshold of her manor?"

Faucon stared at the nobleman in astonishment. He hadn't even considered that Lord Rannulf might be one to ask about shire gossip. "Apparently so."

"Huh, wonders never cease," the nobleman said with a laugh. "As far as I know, his wife has never once let him step a foot inside that gate until now."

Stephen had said something similar about the sheriff and Aldersby. "Why not?" Faucon asked.

Lord Rannulf laughed at that, this time displaying the smile that he and his brothers shared. It was one they must have inherited from their father, for there was nothing like it among the de Veres. "Because she enjoys rankling him. Aldersby is her dower from her first marriage, and she holds it in her own right. Sir Alain married her for profit and much against her wishes, when he paid the king to acquire her from among the royal wards. That set the lady on a quest to see the sheriff receives as little profit as possible from her. She's even managed to produce nothing but girls by his seed."

"It's a shame what time wrought of Sir Alain," Bishop William said, his tone subdued. He crossed his arms and shook his head. "Aye, he's a man of much more substance these days, but he's not the man I knew when he was but a landless knight under William de Mandeville, and we all rode out of Essex to make our journey to the Holy Land."

Faucon drew a breath so sharp he coughed. The bits and pieces of information he had in store shifted again. This time, when they came to rest, he could see the end of this trail and knew what awaited him there.

"I'd press Hubert Walter for his removal if there were someone both trustworthy and powerful enough to replace him. Sir Alain has many supporters in this shire, most of them benefitting somehow from his reign as sheriff. What can I do? There aren't many sheriffs as honest as Geoffrey," he finished, referring to Faucon's cousin and Lord Rannulf's middle half-brother.

"My lord, might I ask when you made that journey to the Levant? I can't recall my lady mother ever mentioning it," Faucon asked.

"It was years ago, before you were born, Pery," William replied, "just before I came to be the first abbot of the Waltham Abbey." There was a moment's sadness in his gaze, then it was gone.

Faucon glanced from his uncle to the baron. "Would either of you know anything about a woman named Agnes of Stanrudde? I think she might have been leman to a knight or baron in this shire. She was the murdered miller's wife."

Lord Rannulf shook his head. "Nothing comes to mind for me," he said, "but the subject of kept women isn't one that honest men speak of, one to another." There was strong disapproval in his voice.

"And I'm not from this shire, nor is it likely any man with the rank of less than an earl would dare tell me tales of his mistress," William said with a cockeyed smile and a laugh. It was the first time Faucon had seen his uncle look like a man rather than the polished diplomat and accomplished churchman life had made of him.

"Sir Faucon!" Edmund called out. "The bag worked well enough. What must be scribed has been written. Now it is time to call the inquest jury."

Faucon wanted to groan. Given the look of this land, he guessed the borders of the hundred here were widespread, with some distance existing between farms and hamlets. He didn't want to wait for however long it took all the men of living within this district to gather. He wanted to return to Blacklea and stew over all he'd gathered about Halbert's death. Given a little time to think, he was sure he could return to Priors Holston in the morning to follow his developing trail to its finish.

It was his uncle who made the sound that Faucon had suppressed. "Must we?"

"I think we must," Lord Rannulf replied. "There'll be even less of her by the morrow if we leave her where she is for one more night."

The bishop grimaced. "What if we put up a barrier or some such to keep the predators at bay? We've already waited more than two hours for Pery to arrive. That's another day of hunting gone, when I'd hoped for at least a little respite before I return to my duties."

Faucon leapt to exploit the opportunity his uncle offered. "My lord bishop, here is a matter I intended to address with you. This morning, Sir Alain had already assembled the inquest jury for the miller when I arrived at the village, doing so upon the assumption of a simple drowning. The group was so large that taking their oaths was hardly satisfying. Any other communication with all of them was nigh on impossible. Had I not begun the viewing when I did, Brother Edmund and I wouldn't be here now. Instead, you'd be setting camp, wondering how much longer you'd have to wait for me. Meanwhile Brother Edmund and I would be making our own plans to spend the night in Priors Holston as the commoners still filed past the corpse. Must every man and boy in the hundred come? Can the jury of the inquest not be arranged in the same way the hundred court is, with a smaller number of men representing all the rest?"

"That should not happen here, Sir Faucon," Edmund warned most sternly. "All the men of this hundred must come view the dead child so she can be identified."

"How will they identify her?" Faucon demanded of his clerk. "What will they see of her but bloodied bones and rot and dark hair? Even if we wait the hours or more it takes for every man to arrive, we're not guaranteed we'll discover her identity. It's clear that the one who killed her brought her here from someplace else. What if no child in this hundred is missing? Then we'll have waited hours for no result. However, if a child has gone missing from this area, even if we call only a few men to come as representatives of their neighbors, those men will know this and bring with them the name we seek. Does that not seem the easier route to discovering her identity?"

"But it is the law that all men of the hundred be called to the inquest jury," Edmund protested, although his voice lacked its usual certainty.

"Laws can be changed and your argument has merit, nephew," Bishop William said. "I will bring it up with the archbishop when next we meet. But for the now, things must remain as they are and all men should be called to the jury of the inquest."

He paused. "Except for this one instance. Brother Edmund, please note in your record that William, Bishop of Hereford, did require an inquest jury consisting of only twelve men from the hundred to view the body of this murdered child."

"Aye, my lord," the monk said and bowed his head, complying without his usual resistance.

"Rannulf, send your men to the nearest settlement," William continued. "Have them inform the bailiff or headman of the body we've found here. Your men must tell them that Graistan's lord and the Bishop of Hereford ask them to send at least twelve men for the jury. No fewer than twelve can come, but we will not turn back others if they wish to help identify this child, as long as they are swift in arriving."

Chapter Fifteen

Faucon was right in his guess. The nearest hamlet was more than a mile away, and according to the men who came, the next hamlet more than double that distance from their homes. Once the twelve arrived, the inquest proceeded comfortably. It was easy to address them and easy to hear them when they swore their oath, then confirmed his verdict of 'murder by persons unknown.' Moreover, Edmund was able to collect and write all their names into his record, something that would have been impossible to do at the mill.

None of the jurors recognized the dead child, nor had they heard tell of a missing girl among their neighbors and relatives. The locals assured their betters that had a lass gone missing, it would have been discussed at their hundred court which had been held only a few days past. When all was done, Lord Rannulf paid the commoners to take the child to their parish church. They agreed to do so after Bishop William assured them that she had the right to be buried in the hallowed ground of their churchyard.

The sun was creeping steadily toward the horizon as Faucon and Edmund once more reached the gap in the hedge at the front of St. Radegund's. The ride had been a quiet one, what with Faucon concentrating on turning his bits and pieces of knowledge this way and that.

Edmund more fell off Legate than dismounted. Clutching his sack, he looked up at Faucon. "I'll send that man who watched your horse on the morrow if I have discovered anything regarding the will you seek, sir," he said.

"Nay, I will come to you," Faucon told him. "We have more work to complete as regards the miller's death."

He intended to visit Stephen's wife at her family home upon the morrow. He knew without doubt that he'd find 'Wina there without her husband. Stephen would be at the mill, certain that all was now right with the world, and blissfully unaware of what lay ahead of him.

"You will come to me?" Edmund's words were so filled with astonishment that it startled Faucon out of his thoughts. "*We* have more to do?"

"I will, and aye, we have more to do. I wish to speak with the young miller's wife," he replied, then smiled. "Or perhaps yet another man will die between now and then, and we'll be off once more to view a body, having been cheated of our nightly rest by the quiet dead."

Something shifted in Edmund's face. "Until the morrow then, Sir Faucon." It almost sounded like a friendly farewell.

"Until the morrow, Brother Edmund."

Faucon turned his horse and started back through Priors Holston, keeping Legate at a walk as this man or that woman hurried around them along the lane. The carpenter's workshop was shuttered and dark. The cobbler's woman stood outside her home in the same place she'd occupied while making that boot. This time, she had a babe perched on her hip as she and the cobbler, or so Faucon assumed by the way he had his arm wrapped around her, chatted with another couple.

At the alewife's house, Susanna threw up a beefy arm and shouted "good night" to him. All but one of the customers seated in her foreyard waved with her. Agnes sat at the table closest to the cottage door, her elbows braced upon the table top, no expression on her face as she watched him ride past.

Reaching the edge of the village and the Stanrudde

Road, Faucon put his heels to Legate, urging his steed to a faster pace. They hadn't gone far before he spied a lone man walking the road ahead, his back to the village behind them. This one carried a full canvas sack and moved at an easy, unhurried pace despite the encroaching night. He was tall and broad-shouldered, his hair fair and his tunic dusty.

As Faucon rode up behind him, Alf glanced over his shoulder. "Sir Crowner," he said in greeting, stopping to wait for Faucon to dismount and join him. "Have you sought me out for some reason?"

"I do not seek you at all, Alf. We are but traveling in the same direction. I'm on my way back to Blacklea, my new home. Where are you off to? Has Stephen asked you to leave the mill, as he did his stepmother?"

No caution remained in the former soldier's expression. Instead, his lips curved slightly in amusement. "You ask what you already know, sir, and you know very well that he did not. Shall we step outside of our redoubts and defenses to parlay as honest men? I will begin. Why are you not arresting me for Halbert's murder?"

Faucon laughed. "After the day I've had, an open and honest conversation would be a welcome relief. As you will. I am not arresting you because you did not kill Halbert, no matter how circumstances conspired to make it appear as if only you could have done it."

"Ah, but you wanted to arrest me," Alf replied, still offering him the curve of his lips that served him as a smile.

"I longed to do so," Faucon agreed. "Naming you Halbert's murderer would have been a convenient solution to what has since become a thorny and complicated problem. I have answered your question. Now you answer one of mine. Why did you not tell me you'd spent the night at Susanna's?"

Alf's brows rose at that. "You had already decided

only I could have done the deed. Nothing I said was going to change that. I wanted to let Susanna clear my name, rather than protest my innocence to deaf ears. Moreover, even at this moment, I am none too certain the whole of Halbert's strange death hasn't been arranged so I would be named the guilty one. When we first spoke, I wasn't willing to trust someone unknown to me."

"And now you trust me?"

"More than I did then," Alf replied, the corners of his mouth lifting.

Faucon sent him a taunting, narrow-eyed look. "You don't trust me? Were you not the one who told me to trust that all in the inquest jury would give their oaths, even if I didn't hear everyone? Then you went on to break that very oath. I asked if you heard the millwheel turning in the middle of the night from your bed. You lied to me."

Alf almost winked at him. "You asked the wrong question and did not listen carefully enough to my answer. I said I could not hear the wheel from where I slept. You assumed I meant the mill. I didn't lie. You cannot hear the wheel from Susanna's home."

That made Faucon laugh again. "Aye, Halbert's was indeed a strange death."

Alf nodded. "Today, I am very grateful Simon sent me from the mill last night. Had I been there, I would have arisen when the wheel began to turn and rushed out to confront what might have been a trap set to see me hanged. I gave the fuller my thanks before I left the village."

"Do you know he believes you're a runaway serf?"

The soldier gave a breath of a laugh. "That doesn't surprise me. I suspect he's not the only one in Priors Holston who believes that. But you do not?"

Walking behind them, Legate chose that moment to snort. As he did, he tossed his head, his harness rings jangling. It was as if he chuckled at the comment.

Faucon smiled broadly. "Nay, I knew better, even before Agnes told me you were a former mercenary done with war. A simple peasant would have been far less comfortable holding the tool that had killed a man. Nor would such a man have so easily put his finger into another man's death wound," he said, once again seeing Simon's reaction over finding Halbert's blood on his property. "That sort of ease with killing belongs to those of us who deal out death to earn our daily bread."

Alf cocked his brows and nodded at this, but said nothing. They walked on in companionable silence for a time.

"Tell me something else," Alf finally said. "I cannot puzzle out why Halbert wasn't simply put in the race to be taken by the wheel. Why go to the trouble of piercing his heart?"

"For the sake of vengeance. Blood had to be shed. You see, Halbert had made Agnes bleed," Faucon told him.

The workman looked at him in astonishment. "But how can that be? Stephen despised her."

"Who said Stephen was the one to pierce his father's heart?" Faucon retorted.

That made Alf stare at him. "If not Stephen, then who?"

"I'm not willing to speak that name yet." Faucon dared not. To say the name aloud was to court his own death. Frustration gnawed at him. "I have lingering questions," he finally said, when in truth it was nagging demands for resolution that plagued him.

"Such as?" Alf asked.

Faucon hesitated, torn between the need to speak, as he had done with Brother Colin, and the need to hold close what he knew for safety's sake. He glanced at the soldier. Alf didn't look at him, only strode along beside him. It seemed the former soldier didn't care if he received a response to his question. For some reason that made it easier for Faucon to speak his piece.

"When I think of Halbert's death, I understand the need for his blood to be shed. The one who killed the miller had once loved Agnes, and had put his former love into Halbert's protection, only to have Halbert betray him with his drunken violence. I can only think this was the reason the man dressed Halbert in the tunic Agnes had given him as a wedding present. Perhaps that garment was a symbol of what Halbert had done to earn his death.

"But when I see Halbert beneath the wheel, I get trapped by the thought that he was put there after death so that Halbert's family might be destroyed as well. This, when I am certain Stephen participated in his father's death. I cannot understand why he agreed to assist in his father's murder, when the cost of the deodand for the wheel would send his family into penury."

"Not likely," Alf laughed. "Paying that deodand might well have pinched Stephen some, but it would hardly have stolen the food from his table."

Faucon frowned. "What do you mean? I thought the wheel needed to be given to the Church for cleansing, and a new one built to replace it."

Alf was still smiling. "Perhaps that is how it works in some vales, but that is not how I've ever seen it happen. Aye, if the deodand is a small item, say a woodcutter's axe or the awl used on Halbert, then the Church takes it and a fee is charged. But that amount is usually nothing, a farthing or two. Something large or immovable, like a well in which a man drowns, is different. The owner is required to pay the value of the item as assessed by the inquest jury, then a priest comes to cleanse it while it remains where it is."

"But, the value—" Faucon started.

Alf held up his hand. "Let me finish, for this is the

piece that you, being no commoner, will have missed. If you think any member of that jury is going to ruin his neighbor for the benefit of either the Church or crown, you are sorely mistaken. Those times that I have participated in juries that value deodand, I have every time confirmed a value for the item that is but a shadow of its true cost."

Faucon stared at Alf, hearing again the subtle laughter that rippled over the inquest jury as Stephen protested how the cost of the deodand would ruin him. Halbert was put beneath the wheel for the exact reason that Faucon had stared at all day: to disguise the fact that he'd been murdered.

"Mother of God. A simple, drunken accident, one that wouldn't even raise eyebrows in the village. At almost no cost to himself, Stephen allows another man to take his father's life, thereby winning this one's favor. And Agnes is freed from the trap of her marriage."

Here he paused to look at Alf. "Only there never was a trap for Agnes, was there? You are leaving Priors Holston too soon, you know. I'm told that Halbert committed his will to parchment a few weeks ago."

Alf kept his gaze focused on the road. "Did he? What import has that for me?" His voice was even, his tone seemingly uninterested.

"I thought we were speaking honestly. You are Halbert's elder son," Faucon replied.

This time when the former soldier looked at him, he smiled. The spread of his lips was slow, and it didn't stop until he was full-out grinning. In doing so, he revealed a line of healthy teeth which had the same snaggled arrangement Faucon had noticed in Halbert's mouth.

"Not just the elder, but his only legitimate son," Alf replied. "My mother still lives, and, as she never sought to claim Halbert dead after he abandoned us, she is yet Halbert's true wife. Or rather, his widow."

That made Stephen Halbert's bastard, and Agnes a wife who never was. Halbert's marriage was a secret he had never shared, not even with Agnes' former lover, the man who had once been his commander and had led him into the Holy Land. It explained why Halbert had told the village he would not remarry. He had risked all when he'd pretended to wed Cissy, wanting the mill, and the comfortable life it represented, more than he feared discovery.

"Halbert recognized you when you came to Priors Holston?" Faucon wanted to know.

"Nay. Nor did I wish him to know me. I had followed his trail from place to place, even to the Holy Land, as you have learned. By the time my troop had left the blood of Acre behind us and King Richard was marching us past the walls of Jerusalem, I'd long since begun to doubt if the man who sired me was worthy of discovery." Again he fell silent.

"Then you followed him to Priors Holston, and found him living a life of luxury at the mill with his son, his bastard. What then?" Faucon prodded.

"Then I doubted no longer. However humble, my uncle's cottage was a far more cheerful place in which to live than the miller's fine abode." As he spoke, Alf kept his gaze focused on the road ahead.

"Yet you remained in the village. You worked with him for a full year. And in all that time you never told Halbert who you were?" Faucon pressed.

Alf shot him a laughing, sidelong look. "I never said that. A moment arose. We spoke. He was surprised that I would come without ambition and ask for nothing from him save the chance to know him."

"And then what happened?" Faucon wanted to know.

"What happened is that the next day I still called him 'Master' and life went on as it had. Now he's gone, and my life is no longer cluttered with musings about who sired me. Although I must admit I find myself at loose ends. I've come to enjoy milling."

"Then you are walking in the wrong direction," Faucon replied with a laugh. "But this is a discussion for the morrow. For the now, come with me to Blacklea, my new home, and take your ease. I will see that you eat well in the kitchen—I was told there would be mutton tonight—and you may take your rest in my hall. Stay the day tomorrow. If sunset on the morrow still finds you yet at loose ends, I will bid you good journey and see you on your way."

Once again, Alf offered him that grin. "As you chided me, sir, I must now chide you. I thought we were speaking as honest men here. Say what you mean. Tell me you need me to stay for your own purposes."

"I very much need you to stay for my own purposes," Faucon repeated, liking Alf well indeed. "I yet have details to puzzle out before I can finish this."

"Then you are resolved to expose the one who used that awl on Halbert last night?"

Faucon nodded. "I am. But such a man as this one will not easily fall. I cannot think that tomorrow will offer me any success. Instead I suspect his exposure may be years in coming despite my best efforts. After all, there are no witnesses to what happened, save one who cannot speak because he participated. I cannot act against this man if all I do is *believe* I know what he has done."

"Ah, belief," Alf laughed. "That is precisely why you find me here on the road. I am a newcomer to Priors Holston. I do not believe that I can recruit enough men from the village to swear to my innocence, should someone with a stronger purpose wish to prove me guilty. If I cannot do that, then I will likely hang."

He grinned again. "And that, Sir Crowner, I am not ready to do."

Upon their return to Blacklea, Faucon went with Alf to the kitchen to see he got his meal, only to discover that Sir John and Lady Marian had requested he join them for their evening repast. Although there wasn't time for another bath, he did shed his under-armor and dress in his best. As he unrolled the garments from the protection of the oiled skin, he almost laughed. How this day had changed him! His fine linen shirt and dark green floor-length gown with its golden trim—the precious threads embroidered onto the garment by his lady mother's needle—didn't look nearly as rich as the attire Stephen Miller had worn this day.

Following the cook's directions, stopping only at the laundry to ask the washerwomen to see to his under-armor cleaned for the morrow, he walked from the stone manor house to a cottage half the size of Halbert's fine home. Despite that difference, there were similarities.

A curtain divided the home's single room into public and private areas. If there was no fine cabinet, a good number of wooden shelves filled the walls near the hearth end of the house, each one piled high with well-made bowls or carved wooden spoons or some other sort of dining utensil. As in the miller's home, there was a loft—the space that Robert had claimed as his own and now had to share with Mimi. The ladder that led up to this loft wasn't nearly as fine as the miller's.

And just as in Halbert's house, a table sat at the center of the dwelling. However, this table, presently dressed with a white tablecloth, was meant to be disassembled when not in use. If it weren't, there'd be no easy passage from one side of the cottage to the other.

The family had waited for him, the evening's mutton stew kept warm on the hearthstone at the kitchen end of the room. Although it was but a cottage, Marian hadn't dismissed the niceties required of a meal. Looking the sober housewife dressed in a blue gown over a pale green undergown, her head covered in a plain white wimple, she showed him the bowl and aquamanile so he could wash his hands. When he was done, she offered a fresh cloth for drying them, then led him to the place of honor at their table.

Marian's husband sat at the opposite end. Blacklea's former steward was a man more than two times Faucon's age, his skin beaten to leather by time and the elements. Although the older knight's hair and beard still owned a youthful thickness, they were white as deepest winter. He was a big man, but pain had eaten him to just bones. Faucon could see that in the shadows hanging below his pale eyes and the hollows in his cheeks.

The table was set with wooden trenchers to hold the bread that would absorb the night's stew. As the guest of honor, Faucon used the household's finest cup for his watered wine. It was a pretty metal affair, chased with silver. Sir John and Marian shared a small wooden mazer, while Mimi and Robert made do with a worn wooden cup between them.

At first, the children peppered him with questions about the day and the dead miller. Since good manners required a guest to entertain his hosts in payment for his meal, Faucon did his best to make his story worthy of their hospitality, holding back only what he could not yet share. Once he finished, a squabble broke out between the children over the cup. This resulted in them being banished to the loft, although the punishment didn't seem to sting too sharply. Whispering and quiet laughter soon descended from their gaol.

"That's quite the tale, Sir Faucon," Sir John said, his voice deep but quiet. "I think Lord Rannulf will be glad he gave you the position the bishop wanted for him."

The older knight paused, his gaze on his guest. "And I think I am glad that you are the one who will now guide Blacklea. My time here was finished before you came." His final word caught in his mouth as he flinched.

Marian, who sat around the corner of the table from him, reached out to touch his hand. "Shift your legs a little, my love," she said.

He shot her a quick sidelong look. "I am not a child to be ordered about," he retorted, but there was affection in his tone. Moreover, he did as she said, although he had to use his hands to reposition his legs.

Once he was again comfortable on the collapsible stool which served him this night, he offered Faucon a weary smile. "Last year, I fell from my horse. It was a ridiculous accident, one I couldn't repeat if I tried. Since that day, my lower limbs seek to fall from their sockets, running like rats from burning thatch. I have outlived my body."

"Hush," Marian commanded. Fear and grief filled her gaze. "You know I don't like to hear that."

Her husband took her hand, placed a kiss on her fingers, then released her. "Go," he told his wife. "See to those hellions of ours. Sir Faucon and I have matters to discuss regarding the management of Blacklea."

She made an irritable sound. "I am not diverted."

"Pardon, Lady Marian," Faucon said. "Before you go, I'm wondering if you—or perhaps you, Sir John—can help me. I'm yet seeking the name of the knight or baron who might have kept Agnes of Stanrudde as his leman. Is there any chance you know?"

"I wouldn't," Sir John said. "Although I came here more than ten years ago, I am still considered an outsider. No one shares gossip with us newcomers, as you may already know. What of you, my sweet? You were raised in this shire."

Marian laughed. "Aye, I was raised in the shire, but in the wrong class for Sir Faucon to be asking me about the doings of knights."

She looked at Faucon, still smiling. "My father is a wool merchant in Coventry. All I know of Stanrudde, outside of the fact that I love going into the city on market day, is that my father thought the world of a wool merchant who lives there, by the name of Peter. Now it is my turn to ask something of you."

"Marian!" Sir John protested.

"Nay, I must ask him," she almost begged. "I cannot feel comfortable on the road with only a few serving men to see to our safety."

"He owes us nothing." Sir John held up a forestalling hand, but he might as well have been trying to command the tide to recede. His wife opened her mouth to argue, fierce determination filling her eyes.

"I may not owe you anything," Faucon dared to interrupt, "but I would hear the request. Please allow your wife to continue, sir."

Helplessness and the frustration it engendered filled Sir John's face. He sighed in defeat and spoke the words that he would not allow his wife to say. "It was planned last year that during this week of Mimi's saint day, my lady wife and my daughter would travel to Nuneaton. Because the Benedictine sisters at the abbey there—"

"Priory," Marian corrected quietly. "All say 'abbey' when there is naught but a prioress to rule it."

"Priory," John said, then continued as if she hadn't interrupted. "The nuns remember my wife fondly from when she resided there." He raised his voice a little. "Because of that, they have foolishly agreed to attempt to educate our daughter. I fear they have little chance of success. Where my lady wife is sweet-natured and pliable, my daughter is stubborn and thick-headed."

"Papa!" Mimi cried down in complaint.

"I knew you were listening," he called back. Then he added, "And an eavesdropper."

Mimi huffed in irritation.

Sir John lowered his voice as he continued. "When we arranged to do this, I was yet whole. Now I am but half a man, and cannot see to the safety of my wife and daughter as they travel less than five leagues, on tracks that are regarded as safe by most."

"I would be honored to see your family safely to the convent," Faucon replied swiftly. "Might the trip wait until after the morrow? I am expected in Priors Holston and may have to linger there for all the day, until I complete my duties."

That was, unless some other man died unexpectedly. Faucon found himself wondering what happened if he were summoned to a death but wasn't free to immediately attend the body.

Marian aimed that blinding smile of hers at him. "The day after tomorrow will work very well indeed. Nor is the ride any hardship. As my husband says, the convent is hardly more than a dozen miles distant. Thank you, thank you, a thousand times."

Sir John frowned at his wife. "You got what you wanted, now leave us."

His harsh chide didn't prevent Marian from placing a kiss on his forehead. She offered Faucon a quick curtsy, then squeezed behind her husband to climb the ladder to the loft. The children shrieked in pleasure. A moment later they settled, as Marian promised a tale.

"Thank you kindly, sir," Sir John said quietly, his voice thick as he stared at his hands on the table.

He made his fingers like spiders on the wood, then slowly lowered them until his palms were flat on the tabletop, his fingers spread wide. Still staring at his hands, he spoke, his voice was barely more than a whisper.

"I was a fool. I wed too late and married too well. Now I will leave her too soon, when I cannot bear to be parted from her. God be praised that she yet has her family in Coventry, for I am leaving her with almost nothing when I am gone."

The shame in the knight's words made Faucon think of Agnes and her confession of panic at finding herself alone.

When the older knight looked up, his gaze was filled with scorn aimed at himself. "Now, tell me why you aren't sending us from Blacklea, when I can be but a drain on your income."

Seeking to set the man at ease, Faucon laughed. "Because your lord is a worse cutpurse than any I've ever had the misfortune to meet. Yesterday, he set my head whirling with words, and before I knew what was what, I'd agreed to let you stay on at Blacklea for one full year, albeit unpaid, unless you and I agree differently."

Sir John looked at little startled at that. "I thought you were family."

"I am," Faucon replied, still laughing. "Imagine what the gift of Blacklea might have cost me if I'd not been!"

Chapter Sixteen

"**A**re you certain this is appropriate, Brother Edmund?"

Brother Heymon was short and slight, his fingertips stained with ink. So was the corner of his mouth. Faucon wondered if the brother had a habit of sucking on the tip of his quill. If that was so, then the stain was a reminder of yesterday's work, since the monk hadn't been at his desk yet this morning. Instead, he'd come to meet his crowner with his hoe still in his hand. According to Brother Edmund, the monks would be working their fields for the whole of this day.

The three of them stood in the circle of gravel at the center of the cloister garden, where the traditional four paths met. Faucon now understood why the new cloister had arches so deep and narrow. They kept the weather at bay. What might have been a covered walkway at other holy houses was the scriptorium at St. Radegund's. Twelve desks, each with its own stand on which to place the piece a monk might be copying, filled the space. Here, with the sun to light their work, the monks did their scribing and transcribing.

Only today there was no sun. The day had dawned overcast and threatening rain. But of course. Did he not wear his chain mail once again, with all muck, mud and rust sanded away?

"I am most certain," Faucon's clerk replied, "as are you, Brother. Prior Lambertus gave you his leave to speak with Sir Faucon this morning when we approached him regarding the matter."

The smaller monk made a face in chagrin. "So he did. It's just that this is all so unusual, you asking me about it, the prior agreeing that I might speak about it. That the miller even came. And then what he had me write!"

The monk looked at Faucon. "Aye, the miller did come two weeks ago and he did ask me to write for him, but it wasn't a will." Brother Heymon looked at Edmund. "That's why I told you 'nay' yestereven when you asked about it, Brother Edmund. I had not written a will for him. It wasn't until we were singing our Matins prayers that I realized you only thought he might have written a will. You didn't know that wasn't what he had wanted scribbled at all."

"What did he want you to write for him?" Faucon asked, trying to prod the monk in the right direction. As he spoke, a cool breeze swirled around him, lifting the hem of his surcoat.

He pushed it down. Without his sword at his side, there was nothing to hold the slit-sided garment in place atop his armor. As custom and the law required, he'd left his sword and scabbard hanging on Legate, along with his helmet and his shield, all of which he hoped he'd have no use for this day.

The small monk looked at him again, shaking his head as if befuddled. "As I said, it was the strangest thing. It was only a few lines and he took the skin with him when he left. I remember it all. I doubt I could forget it."

Just as Edmund had done when recalling the pronouncement about the Keepers, Brother Heymon tucked his hands into his sleeves, shut his eyes and leaned back on his heels. "'I, Halbert Miller, now of Priors Holston, do admit that I had no right to marry Cecilia, daughter of Oton, even as I traded vows with her. At the time of our marriage, and to this day, I remain married to another. I regretfully pronounce Stephen, her son by me, bastard-born.'"

The monk breathed out in satisfaction, then opened

his eyes again. "That was it. Only those few lines."

Edmund stared at him, round-eyed in surprise, then looked at Faucon. "By all that is holy, why would a man write such a thing?"

Faucon smiled at him. "Because he had committed bigamy and knew it. Thank you, Brother. This has been very helpful," he said to Brother Heymon.

The monk blinked at him, then tapped his ink-darkened fingertip to the stained corner of his mouth. "Now that he is dead, I don't see how it could be of assistance to anyone save our Lord, sir, but I am glad you find it so."

Then, shouldering his hoe, he made his way down one of the paths. Only after he'd left the cloister to circle around the church on his way back to the fields did Edmund speak.

"But why reveal such a thing now? This is especially so since it seems the miller had kept his secret for all his years in Priors Holston," asked the man with the 'honest' tongue.

"It was the final act of a vicious man, who knew he was doomed and wanted to punish the ones he blamed for destroying his life," Faucon replied. "It's the sort of thing a sot does, striking out at others over what is his own responsibility."

"But if Stephen is a bastard—" Edmund started.

Faucon finished the sentence for him. "Then he can inherit nothing, not that there is anything for him to inherit. Halbert had no right to claim ownership of anything that belonged to Cissy before their marriage, because he was never married to her. Susanna has herself a new cottage, I think."

"This does not bode well for what we'd thought to collect on the king's behalf," Edmund said with a shake of his head. There was neither disappointment nor frustration in his voice, or in the movement of his head. "Ah well, there will be other deaths, and other estates to value and confiscate."

Faucon eyed his clerk in astonishment as the monk picked up a knee-high tubular basket by the leather strapping knotted into its weave at top and bottom. Edmund patted its lid. "This is a far better way to transport my supplies. I found a piece of an old lectern to use as my desk for the time being. If you are finished here, sir, I am ready to be on our way to collect whatever confession might come forth this day."

"I am ready," Faucon replied, still battling his astonishment. Who was this stranger?

As they started from the cloister, Edmund added, "I hope you don't mind, but I had enough of your horse's rump last night. I'll be riding my own donkey today."

This time, Faucon let his laugh fly. Whoever Edmund was becoming, Faucon thought he liked him well enough. "I do not mind at all, Brother. Let's be off."

Following Susanna's directions, and carrying her greetings to her niece-by-marriage, Faucon and Edmund found the hamlet and the farmhouse with ease. To call 'Wina's family home a simple farm was to do it an injustice. Then again, 'Wina and Stephen wouldn't have wed unless they each brought equal value into the marriage. Halbert would never have accepted anything less.

Surrounded by barns and sheds, paddocks and fields enclosed by tall hedges, the main house was three times the length of any cottage Faucon had ever seen. With walls of piled stone and a thatched roof that reached almost to the ground, it was an ancient construction. It also appeared to be too short to allow a man to stand upright within doors.

They rode through the opening in the withe-walls that separated the front of the place from the track, to be greeted by a great crowd of children. Oxen, more than necessary for a single team, and a flock of sheep wandered to the closest edges of their paddocks to study the newcomers. Chickens scattered, ducks eyed them in suspicion, while the geese came dashing toward them, ready to defend their home with beak and wing, if not their lives.

Once the children had chased off the geese, Faucon and Edmund dismounted and were invited to enter the main dwelling.

They stepped down to enter; the floor of the structure was well below ground level. The air inside was warm and smelled of smoke. The massive beams which held the roof aloft were themselves held aloft by what seemed whole trees, buried deep into the earthen floor and set like columns down the middle of the structure. The spaces between the tree trunks were set off by more woven walls so they could be used as individual chambers.

It was obvious that the back half of the house was used as a barn for the animals; the heat of their bodies went far to warm the interior in deepest winter. The more forward of these walled bays were used for either food storage or sleeping. The kitchen end included a massive hearthstone, the walls behind it filled with shelves on which stood pots, jars, utensils and more. Bulky and misshapen with what they held, hempen bags were piled in one corner surrounded by barrels and large ceramic pots. Smoked meats, strings of garlic and onions, and drying herbs hung from the rafters above the hearth.

A large table with benches and stools of all sizes filled the central portion of the house. Four women sat at the table, all of them willowy, fine-boned beauties with honey-colored hair. None of them looked capable of pouring boiling water on an abuser. Only one looked distressed.

It was she who rose to her feet as Faucon entered. As tall as he, her eyes were red-rimmed from crying and her otherwise flawless skin was blotched with grief.

"You are this new crowner folk are talking about?" she asked before he could introduce himself.

It startled Faucon that she might have heard of him, until he realized she'd no doubt had visits from neighbors and friends after the inquest jury disbanded yesterday. Faucon would have wagered all he owned that she hadn't heard of him from Stephen.

"Don't forget," Edmund whispered from behind him. "She must swear an oath that she will speak the truth even though she is but a woman."

"I am," Faucon replied, ignoring his clerk for the moment. "I am Sir Faucon de Ramis, Keeper of the Pleas for king and crown, but you may call me crowner if you wish. I have questions about your husband."

"So do I!" 'Wina cried, her eyes glistening with unshed tears. "He has gone mad!" One of her sisters came to put an arm around her shoulders.

'Wina caught back a sob. "Yestermorn, I thought I could breathe again. I admit it. I was glad that Halbert was dead. He was a hateful man."

"Not hateful," her sister interrupted. "That man was purely evil. I don't know why my parents allowed our 'Wina to marry into that family."

"She was smitten by Stephen, more's the pity," another offered.

"He wasn't like his father when we wed," 'Wina protested, then once more looked at Faucon. "It's certain these last months have been the worst since I married Stephen, what with his father and Aggie locked in that horrible union of theirs. But I didn't expect–" she drew a ragged breath as the tears that filled her eyes spilled over to track down her cheeks.

"I didn't expect Halbert's refusal to speak to us about why he'd married Aggie to eat at my husband until the man I thought I knew was no more. I cannot bear what he has done!"

"Then Stephen left last night after the wake?" Faucon prodded gently, trying to lead her where he wished her to go.

"She must swear," Edmund hissed from behind him. Again, Faucon ignored him.

"He didn't stay for the wake. He left us to mourn on our own as the sun began to set," another of 'Wina's sisters said, her tone snide.

This one rose from the table to go to the hearth. As she stirred whatever bubbled in the pot, she looked over her shoulder at Faucon. "He opened yon door," the jerk of her head indicated the only entrance or exit from the house, "then walked the opposite way from Priors Holston on the track. Poor 'Wina went running after him, calling her questions and pleading with him to tell her where he went. He never once looked back. He didn't cross our threshold again until nearly dawn yesterday."

'Wina buried her face in her hands. Her shoulders shook for a moment, then she raised her head. Catching another ragged breath, she used the backs of her hands to dry her cheeks, then looked boldly at Faucon, her shoulders squared and her spine straight.

"Wife I may be, but I will not—cannot hide what he has done, not even to preserve our marriage. My soul will not carry it," she said, her lips quivering as she spoke.

In that instant, Faucon saw what Susanna so admired. No matter what the world sent 'Wina's way, she would do what was right, the consequences be damned. Stephen had married the wrong woman.

"Come with me, sir," 'Wina almost commanded, then threw off her sister's embrace. When she walked past Faucon, her long-legged stride was as confident as any man's.

As Faucon turned to follow her, Edmund looked at him, his raised brows adding emphasis to his disapproval. "She hasn't sworn to tell the truth," he complained, still whispering.

Faucon stepped up out of the long house, then waited for his clerk. They walked together as they followed 'Wina, who was heading toward a nearby byre.

"Brother Edmund, can you not see?" he asked of the monk, his voice lowered to keep his words between them. "It is not in that woman to tell anything but the truth. Let her cleanse her soul as it demands of her. When she is done, we can ask her to swear, telling her that this is what the law requires. If we ask it of her now we only add insult to injury. Her heart is already battered almost beyond bearing."

Although Edmund still frowned, his disapproval now like a cloud over his head, he held his tongue. As they stopped at the byre with 'Wina, Faucon could hear the grunting of pigs. Just outside the enclosure was a pile of what seemed rags, until she lifted her hems, and, using her foot, spread them out onto the ground before her crowner and his clerk.

"These are Stephen's garments. I know them well, having washed them often these past years, which is why he didn't dare bring them into the house. My nephew found them at the back of the byre yesterday morn when he came to feed the pigs. I cannot know if Stephen buried them and our sows pulled them out, or if he gave them to the pigs, thinking they would tear them to pieces or eat them. I do know what they mean."

It was a yellow tunic and a pair of red chausses. The brightly colored stockings were darkened with a thick coating of ashes but the tunic seemed only torn and stained by the action of the swine. Squatting, Faucon straightened the mangled garment until it lay flat on the ground, front up. Reddish marks smeared its left shoulder. He lifted it by that shoulder and folded it over until the back of the garment could be seen. There was no mistaking the blood that darkened its back.

"God help me, I know what this means," 'Wina repeated, her voice trembling. As she spoke, she rubbed her hands on the skirt of her blue gown as if to scrub them clean, even though she had not touched the garments.

"Mama!" A child dashed up to her. The lass's face was the reflection of her mother's fair features, her creamy skin without a single mark; her hair was a glorious deep red.

'Wina grabbed up her daughter. Then, tucking her babe's head into the curve of her neck, she bowed her head and began to cry in earnest.

Chapter Seventeen

Once 'Wina calmed, they returned to the house. The two sisters who yet lived with their families at the farm sent their eldest children to fetch their fathers. Only then did Edmund put quill to parchment.

To a one, men and women, they swore Stephen had not been in the house during the night of Halbert's death. They stated that he had instead arrived just before dawn, coming within doors already dressed in his finery. By the time Faucon and Edmund were leaving, 'Wina had returned to weeping.

"Why are we turning in this direction?" Edmund asked as he sent his donkey out of the gate, following Legate. He drummed his heels into the sides of the small creature, trying to bring the ass alongside the courser. At just a walk, Faucon's mount was almost too fast for Edmund's donkey to keep pace.

"We are going to Aldersby. I am hoping the sheriff hasn't yet departed."

"Ah, of course. You wish him to arrest the miller's son," Edmund said immediately, mistaking Faucon's intention for seeking out Sir Alain. "Know you, it is no matter if the sheriff has already gone. If it is our duty to discover who did the murder, then it must also be our right to arrest the one we identify." He paused in thought for an instant. "Although, if the sheriff is gone, it might be best if we seek out the village bailiff to assist us, just to be certain."

They rode for a bit in silence, then Edmund cleared his throat. He looked up at Faucon. "I don't understand how you could know the miller's wife would speak only the truth." His tone was both hesitant and wary.

"I don't see how you didn't know it," Faucon replied, again listening to his clerk with but half an ear. His thoughts were already at Aldersby as he prepared for battle, although he prayed this would be no more than a mere skirmish of words. "It was written on her face for all to read."

"On her face?" The clerk made a disbelieving sound. "How can you say that? There was nothing on her face save eyes and nose and mouth."

Then he sighed. "But that matters not. You were right. There was no need to get her oath beforehand. It is a shame there were but two men to add their voices to those of the women. So few men speaking to Stephen's actions may not convince a justice of his guilt, not if he brings enough of his own witnesses."

That teased Faucon out of his twisted musings. Edmund was right. No one but the two who committed the murder had witnessed Halbert's death. Because of that, not even the testimony of Stephen's wife about blood-stained clothing would be enough to prove his guilt, not if Stephen could bring enough men from Priors Holston to swear that he was a good man and true, and not capable of murder.

Then again, once Stephen was arrested, he'd be bound for the gaol at Killingworth. In that instance, Faucon doubted the young miller would survive that journey or his incarceration to stand before a justice.

'Wina's directions led them without event to Lady Joan's dower house. Faucon eyed the place in surprise. The farmstead–and this manor was in all truth nothing but a farmstead–was surrounded by a staked palisade and a moat.

Trapped within that wide, water-filled ditch was a square island of land that included a dovecote, a stable and what looked to be a separate kitchen building, and

Lady Joan's dower house. The house itself was no bigger than the miller's abode, and as any other cottage, was built of sticks, mud and manure, with thatch for a roof.

He and Brother Edmund drew their mounts to a halt at the tongue of wood that bridged the moat. The gate on the other side was open. Through it, Faucon could see the sheriff and a half-dozen men in the courtyard with their horses. All the men, the sheriff included, wore leather hauberks sewn with metal rings over their tunics, and swords belted at their sides. He and Edmund had arrived just in time. Sir Alain was readying to quit his lady wife's manor.

"Who comes!" shouted one of the sheriff's soldiers as he stepped into the gateway. Behind him in the courtyard, all the men paused to turn their gazes toward the gate.

"Sir Faucon de Ramis, Keeper of the Pleas for this shire," Faucon called back. "I have come to discuss the death of Halbert Miller with Sir Alain."

At his call, Sir Alain lifted his head and stared at Faucon. Once again, no expression softened the harsh features of the older knight. He gave no sign of welcome or refusal, simply watched Faucon as the soldier in the gateway walked back into the courtyard toward his lord.

"He'd better agree to speak with you," Edmund grumbled. "Just as we have done our duty and found what is necessary to prove Stephen guilty of his father's murder, the sheriff must now do his duty and convey the miller's son to the gaol, so he doesn't run and become outlaw."

Faucon eyed his clerk. Edmund couldn't be allowed to alter the pattern of this conversation as he'd done with Agnes. Too much depended on the words that would be spoken.

"Vow to me, Brother," he said. "Swear upon your love for our Lord that you'll say nothing whilst I speak with the sheriff. As you vow, do so as if you believed my life depended upon it."

The request set Edmund to blinking rapidly. Then he frowned, although not in disapproval. His gaze caught and held Faucon's for a long moment. Awareness, if not understanding, stirred in his gaze.

"What is this?" he asked

"It is what it is," Faucon replied. "Ask me no more, only remember the law. It allows for a man to use more than witnesses and oaths to prove his innocence."

Edmund's eyes widened slowly, as he struggled with what his employer had said, and what he had not. Faucon held his breath. A moment later, the monk's jaw tightened and his eyes narrowed. He reached within the neck of his habit and pulled forth the wooden cross he wore against his skin.

"I so swear, upon my vow to serve our Lord for all my days," he said, the crucifix clutched in his fist.

Inside the courtyard, the soldiers mounted. Sir Alain rode at their head, leading them out of the manor gateway. Faucon and Edmund maneuvered their mounts so they no longer blocked the exit from the bridge, and as the sheriff crossed, he brought his mount to a standstill alongside Legate.

"We will let them ride ahead so we may speak," Sir Alain said, his voice no more or less gruff or dark with violence than it had been yesterday.

Together they waited, until the last soldier crossed the bridge and turned in the direction of Priors Holston and the main road that lay beyond the far border of the village. Only then did the sheriff put his heels to his mount. Faucon did the same, and they joined the back of the plodding, jingling cavalcade. Brother Edmund's donkey brought up the end, pitter-pattering behind them, doing its level best to keep pace.

"What is it you desire of me, Keeper?"

"Crowner," Faucon replied. "That seems to be what

folk are comfortable calling me. As for what I desire, it is the resolution of Halbert Miller's murder, which I now believe within my grasp. I would like you at hand when I confront the one who committed this foul deed, so you can take him into custody."

"What murder? It looked to me yesterday that Halbert Miller drowned." The sheriff kept his gaze focused on the men ahead of him.

"So it did to me, as well," Faucon agreed, "until we removed the miller from the race and examined his body, to discover that his heart had been pierced. It was a tiny wound, barely noticeable. Indeed, it was so small that I might well have dismissed it as inconsequential, save that the brake on the waterwheel was set yestermorn. If you recall, your man was trying to release it when I arrived. If the miller had been alone when he drowned, pinned beneath the wheel, then he could not have set that brake."

The sheriff shot Faucon a sidelong look. His brows were lowered over his eyes. As he studied Faucon, he ran his gloved hand over his beard in what seemed an unconscious gesture.

"How clever of you," he finally said, his voice still flat. "And how foolish of the one who set that brake. There cannot be many who have access to the miller's tools."

Faucon nodded. "There are not. The man you will be arresting is the miller's son. There is no other save he who could have used that wrench two nights ago when the miller died."

"Ah, I recall now. When I arrived at the mill yestermorn, the man did not seem much aggrieved over his father's passing. Do you know the reason the miller's son killed his sire? To win his inheritance sooner than time was offering it, perhaps?"

Faucon drew a steadying breath. This must be how a rope dancer felt, toes curled tightly to the one thing that prevented him from crashing to the earth so many feet below.

"Nay, not to take his inheritance sooner, but to confirm his inheritance. Stephen Miller was unwilling to lose what he believed was his by right of birth, but in truth, was not. He was desperate to keep his father from revealing to the world that Stephen had been bastard-born."

So sharply did Sir Alain shift toward Faucon in his saddle that his mount danced, trying to buck. The soldiers ahead of them looked back, startled by the commotion. Once the sheriff steadied his mount, he again looked at Faucon. The man's eyes were yet wide in surprise. His mouth opened and closed a few times, as if words bubbled onto his tongue, only to dissolve before they could exit past his teeth.

"Bastard? How—?" Sir Alain finally managed to spew.

"How is it possible that Stephen is a bastard?" Faucon offered, keeping his gaze on the rump of the horse in front of him. "It turns out that Halbert became a soldier to escape his rightful wife. The wife he abandoned never tried to free herself from their vows, and yet lives. Thus Halbert was never wed to Cissy, and that makes Stephen a bastard.

"A few weeks ago, Halbert had that exact confession scribed onto parchment by one of the monks at St. Radegund's. I suspect Stephen found the skin—" something Faucon was certain Halbert had intended his son to do "—and took it to one he trusted to read it for him. I believe Stephen thought what he'd discovered was the marriage contract between Halbert and his new wife, Agnes of Stanrudde. That marriage had quite upset him. He feared his father had given his new wife a substantial dower. He said as much to me yesterday. It seems his father refused to speak to him about his new union, threatening disinheritance if Stephen pursued the matter."

Faucon said no more. It wasn't necessary. He knew the rest, as did Sir Alain.

Stephen hadn't approached the sheriff to help him kill his father, because Sir Alain had been Agnes' lover. Stephen had never known that. Instead, he'd gone to Sir Alain because he was Halbert's lender. Stephen, protesting that his father was ruining their trade with his drinking, and how that would soon affect their ability to make payments on what was owed, had given the sheriff the opportunity he craved to correct the error of Agnes' marriage, a marriage that never was.

The sheriff once more stared ahead of him. "What proof have you that it was the miller's son who did this deed?"

"He left his bloody garments at his wife's family home, and the pigs found them," Faucon replied.

"And there is no abettor? The man did this on his own?"

It was Faucon's turn for surprise. He hadn't expected so direct a question. It was a potent warning. The sheriff would use every tool at his disposal to protect himself from one he considered an interloper.

Faucon kept his gaze focused ahead of him, his thoughts scrambling. The quiet lasted long enough that Sir Alain once again shifted to look at him.

"Nay, no one aided Stephen as he put his dead sire into the race, then released the brake so the wheel would take him," Faucon said carefully. "By the by, Bishop William of Hereford remembers you with admiration from the journey the two of you shared to the Holy Land. I spoke with him about it yesterevening, when I went to view the remains of a murdered lass who had been left in the open to rot. He and Lord Graistan discovered her body while hunting. There was so little left of her that we buried her, having no hope of discovering her identity."

Still Sir Alain stared at him. Faucon battled the urge to touch his sword hilt, to reassure himself it was still within reach.

"A murdered child, was it?" the sheriff asked at last. "On Lord Graistan's lands?"

"Aye, a girl of perhaps a half-dozen years," Faucon replied.

"Well, if she's on Lord Graistan's land, then she's his problem to resolve," the sheriff replied, turning his attention back to the track ahead.

They completed the ride to Priors Holston in silence. It took almost that long for Faucon's muscles to relax. Nay, Stephen would never see the inside of the gaol at Killingworth.

Nor would Faucon be called to meet Sir Alain sword-to-sword in judicial combat, as the sheriff sought to prove himself innocent of the miller's death.

Not yet.

As they entered Priors Holston and started toward the mill, their troop acquired a following. The men, women and children kept a respectful distance as they trailed the soldiers. Just as Faucon had done yesterday, the soldiers stopped at the end of the lane near the coppiced trees and dismounted, walking the remainder of the way to the mill. Across the race, Simon and his boys straightened from the fabric they were stretching to watch the soldiers and monk as they made their way through Stephen's toft and croft. Faucon watched Simon glance from the mill to Faucon, then shoot a look heavenward. After that, he called his boys back to work.

The stones were turning. The air in the yard was alive with the rumble of the wheel as it spun on its axle, the constant splash of water and the unrelenting grate of stone on stone.

As Faucon opened the gate and let the sheriff step into the mill yard ahead of him, Stephen exited from the three-sided shed where he'd sat yesterday, the wrench in his hands, no doubt to brake the wheel as he took his midday repast. Halbert's son wore a dusty red tunic, and green chausses just as flecked. Although his head was down, Faucon could see Stephen was smiling to himself.

Only as he stepped outside of the shed did he realize he wasn't alone. He raised his head and his smile died. All the color left his face as he froze where he stood, the wrench cradled close to his chest as if precious beyond silver.

"Wait," Edmund called out from behind, trying to catch up to Faucon. "Wait, you must wait for me!"

"What is this?" Stephen cried out, his voice thready and weak. "Why are you here?"

Faucon glanced at Sir Alain. The sheriff watched him, his expression as flat and dead as always, his arms crossed.

"Well, Keeper," he said, "if you now keep the pleas, then I think it is no longer my duty to make the accusation. Accuse him, and let the man refute or confess. I will take him after that."

Of a sudden, Faucon was once more dancing on that taut rope, high above the earth. Only now it swayed as if in a storm. He had expected Sir Alain to make the accusation, doing so to protect himself. Stephen would never dare directly accuse the man who had helped him end his father's life. Such an attempt would be pointless. Sir Alain would simply deny it.

But that wasn't true if Faucon made the accusation. If Stephen spewed a counter accusation at his sheriff, Sir Alain would demand that Faucon either refute the charge or offer proof that it was true. To lie and say the sheriff was innocent was not only cowardly, it would prevent him from ever pursuing the matter further. But to suggest Sir Alain was guilty was to put himself in death's way before he was ready.

Faucon's throat closed. He was too new and unknown in this shire. Edmund came to a panting halt beside him.

"Stephen, son of Halbert," the clerk sang out, the sound of his voice rising above the thundering racket of the working mill, "I have the sworn oaths of your wife, her sisters, and two of their husbands that you were not in their house the night your father died, and did return to their home just before dawn on the morning your father was discovered in the millrace. They swear they found your garments in a byre, and that your clothing was stained with blood. Will you confess that you are the one who placed your father beneath the wheel, so it might seem as if he died by accident?"

Stephen screamed, the sound high-pitched and filled with panic. He leapt off the step, running even before his feet found the earth. He sprinted past Faucon as he headed for the corner of the mill.

"Catch him!" Faucon shouted, grabbing for the miller and missing.

The soldiers behind Sir Alain exploded into motion, toppling Brother Edmund. Still shrieking, Stephen flew around the corner of the mill. Faucon followed, only to stop at the edge of the race, cursing his own fear of water, made worse by the weight of his armor.

The fastest of the soldiers pushed past him, leaping the race to give chase. In the lane, the commoners raised the hue and cry, shouting for their neighbors to catch Stephen the Miller. Some dashed into the mill yard to join the chase. As required by the law, Simon and his sons came running toward the race to do their civic duty.

Stephen was halfway up the channel, on his way to the pond. The soldier was right behind him.

"I've got him!" this one shouted, reaching for the

back of the miller's dusty tunic.

Halbert's bastard son jogged to the left, half-leaping, half-stumbling, and threw himself across the race.

Those who retained some fondness for him would later say that he simply misjudged. Those who did not would swear they saw Halbert's hand reach out of the water and pull his son down into the race. They would say they saw Stephen struggle as he sought to free himself from that ghostly grip. They were telling tales.

Faucon watched Stephen slide into the water and tuck the wrench that could save his life even closer to his chest. He rolled to face the stones at the bottom of the channel.

Sir Alain's men tumbled into the water after him, but the torrent that fueled the wheel already had the man they sought. Water glistened, spraying off the paddles as the wheel turned its clanking circle. A moss-dabbled paddle sliced toward the bottom of the race. It caught Stephen on the back of his head, holding him down in the water just as its broken mate had held his father.

The soldiers splashed and shouted. One had the big man by the feet, another took his free arm. The wrench floated free, rising in the water. From the edge of the race, another soldier reached in to snatch the tool and slipped. As he went under, he knocked over the man trying to winnow Stephen free of the wheel's hold.

The wrench tumbled through the wheel, then cartwheeled down the race, driven by the power of the water. Faucon watched it go. When he could see it no more, he looked up at Simon who stood across the channel from him. They watched each other as more soldiers, both in the race and out of it, made their way downstream in an effort to catch the missing tool.

"Good riddance," the fuller said, his tone bitter. "I should have known it was him who did it. I shouldn't have let him woo me with the promise of that fulling mill. I suppose this means 'Wina will not be back. I'll miss her, and Alf as well."

Faucon shrugged. "Someone will have to run the mill, else you'll have no flour to make your bread."

"Aye, I suppose," the man replied, then sighed. "I suppose this also means I'll lose another day's work because of yet another inquest jury. Perhaps I should curse the day my grandsire escaped his lord and came to own a cottage next to a mill."

Chapter Eighteen

It was late afternoon by the time the inquest jury had finished its work. By then Sir Alain had long since departed, and thankfully so. The jury not only confirmed Stephen's death caused by misadventure, but they confirmed, at Faucon's insistence, that Stephen had only abetted another yet unknown man in the murder of his father. It was a hard-fought resolution, for there had been no end to the muttering the moment the jurors had heard the tale of Halbert's bigamy. Once they heard that tale, the jurors had no difficulty acknowledging that, as his father's bastard, Stephen had no right to inherit his father's property; therefore, there was no property for king and crown to collect. They went on to declare the millwheel deodand for causing Stephen's death, and set its value at the pittance Alf had warned they would.

After hiding meekly behind a thick layer of clouds all the day, the sun finally slipped out of concealment as it neared the horizon. Faucon and Edmund tied their mounts to the fence at Susanna's alehouse. It seemed this was where all the jurors had flown after being dismissed. Men filled every table. More made themselves comfortable on the ground. Faucon wondered how many had come to commiserate with her over the loss of her nephew, and how many to taunt her over her sister's misfortune in meeting Halbert. Or maybe they'd all just come to drink up Susanna's fine ale.

She'd recruited help to serve them. A grandmother and two girls young enough to be her granddaughters were moving around the yard with pitchers, the women laughing and chatting with those they knew. Susanna waved Faucon and Edmund into her foreyard when she saw them.

"Up!" she shouted to the group of men sitting at the table Faucon had used the previous day. "Sir Crowner and his clerk need a place to sit, and I need to sit with them. Godiva," she motioned to the grandmother, "see to it these surly curs get their cups filled once again at no charge."

That stopped the complaints of the evicted, who went to sit on the ground near the cottage door. Faucon and Edmund shared the bench on one side of the table, offering their cups to be filled as they did. After emptying her pitcher into them, Susanna sat upon the opposite bench.

"I cannot believe my ears," she said, her eyes round and her expression astonished. "I mean, I knew Halbert was a stinkard, but to pretend to marry Cissy, and make Stephen a bastard, and all of us none the wiser? That's madness. And then Stephen! I was sure he'd killed his father. There was something different, something in his eyes these past weeks."

"Indeed," Faucon replied. "Where is Agnes?"

"Gone. She left this morning," Susanna said with a sigh. I begged her to stay, but a carter stopped by last night and offered to take her to Stanrudde."

Faucon sighed as well. He would never find her again. Sir Alain would make certain of that.

Then Susanna returned to matters closer to her heart. "Poor 'Wina. She's lost both husband and home, and Little Cissy is tainted by no fault of her own. Well, at least there'll be no heriot for them to pay. The king can't have his death tax from one who the law says cannot inherit." She grinned at that, but it swiftly faded.

"But what happens to the mill now? Is it mine, as you suggested when last we spoke?"

Faucon shook his head. "The cottage at the mill and all that it holds within its walls is yours, as it was Cissy's through Jervis. That means you'll be the one paying that heriot."

That made her bray in laughter. She slapped her hand on the table top to emphasize her amusement. "I'll sell some of Halbert's pretty things to do that, won't I just?"

"As for the mill," Faucon continued, "it cannot be yours as it never belonged to Cissy or Halbert. According to Prior Lambertus, all Halbert purchased with that great sum was the right to use the rented mill for his sole profit. The prior also told me that their agreement with Halbert stipulated that only his legitimate heirs could continue renting the mill after his death. If Halbert had no legitimate heir, then the right to operate the mill would return to the priory's control."

"Well then, it seems the monks once again are millers," Brother Edmund said, as he swallowed another mouthful of ale. Then he winced. Edmund's nose was crusted with dried blood, and there was a darkening bruise where his cheek had hit a stone in the courtyard when he had been overrun.

"If that's so, then Prior Lambertus best take a lesson from his predecessor and swallow his objections to a woman running his mill, if he has any," Susanna declared. "The only one left in Priors Holston who knows how to work those stones is 'Wina."

"You'll have to help her the way you told Stephen you'd help Agnes," Faucon replied, laughing. "You'll likely have to give up brewing to do it."

"The devil will die first," Susanna snapped back, smiling. "Aggie needed help. 'Wina will do fine on her own, that girl, hiring as need requires. You look miserable, Brother," she said to Edmund. "Do you want a cloth to clean that? I have a salve for your cheek."

"That would be a kindness, goodwife," the monk

replied respectfully, but with his nose stuffed and swollen, the words broke into bits and pieces as he spoke them.

That made her bray again. "That's me, a kind of good wife. Enjoy your drink and I'll be back in a moment."

As she left them to enter her cottage, Faucon leaned forward, this being his first opportunity to speak privately with his clerk. "You broke your oath to me," he said, smiling at the monk. "You spoke when you swore not to."

Edmund's eyes widened in surprise. His mouth opened, no doubt to spew some harsh word.

Faucon laughed. "Nay, say nothing. That was but a poor jape on my part. I cannot thank you enough for accusing Stephen on my behalf. I went tongue-tied, with no idea of what needed to be said."

Lifting his cup, Edmund watched his employer over its rim for a long moment. He sipped, then set the wooden vessel back on the table. There was a new intensity in his gaze.

"I could see you were struggling," he said, when he couldn't have seen Faucon at all, not when he was running up from behind. "I knew how important the words would be, what with the sheriff standing right beside you. You are still new to the law. I thought it best that I make the accusation this time." He paused, then whispered. "No one challenges a monk to judicial combat."

It was Faucon's turn for surprise. Edmund had understood his warning for what it was. Then he'd curbed his 'honest' tongue, put aside his rigid rules, and broken an oath he'd made upon his love for the Lord God to protect the man he thought of as his 'penance.'

Disrespectful, aye. Arrogant and inconsiderate, for certain. But courageous enough to put himself between two warriors with no thought for his own safety. There was much to be said for a man with that much heart.

"I think we will do well together, you and I," Faucon told him, lifting his cup in salute to the monk.

"I think we shall, sir," Edmund replied, and emptied his cup. He almost smiled. "I do think we shall."

"My lord prior," Faucon said, turning in the center of the garden to face Prior Lambertus as the churchman entered the cloister from around the corner of the church.

Faucon had escorted Edmund to the priory, only to be met by Tom, Legate's great friend. Lambertus had put the man at the gateway with the message that he wished to see the shire's new crowner, should he come.

From the look of it, the prior had been working with his monks all this day. His habit was sweat-stained, and his feet in their sandals were dark with dirt. Grime streaked his face and his forearms; he'd rolled his sleeves above his elbows.

"Sir Faucon," Lambertus said, that strangled smile of his lifting his lips. He didn't offer his hand, suggesting he'd set aside his ring while he labored, but accepted Faucon's bow instead. "I hear it has been quite a day in the village. I'm told that Stephen Miller is dead by misadventure, but before he died, you were able to accuse him of his father's murder."

Faucon gave a single shake of his head. "Stephen was only accused of placing his dead father into the millrace to make murder seem an accidental death. In doing so he aided the one who killed Halbert. For that, I'm sure he will answer to our Lord."

A tiny crease marred the prior's smooth brow. "But if Stephen had not done the deed, why did he run when he was confronted with the charge?" As he spoke, he unrolled his sleeves, then crossed his arms over his chest and tucked his hands into the sleeves.

"Stephen ran because he couldn't bear to lose the identity and the life he had always believed belonged to him. He didn't wish to be exposed as Halbert's bastard son."

The corners of Faucon's mouth lifted into a grim smile. "But I do not tell you anything you don't already know."

Lambertus had known full well yesterday that there was no will. Where else would the illiterate son of Prior Holston's miller have taken the parchment he'd found, save to the prior who offered the villagers support and counsel?

Lambertus tilted his head to the side as his shoulders lifted slightly in a show of helplessness. "What is given in confidence cannot be breached, not even to aid in seeking out a murderer. It's a shame you weren't able to identify the man who actually killed the elder miller."

"The time for that has not yet come, but Brother Edmund tells me there is no limit to how long I may take in resolving the matter," Faucon offered, then paused for a breath. "I fear I must warn you that the right to operate the mill will not be coming back to you."

"You are mistaken," Lambertus said smoothly. "Stephen is a bastard, and by the terms of our agreement with Halbert, the mill now returns to our control."

"Come now," Faucon chided gently. "All of Priors Holston knew Halbert as a churl, a man who wouldn't give another so much as a piece of straw if there was no profit in it for him. Why else would he have allowed those damning words to be scribed onto parchment, save that he believed he had a son who could inherit all he'd built?"

The prior's arms opened. His eyes widened. He pressed a hand to his brow as if in pain. "Nay. That cannot be true."

"You read the words," Faucon persisted. "Halbert admitted that he was married to another. Did you not stop to wonder if there were children from that first union? As it turns out, Halbert's elder son, his legitimate heir, presently resides as my guest at Blacklea."

What Faucon took from Lambertus with one hand, he now returned with the other. "But take heart, my lord prior. I think this man will be a far more honest miller than Halbert ever was. He doesn't need to make the same profit. Remember, all obligation to repay the money Halbert borrowed died with him. More's the pity for his lender, if that amount was as rich as you suggest."

Here was Halbert's revenge at being forced to wed Agnes. Not one more shilling would the sheriff see in repayment of that loan, nor a single penny of whatever Stephen had promised to pay in return for Sir Alain ending his father's life. The sheriff couldn't even claim whatever collateral Halbert might have promised him. The slate had been wiped clean with the death of Halbert and his second son.

"Now, my lord Prior, the day dims and I still have miles to ride to Blacklea. I'll bid you good health in our Lord, and good night."

Lambertus said nothing as Faucon bowed, then turned and made his way back through the priory to where Legate waited.

Chapter Nineteen

The next day dawned overcast again, but the air was warmer and dryer. Once more wearing his armor, he rode out of Blacklea on Legate. At last he'd had time to arrange for a man to take the news of his great good fortune to Faucon's home, along with a request to send his personal belongings to Blacklea. It would be at least another two weeks before he saw them.

It turned out that in the whole village of Blacklea there were but two riding horses. Perhaps the day would come when Faucon could afford to make such a ride as this dressed more comfortably, and on a proper traveling horse. That day had yet to arrive. Until he had the coins he needed to buy and maintain his own palfrey, he'd ride Legate.

Marian rode one of the riding horses, the palfrey. It had an ambling gait that wouldn't be challenged, but didn't mind the baskets filled with Mimi's possessions tied to its saddle like saddlebags. Marian proved herself a capable and no-nonsense horsewoman. Her traveling gown, cut so she could ride modestly astride, was sturdy wool, dyed a dusty brown.

The other mount was the pony on which Mimi and Robert had learned to ride. Mimi had no riding attire. She sat astride, with her gowns hiked above her knees. When the spirit moved her, she'd drum her heels into the little creature's sides, sending it racing ahead, then racing back again, until Legate made his disapproval known. The outcome was the pony's reins tied to Marian's saddle, and a sulking Mimi perched behind her mother, her knees high as she rested her feet on those baskets.

Over the course of the hours, their conversation flowed like a river. They began by discussing Blacklea. As Susanna had suggested of women, Marian turned out to be as much Blacklea's steward as her lord husband. She knew from whence its income came, which of its folk did what was required of them and more, and which found ways to avoid labor.

Then she began to speak passionately about sheep and wool, about how her father's business continued to grow with no end in sight. When Faucon asked why her husband or Lord Rannulf hadn't already put more sheep on pasture, she admitted that neither of them had much interest, being content with matters as they were.

As Faucon stewed over that information, Mimi asked her mother about the nuns, and their conversation shifted. Where Marian fondly recalled the years she spent at her convent, Faucon told tales about his time with the monks, until Marian chided him for scaring her daughter. He then diverted them both with memories of his squiring, tales of their king, and his travels to the Holy Land.

They reached Nuneaton late in the day. By then, Mimi was seated in front of her mother, dozing.

Upon entering the town, they left behind the tofts and crofts of farmers, and now rode along a lane crowded on each side with homes, each standing cheek-by-jowl to its neighbors, right up against the edge of the lane. The smells and sounds of a town at rest filled the air. Beneath the ever-present smell of wood smoke he caught the scent of cabbage, onions and apples being boiled from one place. A sheep bleated from someone else's back garden. Raucous laughter, the amusement of a least a dozen folk, rolled out of another home, then one man began to sing, his voice deep and a little off key.

Although these townhouses had been constructed in

the same manner of the more rural cottages, with flimsy walls and thatched roofs, they rose to two- and three-storeys tall. Each one seemed to have a placard hanging above its door, proclaiming some sort of trade, as well as a lower storey dedicated as a shop.

"Which came first, the holy house or the town?" Faucon asked.

"A village," Marian replied with a smile. "My father told me that, until the nuns came some thirty years past and our old king gave them the right to hold their market, this was only a village, not much larger than Blacklea. Look what's happened in so short a time!" She pointed out a goldsmith's establishment, then shot that smile of hers at Faucon. "As coins change hands, miracles happen, or so my father always says."

She laughed. "It can only be true. Coins changed hands, and I married a knight."

"Miracles, indeed," he replied in agreement. Coins had changed hands, and he became a Keeper of the Pleas, the crowner for this shire, and a man of sudden substance.

Marian led the way onto another lane. At its end stood a tall red stone wall. He could see the roof and tower of the church rising above the wall. Unlike St. Radegund's leafy fence line, this wall had a proper arched gateway built into it, complete with a pair of iron-bound wooden doors, one door thrown wide. A nun—the portress—stood in the opening speaking with a monk, a fellow Benedictine who wore a broad-brimmed hat and had a leather pack upon his back.

"Brother Colin?" Faucon called, as he and Marian drew their tired mounts to a halt before the gateway.

The elderly monk turned in surprise, then grinned in pleasure. "Sir Crowner! Do the living or the dead bring you to Nuneaton?" he asked as the portress hurried off to fetch the help she needed to accommodate her new visitors.

"The almost-living, Brother." Faucon pointed to the child stirring in Marian's saddle. Yawning, Mimi slid to the ground and leaned sleepily against the palfrey's side. "Lady Marianne of Blacklea comes to be educated by the nuns, just as was her mother, Lady Marian, wife of the steward of Blacklea."

Dismounting, Faucon went to help Marian from her saddle. With his hands at her waist, he steadied her as she worked to free her feet from the bulky gown and stirrups. When she was ready, he lifted her down. She was lighter than he expected. As she found her feet, she discovered the joys of a long day in the saddle. Groaning a little, another man's wife leaned against him for an instant.

He smiled at her, his hands still at her waist. "Pins and needles?"

"Oh Lord, save me," she complained with a laugh, then stepped back from him. There was nothing but gratitude in her gaze.

Faucon let her go, then indicated Colin. "Lady Marian, wife to Sir John of Blacklea, this is Brother Colin of Stanrudde, the monk I told you about last night, the one who can tell how a man has died by looking in his mouth."

Marian offered the elderly monk an unsteady bend of her knees. "Quite the feat that seems, the way Sir Faucon tells the tale," she said. "What brings you to Nuneaton, Brother?"

"Herbs, my lady," Colin replied. "I am away from my house in Stanrudde all the growing season, harvesting what is needed for treating ills. There is much to be found in this area, and the infirmaress here enjoys tramping through brambles and bracken with me. Only it seems she's away from the house at the moment, and not expected back until the day after the morrow."

Just then the portress returned with stable hands

and a maidservant. The lads took all three horses, after being assured Legate was safe without his rider. The portress called for Mimi and Marian to follow her. Mimi waved her farewell and Marian called back a promise that she'd be ready for an early departure in the morning.

"This way to the guest house, sir." The waiting maid servant pointed to a fine, two-storey structure that clung to the outside of the convent wall only a few dozen yards distant. It had a second-storey entry door, reached by an external staircase. "I'm to help you disarm, then I'll see you get a warm meal."

As she started toward the guest house, Faucon looked at the older monk. "If you are at loose ends this night and have no prayers to say, I would enjoy your company."

"I do have prayers to say, but I would be pleased to join you for a time, until I retreat for the night to the chaplains' house," Colin replied with a smile and a nod.

It wasn't until they were climbing the stairs to the guest house door, the monk trailing Faucon, that Colin asked, "So, have you come any closer to resolving who murdered the miller?"

"I have indeed, and it's a strange tale for certain. I even know why Halbert Miller was killed."

"Why?" Colin asked.

"Because the Priory of St. Radegund is short of money, while in the middle of building," Faucon said as he stopped on the porch at the top of the steps and looked down at the monk.

"I beg your pardon?" Colin gasped, his eyes wide in shock. He stopped where he stood, midway up the stairs.

"Come up. It is a complicated tale, and I'll need to be out of my armor and filling my belly if I'm to tell it properly."

The chamber set aside for the convent's male visitors to use was a rich one, complete with a curtained bed. As it should be. The place had been founded by an earl who had come often to visit his sister.

Not only did the room have a line of narrow windows in its outer wall, but its hearth had an odd arrangement, with bricks built into the wall above the stone that formed a channel of sorts to lead the smoke up through the roof where it vented to the out-of-doors. When Faucon asked about it, the maid said as long as the shutters were open on the windows for air flow, the smoke wouldn't leave the channel.

She was right. Faucon and Colin brought their small backless chairs up to the hearthstone and savored the heat without the sting of smoke in their eyes.

The meal the nuns offered was richer than he expected, with a thick and tasty fish stew, bread and a wedge of fine cheese, and fresh cider to drink. Dressed in nothing but his braies and seated on one of the two backless stools in the room, Faucon savored the warmth and the company as he warmed his bare toes on the edge of the hearthstone.

"Prior Lambertus has always been a man eaten alive by his ambition," Colin admitted with a shake of his head after Faucon finished explaining the priory's connection to Halbert's death. "I see God's hand in sending Alf to Priors Holston, and am glad to hear he will become the village miller. I think each day that Prior Lambertus has to look upon him is one less day he will spend in purgatory, cleansing himself of sins."

Colin leaned forward on his chair to set his cup of cider on the edge of the hearthstone. "So tell me how you can be so certain it is the sheriff who murdered Halbert with Stephen's aid."

"Would that I were completely certain," Faucon replied, then sighed. "If I were, I would leap wholeheartedly into the accusation, more than ready to face Sir Alain in judicial combat."

The monk's brows rose high on his forehead, his dark eyes alive with surprise. "Do you truly think he would challenge you?"

"Of course he would," Faucon replied with a quiet laugh, "doing so not because I believe he killed Halbert, for he knows I will never prove that. I cannot. Nay, he'd do so because I am now the 'sheriff's bane.' That is how Lord Graistan named this new position of mine. To be the Keeper of the Pleas is to be the man who is tasked to see the sheriff gets nothing more from his position save his due, which is a pittance. I'm an even worse threat to Sir Alain, because I'm unknown to him. From this moment forward, he must watch his every move. How much easier his life would be if he were to challenge me to judicial combat over the miller's murder and either end my life or leave me so injured that I could no longer serve the royal court. If that happened, he'd see to it some neighbor or friend was elected in my place and his life would continue as it had."

"You don't think you'll ever prove our sheriff murdered the miller?" Colin asked, elbows braced on his thighs, his cup cradled in his hands.

Faucon sighed at that. "Not if I cannot find the woman who was his leman and convince her to speak against her love. Neither one is possible, not now that Sir Alain is aware of what I believe I know. I have no doubt she is once more in his protection. Sir Alain will keep her safely hidden. Nay, I will never again see Agnes of Stanrudde."

Colin shifted his gaze from the crackling, leaping flames on the stone to look at his host. He frowned a little. "A small woman, and plain?"

"Aye, didn't you see her at the mill?" Faucon replied. "She was dressed in red and her eye was blackened."

Colin only shook his head. "I saw no woman at all, only you and the other men of the inquest. Would you know if this Agnes is a woodcarver's daughter?"

"You know her?" Faucon blurted out, straightening in his seat. "Aye, Agnes of Stanrudde."

"Of course I know Aggie," Colin replied, as if surprised by Faucon's surprise. "Did I not tell you I'd been the apothecary in Stanrudde for almost all my life? I was at her father's side when he died. Her sister never forgave Aggie when she took up with Sir Alain, even though his coins were what kept food on their table before their mother remarried. She said that Aggie brought nothing but shame down upon their family. I think that's why Margery left Stanrudde for Banbury, marrying as far as she could from those who knew her sister had become a rich man's poppet."

That made Faucon laugh. "Information come too late to do me any good," he said. "That leaves me only one final mystery to solve."

"Glad to be of service, however belated, Sir Crowner," Colin said with a scornful breath. "So what is this final mystery? Mayhap I have a solution for it hiding somewhere in the recesses of this old head of mine."

"It's Halbert's fine tunic, the one Agnes gave him as a wedding gift," Faucon said. "I cannot believe that Sir Alain stayed long enough at Priors Holston after killing Halbert to put that tunic on him for vengeance's sake."

"What do you mean? Explain it to me," Colin urged. "Better yet, tell me everything you know–or believe–of how this murder happened."

"Aye, then. I'll start where I think this all began," Faucon said. "I think that just before Sir Alain left for the Michaelmas court in Rochester, he received word from Agnes that the prior would not help her escape her marriage to Halbert. She had gone to Lambertus, hoping he would dissolve the marriage when she claimed Halbert wasn't doing his marital duty. I'm not certain she knew that prior was aware of her former relationship with Alain."

He shot Colin a smiling sidelong look. "She was when she left the priory. No matter how she argued, Lambertus rebutted her every request, even claiming the possibility that Halbert might miraculously put life in a womb where none had ever before stirred.

"Now this I can never prove, but I believe Lambertus has also taken advantage of the sheriff's quest for profit and borrowed from him. That momentary lapse on his part now pinches him most dearly. But that has nothing to do with this story."

Faucon once more stretched his toes out to the hearthstone as he continued his tale. "Left with no other avenue to save the one he loved, the sheriff sent word to Halbert that he would come to Aldersby upon his return to the shire from the royal court. I can only guess what threats might have been made, but I suspect it had to do with the loan Sir Alain had made to the miller. Perhaps he was demanding full payment of what was owed to him or to collect whatever Halbert had promised for collateral.

"Any such threat would have panicked Halbert. Again, this is nothing I know for certain, but I wager Halbert was spending coins he should have been paying Alain. Priors Holston is nothing but a large village, not even as big a town as this one, yet Stephen's attire and their home rivals those of the grandest of London merchants.

"Thus, rightly believing himself doomed, Halbert went to the priory where he had the truth scribed on that parchment, which he left for Stephen to find and decipher, injuring two birds with his one stone. Stephen was pressing him about Agnes' dower, generally making life miserable for Halbert. And, if Alain was going to kill him, Halbert was going to make certain the sheriff never received another penny from his loan.

"Then Alain arrives at Aldersby, and before he knows it, there is Stephen, coming to offer just the resolution he craves to the problem of Agnes. I'm wagering Stephen offered to continue paying on that loan if Sir Alain would do the deed that Stephen couldn't bring himself to do. It's my guess that Stephen suggested drowning. Put his father in the race while he was in a drunken stupor, and let the wheel take him. But Alain craved Halbert's blood for his betrayal."

He smiled at Colin. "To simply drown Halbert would have been very unsatisfying," he said, and was rewarded with the monk's laugh.

"Thus the scheme with the pig and the blood, because Stephen wanted his father's death to appear only as an accident. Anything else might lead just where it has, to the revelation of the truth of his birth," Faucon continued.

"The death of 'Wina's mother was but a happy accident, or so I believe. It made no difference if Stephen was in his home at Priors Holston or gone when Halbert died. All the village knew that Halbert had taken to drinking outside by the wheel. And, as Simon the Fuller said, Halbert would release the brake just to spite his neighbors. No one would have raised an eyebrow when a drunken Halbert slipped into the race and drowned."

Here, Faucon paused to grin at his guest. "And all would have gone just as planned—Stephen would yet be milling, Sir Alain would yet have payments to collect—save for the meddling of two monks—Brother Edmund and you."

That set Colin laughing again. This time, the sound of his amusement was a low and very satisfied chuckle. "That is how it is with monks. We meddle. Although he and I should take warning. See what it cost Prior Lambertus to put his fingers where he shouldn't have? Now, about that tunic?" he prodded.

"Ah, that bedamned piece of cloth," Faucon said with no little frustration. He took the pitcher of cider left by the maid from the floor beside his chair and refilled both their cups before continuing.

"So there is Stephen and Alain, returning to the village in the dead of night. No doubt, the use of that awl had been discussed and planned, in keeping with Stephen's goal to make this look like accident. That morning, before Stephen left for 'Wina's home, he goaded his father with his departure, battering his father, knowing his refusal to stay would drive Halbert to drink more than usual.

"The workday ends, Halbert begins drinking. He's angry at Stephen and expects Alain at any moment. In his drunken rage, he brings out the tunic he doesn't wear, the one that Agnes gave him, the symbol of all that will destroy him. Simon intervenes, sending Agnes to the alewife's house. Halbert drops that tunic on the side of the race, and there it stays as Halbert spews his curses at the wheel, then finally falls asleep on the side of the race."

Faucon breathed out, staring into the fire, as the information he had in store shifted and turned in his mind.

"Then, in the dead of night, the miller's son and the sheriff come," Colin said, prodding. "They carry Halbert into Simon's croft. The sheriff pierces Halbert's heart and...?"

"Nay, they undress Halbert on the race side," Faucon corrected, "then carry Halbert into the croft. Remember, there were no stains of any kind on Halbert's braies or shirt when there would have been, had he sat or lain in the ashes," he told the monk, then took up the story once again.

"Alain pierces Halbert's heart, getting the vengeance he craved for Halbert's betrayal, then he leaves, not knowing that I've been given the Crowner's position. He expects no difficulties with the inquest on the morrow. That's why he left it up to Stephen to finish the night's task, not realizing that out of habit Stephen would brake the wheel after his father's body had already stopped it from turning."

"As I said," Colin offered, "a liar always missteps. So when Stephen carried his father's body back to the race, he washed him and dressed him—"

Faucon caught his breath as the meaning of the tunic hit him. "He dressed in the clothing left on the edge of the race," he interrupted. "In his hurry or his nervousness, he put his father in his shirt and braies, then the tunic. Because it was there."

Colin shook his head. "Nothing more than that?"

"Nothing more than that," Faucon replied, smiling. "Then he put his father in the race and when Halbert was up against the wheel, released the brake. Halbert was swept beneath the wheel and it stopped. Then, as I've said, he braked the wheel out of habit, dropped the wrench and fled, expecting Alf to appear from the mill."

Here, Faucon paused. "Alf suggested it might have been intended that he would be accused of Halbert's death. If Stephen had any inkling that Alf was also Halbert's son, this might have been the plan, but that's something we'll never know, not now."

Rolling his cup between his palms, Faucon continued. "I think I'm going to like this crowner's position. But I see I must accustom myself to these murders that may not be resolved."

"These? There is more than one you cannot resolve?" the monk wanted to know.

"Aye, one more already. After you left me at Priors Holston, a child's body was discovered some miles away. It was clear she'd been carried to where she was left, as there was no nearby village or hamlet. Her throat had been slit, but the scavengers had been at her for a time before she was found that there was no knowing who she might have been."

The color drained from Colin's face. He bent to set his cup upon the hearth stone, then looked at Faucon. "Was she dressed in a fine linen shift with a crown of flowers upon her head?" His voice broke as he spoke.

Faucon eyed him in surprise. "The flowers, aye. But her attire was more shirt than shift. Why?"

"Lord save us, it's happening again," the monk breathed, a hand pressed to his mouth. "I thought it was finally over."

Faucon lowered his feet to the floor, then straightened in his chair. "A child has been killed in this same way before this?"

Colin nodded, sadness filling his gaze. "And just as you describe. There have been six. Sir Alain brought their remains to my abbey, where we kept them in the ice house, hoping to identify them before they were naught but bones. When he stopped bringing them, I breathed in relief."

Folding his hands in his lap, he stared at his entwined fingers. "Here is all I know of them. The child is always found in the open, her hair loosened and a crown of flowers upon her head. Her throat is slit. The lasses I've seen have each been dressed in a fine linen shift. None have been known by anyone in Stanrudde, nor has any family complained of a missing girl."

"Six?" Faucon said in welling disgust. What sort of beast murdered innocents?

"Six, only if every murdered babe has been found," Colin corrected gently. "You know how folk will do when they find the body of one they don't know. They'll move the corpse outside their boundaries or bury it, all to avoid the murdrum fine. We haven't seen a girl now for more than two years. I thought—nay, I prayed it had ended."

Colin looked at him, hollow-eyed. "We need a good knight and true, Sir Faucon. One who cares not if the child is but a girl and worth nothing, as was Sir Alain's complaint when my abbot pressed him to take action. Pursue the one who does this, because it is the right thing to do. Stop him."

St. Osyth's Day

I catch my breath in stunned surprise. She is exquisite! I vow I've have never seen such beauty in one of her lowly birth. Her hair is the color of holy fire. The fine strands waft in the air, shifting and shimmering as they catch what remains of the day's light, encircling her with a glow that proclaims her purity.

That stirring I know so well begins, welling until it fills me from my head to my toes. Our holy Father has claimed this one as His own.

I pause at the gate to the place, waiting to be seen. Folk of their sort are always hospitable to those of mine. I have never been refused a bed and meal when I am on the road.

It takes but a moment before they see me. The children come dashing, calling for the elders to join them. I watch as the child's mother lifts her daughter and cradles her close. Her head bends over the babe's shoulder as tears start from her eyes.

My heart breaks for her. So it is with those like her. They are so often worn to exhaustion by the hardships of their lives. It's a shame that they cannot see beyond their earthly sorrows to the promise of joy that awaits in their Heavenly home.

That is why it so important to find His maid servants when they are yet young, before these girls are emptied of all faith and joy, left bitter by the grinding poverty of their lives.

As the mother draws close to the gate, I see that her daughter is younger than I first thought. It makes me pause. I've never been called to one so young.

Then again, if her Lord and mine has led me here, I may not question. I draw a sustaining breath and set my heart to the task required of it. With this one hardly more than a babe, it will take more time than usual to convince her mother to release her into her Lord's custody.

A Note from Denise

Thank you for reading this first book of my new mystery series. I hope you enjoyed Faucon and his adventure as a Crowner. If you liked the book, or I suppose even if you didn't, consider "liking" the book or leaving a review. If you've found any formatting or typographical errors, please let me know by email at denisedoming@gmail.com. I appreciate the chance to correct my mistakes!

I have to admit I had much more fun than I expected following Faucon's appointment to the Crowner's position. I'm looking forward to starting on the next book in the series. A part of me wants to write the book from Sir Alain's viewpoint. Truth be told, when I first conceived of this series, his was the voice in my head. Then Faucon came along and everything changed.

If this is the first book of mine you've read, I do have others. Except for Monica Sarli's memoir, which I co-wrote, they are historical women's fiction. By the way, you'll find Lord Graistan and Bishop William in the first four Seasons books.

Glossary

This book includes of number of Medieval terms. I've defined the ones I think might be unfamiliar to you. If you find others you'd like defined, let me know at denisedoming@gmail.com and I'll add them to the list.

Amercement   "being at the mercy of". An arbitrary fine commonly used as punishment for minor offenses and as an alternative to imprisonment.

Braies   A man's undergarment. Made from a single piece of linen that is tied around the waist with a cord. Worn more or less like a loin cloth but more voluminous so the garment can be arranged to cover the hips and thighs.

Chausses   Stockings made of cloth (not knitted). Each leg ties onto the waist cord of the braies.

Crowner   From the Latin *Coronarius,* meaning Servant of the Crown. The word eventually evolves into 'Coroner'

Deodand   Derived from the *deo dandum*, meaning "to be given to God." An object is declared deodand if it has been used to kill someone. The inquest jury is responsible for appraising the object's value and the owner is expected to pay a fine equal to that value. If the owner cannot pay, the hundred or village must pay in their stead. Theoretically, once the crown has taken possession of a deodand, it must sell it then use the profit for a religious or pious purpose.

Dower

The bridegroom's offering to his bride. Generally dower should be one-third the value of the bride's dowry. Dower is an annuity for the wife, meant to support her after her husband's death. She holds her dower for her life time, and can accrue dower over the course of multiple marriages. Upon her death, her dower returns to the heirs of the original owner.

Dowry

What the bride brings to her husband upon marriage. Depending on her class, this can be a throne, estates, a skill (such as milling), or in the case of peasant brides, pots and pans and other household goods.

First estate,

Ordained first by God, this is all clergy, from the pope to the lowliest clerk.

Second estate, Ordained by the clergy, the royalty and nobility

Third estate

Ordained by the nobility, the commoners and merchants, or working men in general.

Fee Tail

From Medieval Latin *feodum talliatum*, which means "cut-short fee". Used to make certain an estate remained in the family line. Mortgaging land (or in the case of this book, the operation of a mill) in fee tail was a risk, since the heirs had no obligation to the lender.

Fulling	Fulling involves two processes applied to newly woven woolen cloth. Scouring removes oils, dirt and impurities while milling thickens the cloth. This is done by pounding the woolen cloth with the fuller's feet, or hands, or a club, or, eventually, with a water-powered fulling mill.
Gambeson	A heavy padded, long-sleeved tunic usually hip length worn beneath a chain mail tunic
Hemp	A soft, strong fiber plant with edible seeds. Hemp can be twisted into rope or woven for use in making everything from storage bags to mattress covers.
Hundred	A geographic division of a county or shire. It likely once referred to an area capable of providing a hundred men at arms, or containing a hundred homes.
Koren	The Old English word for "corn", meaning kernels as in wheat, barley and other grains. Modern corn, as in sweet corn, is rightly referred to as maize.
Mazer	A large wooden drinking bowl commonly used for celebrations
Murdrum	From which the word "murder" comes. Established after the Norman Conquest when the English were actively killing their conquerors. If a dead person cannot be proved to be English, said person is assumed to be Norman and the fine is levied. By the 12th Century the

fine is more about raising revenue than punishing the citizenry.

Pleas of the Crown

To plead for justice from the royal court, or representative of the court. Like going to your local police station and filing a complaint.

Prebendary   A senior member of the clergy who is supported by the revenue from an estate or parish. He generally had a role in the administration of a cathedral.

Toft and Croft A toft is the area of land on which a peasant's house sits. The croft, generally measuring seven hundred feet in length and forty in width. It was in the croft that a serf would grow their personal food staples, such as onions, garlic, turnips and other root crops, legumes and some grains.

Withe   A thin, supple willow (but also hazel or ash) branch

Made in the USA
San Bernardino, CA
13 September 2014